Sonata FOR A Scoundrel

ANTHEA LAWSON

Fiddlehead Press

Also by Anthea Lawson

"A new star of historical romance." – *Booklist*

~ Novels ~
Passionate
All He Desires

~ Collections ~
Kisses & Rogues: Four Regency Stories

~ Short Stories & Novelettes ~
Five Wicked Kisses
Maid for Scandal
The Piano Tutor
The Worth of Rubies
To Wed the Earl

Sonata *FOR A* Scoundrel

 NTHEA LAWSON

Cover photo from Jimmy Thomas. Used with licensed permission. Cover design, Kim Killion at The Killion Group.

Edited by Laurie Temple, copy editing by Arran at Editing720, Final Oops Detection by Victory Editing.

Discover more at anthealawson.com, and please join Anthea's new release mailing list at *www.tinyletter.com/AntheaLawson*. Anthea also writes award-winning YA urban fantasy as Anthea Sharp.

All characters in this story are fiction and figments of the author's imagination. To obtain permission to excerpt portions of the text, please contact the author.

QUALITY CONTROL: We care about producing error-free books. If you find a typo or formatting problem, send a note to anthea@anthealawson.com so that the error may be corrected.

ISBN-13: 978-0615885940
ISBN-10: 0615885942

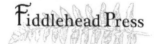

Fiddlehead Press

DEDICATION

To my husband, Lawson—my partner in music, and in life.
I love you.

CHAPTER ONE

The Maestro Arrives!

In a mere two days, that preeminent virtuoso of the violin, Master Darien Reynard, will grace the stage at King's Theatre. Ladies, keep your smelling salts close at hand, for Master Reynard is renowned for leaving a swath of swooning in the wake of his performances...

-The London Engager, November 1830

The melody threading through Clara Becker's mind stopped, snipped by the angry voices penetrating the study door. She sat back in the cracked leather chair and put down her pen, the musical notes wavering on the page before her tired eyes. The ache in her shoulders and hand—distant when she was caught up in composing—now pulsed distractingly, vying with the landlady's shrill tone to fragment her concentration.

"If you don't deliver the rent tomorrow, you're on the street. Out, I say!" The landlady's voice was nearly a shriek. "You've been late one too many times, Mr. Becker. I've a mind to send my sons over tonight to pitch you out!"

"We will have the money," Papa said, his cane thumping the floorboards for emphasis. "But now, you must leave."

The fire in the small hearth had burned down to nothing but sullen embers. Clara covered her ears with her chilled hands and hummed under her breath, trying desperately to recapture the music. If she did not finish this piece, they were ruined.

"Please, Mrs. Tench." Her brother Nicholas spoke. "By tomorrow afternoon you'll have two months' rent in hand. You know we've always managed before."

The voices faded, thank goodness. Nicholas was moving the landlady toward the front door. Clara let out a breath and closed her eyes. The door slammed, and blessed quiet filled the house. It was a strained silence, but it was enough.

The music sprang into her mind once more, bright strands of melody flung against a somber background. She took up her pen and bent to the page, letting the notes inside her mind transport her to a distant, splendid place. A place far away from the reality of their cramped lodging, the worry that shaded her days, the hoarded coals that barely kept the chill of November from biting to the bone.

There was nothing now but the notes unfolding. She sang the refrain under her breath, the dip and scratch of her pen keeping a steady rhythm. Time fell away, until she inked in the final double bar.

Finished. Clara pulled her frayed shawl tightly about her shoulders. The music was complete, the window in her soul shuttered, and she felt like ashes; the dun and dross left by a consuming fire.

She could hear Papa and Nicholas at odds again. Despite their attempt to whisper, her brother's voice rose in counterpoint to her father's gruff tone. She rubbed at her forehead. Papa would win the disagreement, in this as in all things. Though she appreciated Nicholas's support, it would be easier for her to compose if the house were not so often filled with unhappy tension. Still, argument was better than that terrible month when Nicholas had not spoken at all.

She blew lightly across the page until the ink no longer gleamed, then gathered the rest of the manuscript. The chair scraped across the floor as she stood, and the arguing voices stilled. Clara was not surprised to pull the door open and find both her brother and father waiting. Their faces were filled with anticipation, though in Papa's case it took years of familiarity to identify any change in his usual dour expression.

"Finished," Papa said. It was not a question. He did not wait for her nod, but gestured to Nicholas. "Give it to your brother, so we may hear it."

Nicholas gave her a smile, as weak as the light from the single lamp in the room. A lock of his overlong blond hair fell across one eye as he glanced toward the piano.

It was not as though she were incapable of sitting at the instrument and performing the music herself. As children of a music master, both she and her brother were accomplished pianists. But Papa felt it best that Nicholas play the music as soon as she had finished the composition. It was a ritual now. Nicholas would play it, and the music would no longer be hers.

She hesitated, as she always did. Papa cleared his throat and she forced the pages forward, the notes that had been a part of her soul released into her brother's keeping. The sheets of music shook, ever so lightly, as she released her grasp.

Her throat was dry as parchment. How long had she been in the study? Certainly it had been just past luncheon when she began, but now the curtains were drawn against the heavy night, the sounds of the city quiet around them. It must be very, very late.

Perhaps her father and Nicholas had been arguing about letting her stop, letting her rest.

She could not have, in any case. The music had her in its grip. And even if she'd had to scrape and fashion each note with laborious patience, she would have finished her composition before morning broke, cold and hard, over the smudged rooftops of London.

The landlady's visit had been the final goad. They needed the money her work would bring, far more than any of them were willing to admit. It was their only source of income. Her brother's piano students among the gentry were long gone.

"Hm." Nicholas held the first page up to catch the dim light. "It's in E minor."

"A minor composition?" Papa's voice was stern. "Are you certain?"

Clara stifled a sudden, wild urge to giggle. How could the music be anything but in a minor key?

It was winter, almost as cold and dark inside their small house as it was outside in the streets of their dilapidated neighborhood. The pantry was dwindling down to potatoes and cabbages and a sliver of salted meat. They barely had the money to furnish Mary with laundry

4 ~ ANTHEA LAWSON

soap. It was fortunate that Clara's dresses had been drab colors originally, for they were all brownish grey by now.

The only melodies that could possibly find roost in her mind were in minor keys, shaded with melancholy.

"Yes," she said. "E minor." The steadiness of her voice surprised her.

Nicholas lit the candles at the piano. "Have you named it?"

It was impossible not to name her compositions, though Papa invariably changed them. She touched her gold locket, the one that had belonged to Mama, one finger stroking the smooth metal.

"The piece is called *Trieste*." Sadness.

A tap of Papa's cane. "Too feminine. Better we name it..." Another tap while he thought. "*Air in E minor*. Now, let us hear it."

Nicholas settled himself at the keys. He leaned forward, fingers poised, then began.

Slow and quiet at first, the phrases dipped and turned like smoke, like unvoiced dreams, while his left hand kept a steady, tolling beat. Then the middle section—the music seeking the light like a flower, straining upward. Nicholas hit a wrong key and she winced, but held her tongue. Onward... and now to the part where the brightness faded into a series of descending notes, the flower curled into itself, and the piece finally came to rest.

Silence, and utter stillness, followed the last note. Nicholas's hands lay motionless on the keyboard. On the whole, he had done it justice. Clara tugged a strand of her pale hair loose and tried not to look at Papa.

"Well." He gave a sharp nod. "It should fetch a decent price. Nicholas, make a copy, and I will deliver it to the publishers in the morning."

It was the closest he would come to a compliment. It was enough. The landlady would not need to send her burly sons on the morrow. There would be food on the table, with a little left over to keep the creditors at bay.

Nicholas stood and crossed the room to take her hands. "It's lovely, Clara. I know the exact feeling it conveys."

Clara nodded at him. Her brother was familiar with other

feelings, far bleaker than the ones she had set to music. But that was behind them now.

"You should rest," he said.

"Yes." Eyes heavy with exhaustion, she dropped her hands and turned away.

The stairs were steeper than ever, and creaked under her feet as she mounted into the darkness, not bothering to take a light. Behind her, the music began again as Nicholas familiarized himself with the composition. The bright and sorrowful notes twined about her, following her into sleep.

***

The ticking of a metronome in her dream transformed to someone knocking insistently at the front door. Clara blinked at the gray light seeping through the curtains and struggled up, pushing the warm blankets away. Mary, their distant cousin and maid of all work, would answer. And surely Papa was home from delivering the rent by now, but Clara's curiosity was even more insistent than her desire to burrow back beneath the covers.

Cold air against her skin pulled her completely awake. The fabric of her dress was chilly as she hurriedly slipped it over her chemise. She pulled the brush through her hair, grabbed her woolen shawl, and hastened to the landing in time to see Papa open the door. Peeking over the railing, she could make out the legs and shoes of a finely dressed gentleman.

"What is this?" Papa was never gentle with strangers.

Clara edged to the window at the top of the stairs and glanced outside. A large coach was parked before their house, the black lacquered doors and gilt trim as out of place in their neighborhood as a raven among sparrows. In the windows of the row houses across the street, faces stared out like pale, curious moons.

"Sir." The visitor appeared untouched by Papa's manner. "Do I have the pleasure of finding the Becker household?"

"Who is enquiring?"

"I am Peter Widmere, agent for..." He made a dramatic pause, and she could hear Papa's cane thump impatiently.

"Get on it with it," Papa demanded.

"Agent for Darien Reynard."

Papa's cane stilled, and Clara drew in her breath. Darien Reynard! The most famous musician on the Continent! What was his agent doing here?

"Darien Reynard? The maestro?" Papa's forbidding air had faded entirely.

Clara peeked out the window again, trying to see inside the coach. Was it possible Reynard himself was within? She lifted a hand to her hair, the fine strands still dream-tangled. Her heart accelerated, sending a tremble of indecision through her. Should she dash back to her room and finish dressing properly?

But if she left now she would miss everything.

"The very same," Mr. Widmere said. "Now, tell me. Are you Nicholas Becker's father?"

"Yes," Papa said, "I am Herr Becker. Tell me why you have come."

"I was sent to deliver these tickets." The man reached into his coat pocket and drew out an envelope. "As you are no doubt aware, Mr. Reynard performs tonight at the King's Theatre. He directs your family to attend."

Clara covered her mouth, silencing a gasp. She and her brother had spoken of attending Darien Reynard's concert, as one speaks of traveling to Italy, or dining with a duke. It had been as out of reach for them as the clouds.

Papa's back stiffened, as if to deny that any man could command him, but he held out his hand for the tickets. "Very well. We will come to the concert."

"Excellent." The agent made a crisp bow. "Mr. Reynard will be gratified to hear it. Good day, sir."

Papa stood, leaning on his cane as the man marched back to the coach and pulled open the door. The interior was empty. Clara let out a silent sigh of disappointment—or perhaps relief. Of course the maestro would not grace them with his presence, especially not in such a quarter of London.

But they would get to see him perform, this very evening! The clatter of wheels as the coach pulled away echoed the excitement pulsing through her. Darien Reynard, the legendary violinist, had sent *them* tickets. It was dizzying.

She did not care what they said of him, the stories of his excesses and vices, the whispers that he colluded with the devil in exchange for the power to move men's souls with his playing. The only thing that mattered was that tonight, *tonight*, she would see him take the stage and hear him play. A thrilled vibration settled in her chest, then expanded until her whole body hummed, like a piano string struck by a velvet hammer of anticipation.

Papa shut the door, then thumbed through the contents of the envelope.

"Hmph," he said. "Come down, Clara. Three tickets." His tone edged on disapproval, as though their benefactor knew too much about them already.

There was so much that must be kept secret.

Clara drew her shawl more closely about her shoulders as she descended to the chilly parlor. She was so very tired of being constantly cold. Surely the tickets had put Papa in a generous mood? And since he had not said otherwise, he had been able to sell her composition to the publishers and pay the landlady her due.

"May we light a fire, Papa?" It was a shocking waste of coal to light the hearth in the daytime, but her fingers were nearly numb. "I will bring the mending down and work beside it."

He gave a single nod.

She did not wait for more, but bent to the fireplace, carefully wielding the tongs. Perhaps she could send Mary to the bakery to bring home a fresh loaf. What a splendid day it was already. She hardly dared imagine the evening to come.

First, however, was the pressing issue of the mending. Her best gown had a tear in the hem, and Nicholas's good wool coat needed a button. Papa, of course, would be turned out in his usual severe black suit. Though they rarely could afford to attend concerts, Papa insisted they maintain the proper appearances.

They would do well enough. After all, it was not as though they would be seated in one of the grand boxes reserved for the *ton*.

CHAPTER TWO

They were seated in one of the grand boxes reserved for the *ton*. Clara fingered the simple gold locket about her neck and curled deeper into the plush velvet seat, trying to make herself invisible. Sitting in the upper-level boxes changed the entire feel of the theater. The noise and heat rose around them, a dozen conversations buzzing in her ears.

"Do you think the king is here?" Nicholas could not stop glancing into the other boxes. "Look, Clara, surely that is the Duke of Kent, and next to him… the lord chancellor, is it not?"

She did not know, though she was pleased to see Nicholas so animated. The adjacent box was occupied by a grandly dressed lady, gems glittering at her throat and ears, who lifted her lorgnette and surveyed the family with a contemptuous air. The woman nudged her companion, a distinguished-looking fellow wearing a coat decorated with medals. His eyes slid past them as if there were only empty seats in their box. Face heating, Clara pretended to study the program, though she had memorized it already. Beethoven for the first half, then a selection of shorter pieces for the second.

But they were here because Darien Reynard himself had sent them tickets. The thought lifted her chin again, and she met the woman's stare with an even smile. They belonged, because the maestro had made it so.

Nicholas leaned out to view the crowd, his eyes bright. "Everyone is here. There's Mr. Cramer from the publishing company, and Henry Bishop. I hear he's working on a new opera."

"Hush," Papa said. "They are putting out the lights."

Dimness descended and Clara let out her breath. Anticipation pulsed from her toes upward, coiling bright and warm in her chest.

Only moments now, and she would see him perform. Darien Reynard. She tasted the syllables of his name as though they were chocolate upon her tongue.

The gaslights at the front of the stage flared and a hush spread through the audience, the last conversations sputtering out.

A man walked onstage and Clara leaned forward—but no, it was the accompanist, an older, sandy-haired man who took his place at the piano. He swiveled and looked back into the wings, and the audience burst into expectant applause.

Now Darien Reynard strode forward, claiming the appreciation as his due, and there was no mistaking that *this* was the man. Violin tucked easily under one arm, he moved with a contained grace, his tall, broad-shouldered frame poised and full of energy. A shock of wavy black hair nearly touched his shoulders, and his elegant coat was even darker—pure shadow, as though the light could find no purchase upon it.

He surveyed the crowd, gaze penetrating, then halted at center stage and flicked a glance up toward their box, almost as if he could he see them in the dimness. Clara moistened her lips, barely breathing, until his attention sheered away.

His mobile, sensual mouth set in a half smile that only added mystery to his handsome face, Darien Reynard inclined his head to the audience. He set his instrument on his shoulder. With a dramatic sweep of his right arm he raised his bow, then held it motionless above the strings. Instantly the murmurs and rustles ceased.

The first chord sprang from the instrument and rippled into the air, followed by another, another, as he caressed his violin, the notes throbbing with passion. The piano joined in, and the music moved into a sprightlier theme. Clara's heart beat in time; ached and sighed while the figure on the stage led her forward into rapture and mystery. This, *this*, was how she heard music. A doorway into another land, a place where everything was luminous with emotion.

He was never still. Even in the *andante* sections he swayed, as though the music was weeping through him, the notes pulled forth from his body through the gleaming golden wood he held in his hands. Clara was certain her eyes were not the only ones blurred with unshed tears.

The final movement burst like constellations through her, jubilant sprays of notes flung out over the audience. He took the melody at a blistering speed, the bow now flying over the strings so quickly she half expected to see smoke following in its wake. The music exploded about her, rushing upward as Darien Reynard drove the piece forward. The accompanist could barely keep up with him as Beethoven's *Sonata No. 9* thundered to a breathtaking close.

Instantly the audience sprang to its feet, shouting approval, the rush of sound raw and graceless compared to what had just gone before. Clara rose, program fluttering to the floor, and applauded as loudly as she could through the muffling of her gloves. Glorious. Simply glorious.

"That was Beethoven as he ought to be played," Nicholas said. "Reynard could repeat it for the second half and I'd be well satisfied."

Even Papa unbent enough to agree, though his approval was tacit. "The acoustics up here are improved."

"It was much more than better acoustics," Nicholas said. "*That* was a master at work."

Clara nodded. She could not speak yet, not while Darien Reynard's playing still echoed through her, but she was in complete agreement. She had never heard anything so splendid.

"I'm going to fetch some refreshment." Nicholas turned to her. "Coming?"

The thought of journeying through the glittering crowd that swirled outside their box made the skin between her shoulders tighten.

She shook her head, preferring to sit quietly and savor the memory of the man and his music. Clara glanced up toward the gilt ceiling, imagining that the notes were still gathered there, spinning and dancing in the shadows. If she listened closely perhaps she could catch their bright echo.

She closed her eyes, but there were too many voices between her and the trapped strands of melody. Snatches of conversation floated past.

"...in Madrid he couldn't even go out in the street, the crowds followed him everywhere..."

"...the crown princess fainted at his performance. Of course now it is the fashion for everyone to faint at his feet." A feminine giggle. "I wouldn't mind swooning anywhere upon his person, I declare. Such a magnetic man!"

It was true enough. Darien Reynard was impossibly handsome, even without the power of his musical mastery. She did not think any woman could avoid being captivated by him.

Nicholas returned with tea and she sipped at her cup. The warmth of the beverage joined the memory of music still curling about her, the heat of the theater wrapping about them. She was warm from her head to her toes. It was a delicious sensation.

Finally, the house lights were extinguished again and the crowd became an expectant, eager presence in the softly lit dark. This time Darien Reynard strode alone onto the stage, as self-assured as a man entering his own kingdom. He held up his hand, and the audience obediently stilled.

"Ladies. Gentlemen." His voice was rich and resonant, filling the space as effortlessly as his playing had done. "It is not on the program, but this evening I have a special treat for you."

The audience buzzed happily. Darien Reynard waited for silence to fall again.

"Tonight, I am pleased to introduce the work of a composer, little known, but of great talent. This piece moves me deeply, as I know it will move you."

A hum of speculation moved through the audience at his words, and Clara straightened. She did not often have the chance to hear new compositions.

Darien Reynard gave a single nod. "I give you *Rondo*, by Nicholas Becker. Attend."

She fell back against her seat, astonishment pinning her to the velvet. *Rondo*? Her *Rondo*?

The first notes confirmed it. Heat flashed through her as the music *she* had penned surged from Darien Reynard's violin. She was insensible to everything but the man before her, the genius who played her very soul out into the open, who took the sweet, spiraling melody of her piece and transmuted it into pure emotion.

Yearning etched the air as he leaned into the notes, his unruly hair falling about his face. Clara breathed with the movements of his bow, and the entire audience breathed with her. She suddenly believed all the rumors. If he wished, the riveting figure before them could steal all their souls without a single protest.

The last note faded into stillness, an awed hush of perfect quiet. Her heart beat, knocking against the silence, three, four times. Then cries of "bravo!" and wild applause thundered down, like a dam giving way before the torrent. Darien Reynard held his head high and let it wash around him, seeming unconcerned that the force of such adulation might sweep him away. Surrounded by the tumult, Clara sat transfixed, unable to make even a pretense of clapping.

Her music. Her very heart.

Then Darien Reynard raised his arm, palm upwards, and gestured to the box where they sat, bidding the composer to rise and take a bow. Without meaning to, without any thought at all, she gathered herself to stand. Only the weight of Papa's hand landing heavily on her shoulder kept her in her seat. Turning her head, she met Nicholas's eyes.

Wonder and pride shone there. And then guilt. His gaze slid away from hers and he stood, cheeks growing pink as he acknowledged the applause washing over him, the shouts of approval.

Darien Reynard nodded, a sudden smile flickering across his face. Throat tight, Clara swallowed and tried to remember what was most important. It didn't matter that Nicholas must be the one taking the credit. Darien Reynard had played *her* music. Played it before all of London, and played it splendidly.

Eyes burning, she smiled, while her heart twisted equally with pain, with joy.

CHAPTER THREE

Master Reynard Captivates!
All London is abuzz in the aftermath of the maestro's stunning
performance—and the sudden elevation of Mr. Nicholas Becker's compositions
into the public eye. One hopes the attention will not go to the previously unknown
composer's head…
                              -The London Engager

"Are you certain this is the place?" Dare looked out the window
as his coach rolled to a halt.

Underfed children played in the street beneath sagging roofs,
and a blanket of coal soot dimmed all the colors to dullness. It was
too much like the neighborhood he had clawed his way out of at a
young age, vowing never to return to such poverty. Memories
perched on his shoulders like hunched ravens. With a deep breath,
Dare shook them off.

"Yes. Becker lives there, with his father and sister." His agent,
Peter, nodded to the faded house before them. He crossed his legs
and made no move to leave the vehicle. "Dare, are you quite certain
you wish to proceed?"

Frustration beat a rough rhythm through Dare, though he was
careful to make no outward show of it. He valued Peter. In truth, his
agent was one of the few people who would speak honestly to him—
bluntly, if necessary.

"I must. We will convince Becker." Dare's hands ached from
clenching.

He slowly unknotted his fingers. Control. He was in control. He
had proven himself against life for decades now, although it had been
years since he'd wanted something so badly and been unable to

simply impose his will and achieve it. But he could not kidnap Becker and throw him into the coach, away from these dreary environs. No, he must have the man's cooperation.

Dare wrenched open the coach door and dropped to the ground before the footman could set the steps. He could not bear another moment of inaction.

"Come," he said to Peter.

A larger fear pressed against Dare than dusty memories of his miserable childhood. Was Becker indeed the musical genius he hoped? What if he had spent the entirety of his inspiration on that single composition, the *Rondo*? What if there was no more?

The thought spiked painfully through Dare. *What if there was no more?*

Three months ago he had been performing for an exclusive group in the Duke of Salzburg's drawing room. The duke, a music aficionado who collected little-known works, had placed the music before him.

"How about something obscure and English?"

The audience had laughed, but quickly hushed as Dare played the first notes. The music that had lain silent and waiting on the page leapt to his instrument and then into the room, taking life as it took flight, a spiraling twist of melody that held them all spellbound. The brilliance and power of the music caught him by surprise. It was unlike anything he had ever played before. Each note vibrated through him, shook away the soul-deep unhappiness lodged in his heart, the memory of the sacrifices he had made.

When he reached the end, he began again. They told him later that he played it three times in succession. Each time the music gained in power and emotion, becoming more and more his own. At the end he simply set down his violin and walked out of the room. There was nothing else to be said. The *Rondo* had spoken for itself.

That night he retired to the opulence of the duke's best suite. Late, a woman had slipped into to his chamber. A click of the latch, soft footsteps, a cool touch on his forehead followed by a warm, lingering kiss. She was one of the duke's guests, a softly curved woman with dark, unbound hair. He could not remember her name, but it did not matter. He lifted the covers and she slipped in beside him. Warm, feminine, willing.

He had moved on and into her, languorous and dreamy, the music of the *Rondo* still alive and singing in him. They strove together, naked bodies by candlelight, yearning for fulfillment, finding that moment of bliss in the arms of a willing stranger.

She was gone from his chamber when he woke, but the *Rondo* sang on.

Word of his performance in the duke's drawing room spread like flames through dry summer fields. In great halls, in theaters and palaces, they clamored to hear him perform this new work, the *Rondo*. Each time he played it was a new birth. He stood before the multitudes and found his way into that pure, perfect heart of the music. Then he led the audience there, giving them a taste of heaven, leaving them at the end, eyes shining, voices hoarse from cheering.

This was why he had made that impossible choice so many years ago—and lived with the raw burden of its consequence ever since. Music. Not love, but music.

He must find Nicholas Becker. The conviction had grown until it had filled all the spaces of his waking. He must find the composer and see what else the man was capable of. With this music, Dare could be redeemed. He felt it in the depths of his soul.

Their destinies were connected, whether Nicholas Becker knew it or not.

And now here Dare stood, on a worn stoop in a decaying quarter of London. Beside him was Peter, who had steadfastly cancelled twenty-five performances and booked twenty new ones to bring them to this place. Here he stood, Darien Reynard, called the greatest performer of his generation, with his heart hammering in his throat. Unable to lift his hand to knock. The powerlessness infuriated him.

What if he had come all this way and there was no more?

"We won't find out anything by standing on the doorstep." Peter stepped past him and rapped loudly at the door. "And stop scowling so fiercely," he added. "You don't want to frighten the poor man to death."

After an endless pause, an older gentleman answered, his thin silver hair combed back from his stern features. "Yes?"

Peter inclined his head. "Good afternoon, Mr. Becker. Please excuse the unannounced visit. Mr. Reynard would like to have a word with your son. Is he at home?"

The older man's gaze went to Dare, and his eyes widened. "Master Reynard! We are honored. Come in, both of you." He pulled the door wide and called back over his shoulder, "Mary! Bring tea."

Dare exhaled and strode past Peter into a chilly entryway that smelled of mildew. Mr. Becker gestured them into a sparsely furnished parlor where a handful of coals smoldered on the hearth, lending the barest hint of warmth to the air.

"I will fetch Nicholas." Leaning on his cane, the father turned and stumped up the staircase.

Dare listened to the fading notes of the father's passage, the muted sound of voices. Soon. Soon. To distract himself he glanced about the room. The walls were bare, only brighter squares on the dingy wallpaper to show where pictures had once hung.

A piano dominated the back half of the parlor. He went to it and ran his fingers along the cool mahogany, wrestling back the impatience that coiled through him.

"A Broadwood." He nodded to Peter. "No doubt Becker missed meals to purchase the thing." Compared to the mismatched chairs and faded settee, the piano stood out like a sapphire in a box of cheap jewelry.

His agent raised his brows. "That instrument cost a pretty penny."

No doubt Peter was calculating the exact number of pennies it had cost, and the things the family had clearly gone without in consequence.

Dare shifted his attention back to the keyboard. Had Becker sat in this very spot to compose the *Rondo*? The melody tingled in Dare's fingertips. When a single piece of music had such power, just think what the man might be capable of.

And then consider what he, himself, could do with that music.

"Sir!" A young man hurried down the stairs. "Forgive me for

keeping you waiting. I am Nicholas Becker."

Dare stepped away from the piano to shake the composer's outstretched hand. Nicholas Becker—at last.

Becker's clasp was firm, though he flushed and dropped his gaze to Dare's shoulder after his initial greeting. His disheveled hair was the color of wheat, and his dark blue eyes held an expression both reserved and sincere. An odd disappointment moved through Dare. Once again, this was not what he had expected, although he could not say precisely *what* he had expected.

Perhaps it was that the man was so young. He didn't seem capable of composing the intense melodies that had caught Dare's interest.

The father followed more slowly, his cane thumping down the treads. "Offer our guests a seat."

"Yes, please sit." Nicholas Becker gestured to the well-worn settee. "This is just... It's an unexpected pleasure to have you here, sir. My sister will join us shortly. She is eager to meet you, as well."

"Of course. I would be delighted." Dare knew his voice was cold. He did not want to sit about, meeting sisters. "Let me introduce my agent, Mr. Peter Widmere."

"Pleased to meet you," the composer said. He waited for his guests to settle, then perched in one of the armchairs opposite. His fingers were laced taut. "Thank you, maestro, for the concert tickets. And for playing the *Rondo*. You performed it splendidly."

Dare looked the young man squarely in the face. "The *Rondo* is worthy of a far wider audience. It has met with acclaim on the Continent—at least, with the select audiences who have had the opportunity to hear it."

Nicholas Becker's eyes opened wide, and he looked to his father.

"Thank you," he said at last. "We had no idea."

"Have you..." Dare's shoulders tightened, and he leaned forward. "Have you written more?"

He felt Peter shift beside him. It was too blunt, but the question had been burning inside him for so long it could not remain unspoken a moment longer.

"More?" Becker sounded as though a mouse had lodged in his throat. The look in his eyes seemed more panic than pride.

"Other compositions," Dare said. "Have you written other compositions?"

"Um… well, yes," Becker said. "Other published pieces. If that is what you mean."

It was not quite, but Dare nodded.

"May we see them?" Peter's tone was dry.

"Certainly." The composer jumped up from his seat and fetched a small stack of music from a nearby shelf. Wordlessly, he held it out.

Dare took the sheaf. For a long moment, he could not bring himself to open the first piece. He stared down at the frontispiece, an ornately scrolled border that contained the words *Etude, by Nicholas Becker.*

The father cleared his throat, and even Peter leaned over to look, though he would not be able to read the music scribed within.

Inhaling deeply, Dare turned the page. He forced his hands to remain steady, despite the bitter urgency that said *hurry, hurry!*

It was a simple, lovely piece for solo piano. Brief and sweet, something a young lady might play in her parlor for admiring suitors. Not the *Rondo* by any stretch. He felt his mouth turn down in a frown.

"That was written some time ago," Nicholas Becker said. "When, er, when I was practically a child."

Pulse beating in his temple, Dare turned to the next piece, titled *Scherzo*. He scanned the notes within, and let out a breath he had not been aware of holding. The restless mood of the written music stirred him, even unheard.

"Yes." He had not meant to speak the word aloud. "This one has potential."

"Potential?" Peter raised an eyebrow. "We came all this way for potential?"

The composer kept his gaze fixed on Dare's shoes, as if they held the answer to some great mystery. "That one was also written some time ago. I had quite a few, um, small pieces. The publisher sorted through and selected what he thought would sell."

Dare set the printed music aside. Damnation. He wanted to take the composer by the shoulders and shake him until more brilliant music came out.

"Yes. But what about now? What are you working on *now*?" He could not keep the raw demand from his voice.

"Ah..." The composer still did not look up, and for an instant Dare felt panic stab through his chest. He had been wrong.

No. He would not allow it. He fixed his gaze on Nicholas Becker, willing the man to speak.

The silence in the room teetered into discomfort before the father spoke. "Play the *Air in E minor*."

"Yes. Yes, of course." Nicholas Becker stood, one hand plucking at the side of his trousers. "The newest composition. Papa took a copy to the publishers only yesterday."

"Let us hear it." Dare could not look at Peter.

If this new piece was not brilliant, then they had come for nothing. Nothing. All his plans and hopes, dashed. Bile rose in his throat, anger at the universe for showing him a glimpse of perfection, and then snatching it away.

The composer took an inordinately long time to settle himself at the piano. The hush and crackle as he arranged the pages before him was the only sound in the silence. Dare was not certain his own lungs remembered how to breathe as he waited. Finally, after sending another anxious glance at his father, Becker began.

It was a thoughtful, meditative opening, and the room was immediately transformed by the aching sweetness of the melody. Relief flared through Dare, a smoldering ember leaping to flame. He let the music wrap round him, and closed his eyes in fervent gratitude.

As Becker continued to play, two things become quite clear. This newest work was every bit as inspired as the *Rondo*, and the composer was also an excellent pianist. *Now* Dare could look at his agent, his smile laced with triumph. Peter pressed his lips together, but he returned a single nod. Even he must hear the truth of it.

The notes sang through Dare as the piece ascended. His hands ached with the need to play that brightness into being, to sing it with the throat of his violin. It would sound exquisite; himself playing the theme while Nicholas Becker anchored the piece with those bell-like chords. With music like this, they could set the world on fire.

Victory glowed through him. He had been right, and everything would come about just as he had imagined it. The last shadows of fear and poverty slunk away.

His soul would be eased, and his mark made on musical history. Forever.

CHAPTER FOUR

The door to the parlor opened, the draft making the lamp flicker. One of the pages on the piano fluttered to the floor and the composer stopped, the music breaking off so abruptly that Dare caught his breath on that sudden edge. A drably dressed young woman hurried into the room. She paused by the piano and bent to gather the fallen page. With a practiced motion she returned the sheet to its place, then nodded to Becker to continue.

After a brief hesitation he did, and music brightened the air once more. Dare leaned back to listen, but his gaze caught on the figure of the young woman standing beside the piano. She was pale and a bit too thin, but the look on her face arrested his attention. Longing and tenderness filled her expression as she listened to the music. Her lips were tilted up in a half smile that seemed to hold a universe of secrets.

When the last ringing note had faded, she turned her head and met Dare's gaze. Mystery moved through the silver-blue depths of her eyes. Then she blinked, and he saw he had been mistaken; her eyes were plain gray.

"I apologize for the interruption." She bobbed a brief curtsey, then turned and gathered the music into a neat stack.

Nicholas Becker pushed away from the keyboard. "Master Reynard, this is my sister, Clara Becker."

Dare rose and bowed over her hand. The sister, of course. But where her brother was a wheat field under a blue sky, she was the same field seen by moonlight—leached of color.

"A pleasure to meet you," he said.

"Mr. Reynard, you honor us." Her slim fingers were cold in his. "Your concert last night was…" She faltered. "It was glorious. Thank you."

"I'm glad you enjoyed it. You must be very proud of your brother's talent."

"We are all extremely proud of Nicholas." Her expression dimmed, and she slipped her hand from his. "Papa, is Mary bringing tea?"

"Yes," her brother said. "Sit with us, Clara."

Dare nodded at the composer. "Your newest piece is every bit as good as the *Rondo*. I would be honored if you'd let me debut it."

Miss Becker sat down, rather abruptly, in the chair next to her brother.

"I…" Nicholas Becker's ears turned pink. "Thank you."

"In fact, it brings me to the purpose of my call today. I'd like to engage your services as a composer. You have enormous talent, Mr. Becker. If your work had greater exposure, there would be a piece by Nicholas Becker on every piano in England—the Continent, even." Dare leaned forward, allowing time for the words to sink in, and captured the young man's gaze. "I can provide that exposure. You must come on tour with me."

The composer's eyes widened. Clearly he'd no notion of what Dare had been going to say. Beside him, his sister gripped the wooden arms of her chair until her knuckles turned white.

For a moment Nicholas Becker's mouth gaped, and then he collected himself. "That is most unexpected… and generous of you."

"Generous, but unnecessary." The elder Mr. Becker shook his head, his expression severe. "We thank you for the offer of patronage. Nicholas would be happy to write as many pieces as you'd like and send them along—"

"Send them along?" Dare's hands tightened on his knees. "Mr. Becker, I don't think you understand. I do not merely want to *play* your son's works, I want to build my performances around them. My agent here," he gestured to Peter, "has contacts with reputable publishers of sheet music throughout Europe. They will be eager for the compositions of Nicholas Becker, once they learn that I'm featuring them. The *Rondo* has been tremendously well received. There will be a ready market for his new works, too, as the public becomes familiar with the music through my performances. *Our* performances, for your son is a talented pianist as well." He focused back on the composer. "Think of what we could accomplish."

Dare could not keep the enthusiasm from his voice. Surely they would see how crucial it was that Becker himself be an integral part of the performance? It would be a perfect circle of creative effort. Nicholas Becker heard the notes and set them down, Dare transformed them back into music for the world to hear. Two masters of their craft, working together.

Too, there was the impending specter of the musical duel to be held that spring—but to speak of it now would complicate matters far too much. No, he would master each problem as he came to it. He must add the composer to his tour before proposing more.

Becker flushed and he glanced first at his father, then his sister. A curious expression crossed his face; not the elation Dare had expected to see, but something more troubled.

Whatever the composer's reluctance, Dare was not going to fail now. He nodded to Peter.

"Ahem." His agent opened his satchel and pulled out a sheaf of papers. "Mr. Reynard is prepared to compensate you fairly in exchange for premier performing rights to anything you compose while in his employ. The parties will split publishing royalties for contracts, which I will arrange upon your joint approval." He flipped through the pages. "You will agree to accompany Mr. Reynard on his tour of England and Scotland, with the option to continue, terms to be negotiated, to the Continent, presupposing all parties are satisfied with the initial tour. In addition, all expenses of travel will be paid and you will be fed and housed..." He glanced at the pitifully small huddle of coals on the grate, "...appropriately."

Dare was not so subtle. "With the stipend I pay, you'll be able to move your family out of this house. Think of the comforts you could provide your father and sister. Think how your prospects would change." He paused as a girl carrying a tray entered the room.

"I shall pour out," the sister said, rising to take a cup from the tray. She poured with a steady hand. "Do you take sugar, Mr. Reynard?"

Dare glanced at the chipped bowl holding a few forlorn lumps. "No, thank you."

Despite her calm expression, the surface of the liquid trembled as she handed him his cup.

"Well then, how much?" the father asked. "You have not said how much."

Dare smiled to himself. How quickly the old man had changed his tune. "Ten pounds a week."

The maid dropped the tea tray. The pot and remaining cups, the sad lumps of sugar, the mismatched teaspoons, all crashed to the floor.

Dare leapt up and pulled Miss Becker with him, away from the spatter of scalding liquid and broken shards of porcelain. She half stumbled into his arms. She was soft and feminine—more curved than he would have guessed beneath her worn gown—and he was unexpectedly, blazingly, aware of her as a woman. The feel of her burned through him, hotter than the sear of his tea sloshing over the brim of his cup.

"Mary! Take care," the father said.

"I'm sorry, Mr. Becker." The girl bobbed an abject curtsey. "Mistress, masters." She gathered up the wreckage and hurried through the doorway.

Dare took a deep breath and set Miss Becker at a safe distance. He did not need any more complications in this already fraught negotiation.

"We beg your pardon, sir, most humbly." Nicholas Becker's face was red with mortification. "You are unhurt?"

"It's only tea." Dare placed his cup on the nearby table and shook down his tea-dampened cuff.

Judging from the maid's reaction, the amount he offered was a fantastic sum to the family. No matter. He could afford it, and if the performances were received as well as he expected, he would be rewarded many times over. But the financial return was not what mattered.

"As I was saying." Dare looked directly at the elder Mr. Becker. "Ten pounds a week."

He let the words hang in the air, tempting. The older man's eyes narrowed. Then he glanced at his son and shook his head.

"I am sorry," he said. "It is not possible."

"Fifteen," Dare said.

Beside him, Peter shifted as if he would speak, but Dare kept his focus on Mr. Becker. He would succeed in this.

"Fifteen pounds." Nicholas Becker said the words as if they were a hymn.

"No." The elder Mr. Becker's voice was not so firm, this time.

"Twenty," Dare said. "And that includes payment for serving as my accompanist, as well. It's my final offer."

Miss Becker drew in her breath, and the silence stretched one heartbeat. Two. Dare locked eyes with the old man, willing him to accept.

"Indeed." The father cleared his throat. "You make us an offer that is difficult to refuse."

"But Papa..." Miss Becker took a half step forward, her lips pressed tightly together.

The old man waved her to silence. "Let me think."

Sounds drifted into the room: the high voices of children playing in the street, the distant rumble of carriage wheels. At last the father nodded.

"We will accept your offer, but you will take both my children with you." He thumped his cane for emphasis. "Nicholas and Clara, both."

"Are you quite certain?" Miss Becker asked. Her gray eyes were startled, but behind that shock something flared. Yearning. Hope.

Dare crossed his arms. There were undercurrents here he did not understand; some family secret that lay like a sandbar, treacherously close to the surface. Was it going to wreck his plans on the shoals?

He turned his attention to Miss Becker. She met his gaze for a moment, then flushed and dropped her eyes.

"There is no reason to include Miss Becker in the tour," Dare said. "Much as I dislike to say it, I fear she would be an impediment. Her brother and I will be busy, leaving no time to chaperone. This is not some pleasure jaunt, no Grand Tour of the sights where we will have leisure to squire your daughter about."

"Clara would not expect such a thing," the elder Mr. Becker said. "She will keep herself, and her brother, out of harm's way."

Dare raised one eyebrow. "I don't think that will be necessary."

The composer nervously ran his fingers over the back of the armchair, where the finish had worn off. He cleared his throat and met Dare's eyes.

"I must confess. I recently underwent a… difficult period. Clara helped immensely. I am sure Papa wishes her to come along to help see to my well-being."

His words rang true, and there was a tightness about his eyes that indicated the composer was not yet fully recovered. It would explain the family's reluctance.

"I'll see that you are treated well, Mr. Becker," Dare said. "I understand the volatility of the artistic temperament, and I assure you, your sister's presence is unneeded."

"I must insist." Nicholas Becker's hand stilled, then tightened over the back of the chair. "You will take both of us. Or neither of us."

Dare turned to Miss Becker. There must have been something fierce in his expression, for she took a step back, her eyes wide.

"What do you say?" he demanded. "Do you also insist on coming along?"

There was a flash of something—anger?—in her expression, quickly dampened.

"I stand with my family," she said.

Peter set a calming hand on his arm. "Dare, they have laid out their terms. Do you agree?"

Anger pumped through his blood at the damned stubbornness of the Becker family. Why would they not behave sensibly? Dare blew a breath out his nostrils and forced himself to think, though there was only one answer.

He scowled at Nicholas Becker.

"Your sister's expenses will come out of your weekly stipend," Dare said. "I am paying you well enough. I refuse to be burdened with her needs as well."

The composer swallowed, but he nodded.

"It will do," their father said.

"Peter, change the agreements," Dare said.

This was a displeasing outcome… and yet, he had achieved his goal. Nicholas Becker would be composing for him, touring with him, despite the compromise of dragging the sister along.

Dare turned to the composer. "Peter will take your signature and give you a week's advance. We leave for Brighton in two days. I'll send the coach to collect you. Both of you." His gaze went to where Clara Becker stood, pale hands smoothing her skirts.

Shaking his head, he stalked to the door. He could not stand another instant in this cold, shabby house, dealing with the unmanageable composer and his family. Once they were on tour, Dare's word was law. No matter what Nicholas Becker and his sister might want.

***

Clara turned to her father the moment the door closed behind their extraordinary guest. Her heart pounded with excitement even as her stomach clenched at the thought of everything that could go wrong.

"Papa! How could you agree to send us with him? It's impossible. What if Nicholas—"

"Your brother is recovered," Papa said, his tone harboring no room for argument. "There is no choice, Clara. You know this. We cannot afford to refuse. The two of you either go with the maestro, or we will be on the streets within the month."

She folded her arms around herself, palms flat against her ribs. Papa was right. They had sold everything but the piano, and it was still not enough. Nicholas's students had forsaken him during his dark time. The pittance the publisher paid for her works would not keep them housed and fed.

"It is providence," Papa said. "When fate opens the door, one must be brave enough to walk through."

Clara closed her eyes for a brief moment. The tour offered possibilities she could not have dreamed, along with the potential for even greater disaster.

"It's my fault," Nicholas said, his expression pinched with misery. "If I had been able to keep teaching, we wouldn't be in such straits."

Clara slipped her arm around his shoulders. "It's not your fault. It was difficult even before, remember?"

Their mother's long illness had begun the family's slide into hardship; the ineffectual doctors who still had to be paid, the various medicines that had cost all their savings, but in the end had done little except ease her pain.

Nicholas's descent into black melancholy had only locked a door that had already slammed closed in their faces.

"I'm no composer," her brother said. "We'll be discovered. The pretense, traveling with the maestro…" He shook his head, not bothering to brush away the hair that fell across his eyes.

"You will find a way." Papa held up the bank notes Mr. Widmere had left, and shook them for emphasis. "Twenty pounds a week. Twenty! For that, for our family, you must. The contract is already signed. It is your chance, Nicholas, to bring back what we have lost."

Clara felt her brother shudder, then take a steadying breath. There was no arguing with Papa. He always knew just how to force their agreement.

She wet her lips. "How can we possibly manage it?"

Papa began pacing, the thud of his cane a somber, hollow sound. "Everywhere you go, Nicholas will insist on a suite of rooms. He will keep watch while you write, Clara. Compose at night, in your room." He rounded on them, a fierce light in his eyes. "You must swear to never let Master Reynard, or *anyone*, know. Think of what it would do to him—to us. Discovery now will not be a private scandal. If it is found that Master Reynard is promoting music composed by a *woman*, public opinion will turn against him. He will be disgraced… and we will be ruined. You must ensure that does not happen."

She heard his unspoken command as well. *Watch over Nicholas.*

She would, of course, although there had been very little she'd been able to do for him during his debilitating melancholy. It had taken everything she had to keep him eating, to coax him to rest when she heard him treading the floor through the night, to watch with mounting dismay as he grew listless and haunted.

But he had recovered. He was well now.

"You can do it, Nicholas." She gave his shoulders a gentle squeeze. "I'll be there to help. Besides, you are a wonderful pianist. Imagine how the students will flock to you when you return from touring with the master."

Her brother stared at the floor a moment more, then straightened and pushed the hair from his face. "It is madness, but very well. We'll go with him through England and Scotland."

"You will be home again in six weeks' time," Papa said. "After that, we shall see."

They were going with Darien Reynard. They were going with Darien Reynard!

The reality of it sifted down into her soul and left her trembling. She, Clara Becker, was going to be traveling with the most celebrated musician in the world. He might be insufferably condescending, but she could forgive him. Could even forgive his rudeness to her.

After all, audiences would now hear her music the way she did. How would it feel, night after night, to lay her music in the hands of the master? Her heart twisted at how desperately she wanted it, and at how perfectly perilous their scheme was.

Master Reynard was so vibrant, so very masculine, from the set of his broad shoulders to the determination in his shadowy green eyes. So certain that the world would yield to him.

And she had stumbled against him like the most gauche of schoolgirls. The memory sent an embarrassed, thrilled prickle over her skin. No one in her family seemed to notice that brief, intimate contact before he set her on her feet. Likely he had barely registered it himself. But she felt as though something essential had brushed against her for a moment; some dark, beautiful flame.

The man was arrogant and inflexible, but he was *Darien Reynard.*

"Yes," Nicholas said, with more hope in his voice than she had heard for months. "We are going to Scotland, to make our fortune."

He strode to the hearth, took up the coal bucket, and with a flourish upended it into the fire.

"Nicholas!" she cried, from habit.

A half-bucket of coal was a guilty extravagance. But not any more. She could not help smiling at him.

"We can afford to be warm now." The new coals began to glow and a sudden grin lit his face. "Everything has changed, Clara. Everything!"

He took her hand and pulled her into an impromptu polka. "We are going to Scot-land," he sang as they whirled about the room, "with Darien Rey-nard."

The floorboards creaked under their feet, and Clara laughed, dizzy and breathless. Papa pounded his cane, ostensibly to make them stop, but nonetheless keeping perfect time with their steps.

CHAPTER FIVE

With Master Reynard in London, ladies have been observed going to great lengths to snare his attention. Yesterday, in Hyde Park, Miss L_M_ flung herself into his path; and Lady B_ was spotted tapping at his windowpane in the dead of night—one would hope with no success!
-Tilly's Mayfair Tattler

Clara ran her fingers over the silver-backed hairbrush that had belonged to her mother, then tucked it into her valise. She had packed everything she needed; nearly everything she owned, in truth. Her two everyday dresses, her spare chemise and petticoats, her nightgown. Giving in to vanity, she had purchased new ribbons for her bonnet, though they had taken the last of her coins. She fastened the valise closed, glanced once more about her bare room, and stepped into the hallway.

With a pang, she passed the empty corner where their grandfather clock used to stand. Now they had to rely on the timepiece downstairs, which barely tinkled the hours instead of ringing them out with calm authority.

"Nicholas." She paused beside his half-open door. "Are you ready?"

"Nearly."

She heard him open a drawer, then shut it again with a clunk.

"I'm taking my valise downstairs. Master Reynard's note said ten o'clock, and it's rising the hour."

"I know." The drawer closed with a bit too much force. "I'll be there in a moment."

Soon. Soon. Excitement twined with anxiety, the knotted tension coiling up from the soles of her boots. Every step forward from here would be a step into the unknown.

She had hardly slept the last two nights, trying to imagine what it might be like to tour with such a preeminent musician. Before her brother lost his students, he used to describe the grandiose houses to her, the ease and opulence that were simply a way of life to the gentry.

But Darien Reynard was not mere gentry. No, that was like comparing an eagle to a flock of swans. Which she supposed made her and Nicholas little brown wrens. She could not imagine how they were going to fly.

She hurried down the stairs and set her worn valise in the entryway, just in time to catch the unmistakable clatter of a coach arriving.

It was time.

Fingers suddenly cold, she pulled her gloves on, then tied her bonnet beneath her chin. The fresh blue ribbons formed a crisp bow, distracting from the faded brim—at least, she hoped so. Through the parlor window she glimpsed the coach door swing wide.

"Nicholas!" she called up the stairs, then pulled their front door open. A cold breeze rushed inside, the west wind shivering beneath low gray clouds.

A figure emerged from the vehicle and her breath stilled. But no. The slight, dapper-looking gentleman could never be confused with Master Reynard. She waited, but no one else stepped out of the coach.

She breathed a sigh of relief, like a marionette whose strings had suddenly gone slack. The maestro had not come to fetch them himself. Of course not. Instead there was this fellow, dressed with fastidious elegance in checked trousers, a russet coat, and a striking green cravat. He had a thin, beakish nose with large nostrils, and bright brown eyes that assessed her as he strutted up to their door, his ebony walking stick tucked under his arm.

When he reached the entryway he swept off his top hat, made not of the usual beaver, but some odd, silvery fur. He made her an extravagant bow, one foot pointed and extended before him.

"Miss Becker, I presume?" His voice bore a Continental accent.

French, perhaps?

She nodded, unable to muster a reply. Should she curtsey? Was there a certain type of curtsey that answered such a bow? If so, she had already failed the first test, and she had not even stepped out her own front door.

"I am Henri Dubois." He paused, as if expecting some sort of recognition. When none was forthcoming, he gave a shrug and continued. "Monsieur Reynard sent me to gather you and your brother. You are ready?"

"Ah..." She glanced over her shoulder to see Nicholas descending the stairs, his expression quiet and determined. "Yes. We are ready."

The fellow bowed, from the waist this time, and smiled at her brother. "You are the composer, I presume? A pleasure to make your acquaintance."

Papa stumped in from the parlor, and the Frenchman again doffed his hat and introduced himself. He glanced about the entryway, and Clara guessed his sharp gaze missed very little.

"If you are ready to depart," he said to Nicholas, "I will summon the footman to bring your trunks down."

"Our... trunks?" Nicholas shot her a sidelong look.

"Yes, yes." Mr. Dubois beckoned to the servant waiting beside the vehicle. "We must load the coach and be off. One does not keep Darien Reynard waiting."

"But we don't—" she began.

Papa stepped forward. He nodded to Clara's valise, then the traveling case beside Nicholas. "This is all they will bring. A footman is not needed."

"This? This is your luggage for a month of travel?" Henri Dubois's brows climbed alarmingly high, then snapped back down into a frown. With the tip of his walking stick he prodded Clara's worn valise as if were a dead thing. "No, no. It will not do."

"It will have to," Papa said, ignoring the man's disbelief.

Clara gave Mr. Dubois a rueful smile. "Perhaps we can add to our wardrobes as we travel, if necessary."

"If necessary! What do you have in there—a change of

stockings? But now, we must go. Say your farewells." He turned to the burly footman. "Take our guests' handbags. And pray, do not strain yourself."

Mr. Dubois followed the servant out to the coach. A tremor of fear, of lightness, ran through Clara. She turned to Papa and kissed his cheek.

"Be well while we're gone. We'll be home before you miss us. And don't chastise Cousin Mary. I've instructed her to feed you amply and keep the house as warm as she likes."

"Hmph. Impractical." His voice was gruff. "Write me of your travels. Look after your brother. And Clara, both of you," he gripped her arm, "be careful."

"We will, Papa."

"Don't worry." Nicholas shook his father's hand, then let Clara precede him down the walk.

Mr. Dubois was beckoning to them from inside the coach. "Come, come."

Her boots felt soled with lead as Nicholas handed her up into the vehicle. Everything was illuminated with a dreamlike quality: the gleaming lamp sconces, the luxurious leather seats, the gold tassels on either side of the curtains. The interior smelled of polish and privilege. Nicholas settled beside her and she reached for his hand, seeking the one thing that was familiar.

Across from them, Mr. Dubois gave a satisfied nod. As the coach rolled into motion, he closed his eyes, and to all appearances began to nap.

Clara pushed aside the blue velvet curtain at the window and gave Papa a final wave. Their father silently held up one hand, then leaned on his cane, his expression settling back into its usual stern lines. She turned on the seat, watching his motionless figure grow smaller, until they rounded the corner and she could no longer see him at all. She let the swath of velvet fall closed.

They were truly embarked now.

She felt as though she were enclosed in a small, elegant boat. The familiar landmarks slipped away, and she was unmoored, carried along by currents she could not chart. Where would they sleep this night? What would the next month hold? She had very little idea of the towns and cities they were due to visit. Scotland itself seemed very foreign and far away.

Soon enough, Master Reynard would join them. That was the most unsettling thought of all. She twisted her bonnet ribbons between her fingers, keeping time to the rough rhythm of the coach wheels. Mr. Dubois seemed well asleep as the vehicle jolted through the streets of London, conveying them to wherever the maestro was waiting.

She tilted toward her brother, keeping her voice low. "How soon until we arrive, do you think?"

"Let's see where we are." Nicholas pulled the curtain on his side of the coach and secured it open with the gold-tasseled cord. He was more familiar than she with the genteel areas where his former students dwelt.

The neighborhood they were passing through was very different from their own. The streets were cleaner, the buildings more imposing and well kept, the colors brighter. Clara blinked at the violet and scarlet-striped skirts of a passing lady, the colors echoed in her frilled parasol. It was noisier too, the air filled with the clatter of metal-bound wheels over cobblestones, the calls of vendors echoing over the bustle.

"Darien Reynard will be at Mivart's Hotel," her brother said. "Unless he's staying with an earl or some such. In any case, we're heading into Mayfair."

Mayfair. She pulled back her curtain and peered out the window.

They turned a corner, past ornate lamp posts and a swath of green park. Fashionably dressed gentlemen strolled with ladies turned out in stylish perfection from the toes of their shining buttoned boots to the ostrich plumes adorning their high-brimmed bonnets. Clara glanced down at the simple wool of her best gown, the toes of her boots scuffed despite extra coats of polish. They had done the best they could, but it was laughably pathetic—she could see that now.

The graceful terrace houses outside the window began to pass more and more slowly, until finally the coach came to a swaying halt.

"Ah." Mr. Dubois's eyes snapped open. "We have arrived." He brushed invisible lint from the front of his coat. "Remain here. I will inform Monsieur Reynard."

The footman opened the door with a flourish, and Mr. Dubois stepped out. Clara could see him looking archly to either side before entering the gracious building before them.

"Mivart's," Nicholas said. "The best hotel in all of London. Just think, Clara, we'll be staying in places like this as we travel. Can you imagine it?"

"Well, I don't suppose Darien Reynard is planning to house us in the stables. A fine thing that would be, you performing with straw in your hair." She had to smile at the notion; a welcome distraction from the flutter in her stomach.

Though she wasn't so certain the master would be displeased to see *her* bedded down in the straw.

Her brother shook his head at her, the ghost of laughter in his eyes.

"Make way!"

It was Mr. Dubois again, at the head of a cavalcade of uniformed servants bearing trunks and boxes. He led them straight to the coach. The vehicle tipped and tilted as the men began loading the boot and roof.

She was beginning to understand Mr. Dubois's shock, if this was the quantity of luggage he considered normal.

"It's… rather a lot, isn't it?" she asked.

"Darien Reynard tours for months at a time," Nicholas said, as if he were a well-traveled fellow in his own right. "He must bring everything he needs."

She refrained from pointing out that everything *they* needed fit into two small cases.

The activity drew curious glances. When Master Reynard himself appeared at the top of the steps, a crowd immediately gathered.

He was dressed in elegant black, his violin case in one hand. Dark hair framed a face that even without the patina of fame would have been captivating. His strong jaw and sensuous mouth, the faint line between his brows, and his eyes, a particular shadowy green... Would her breath always catch at the sight of him?

With the lift of a hand and a warm smile, he acknowledged his well-wishers and made his way through the admiring throng. He strode to the coach and mounted the steps. A final wave to the crowd, and then he ducked into the vehicle, settling across from Clara and her brother.

"Good morning, Mr. Becker, Miss Becker." He stowed his violin beneath the seat, then sat back. "I trust you're ready to begin our adventure together."

Clara nodded, her voice trapped behind her teeth. That smile, when seen up close, had a rather disturbing effect on her senses. She did not remember him smiling like that before—except, perhaps, at the moment of her family's capitulation. By then she had been too stunned to be much affected by it.

Mr. Dubois hopped into the vehicle and swung the door closed behind him. He nodded at Clara and Nicholas.

"Just look at them," he said. "It is as I have told you."

Master Reynard glanced at her brother, then folded his arms. "My valet informs me there is a problem with your luggage."

"Ah—" Nicholas began.

"Indeed," Mr. Dubois said. "The fact that they have *none*. It simply won't do."

"Your valet?" Clara blinked at the dapper fellow.

"Of course." Master Reynard's tone was wry. "Whom else could I trust to ensure I'm properly turned out for every occasion?"

"No one." Mr. Dubois spoke the words with complete assurance. "But these two ragamuffins—they will not reflect well upon you."

Master Reynard considered for a moment, his gaze growing sharper as he looked first at Nicholas, and then at her. Heat flamed her cheeks as he studied her. Her Sunday best was no match for the understated elegance of his own attire or the fashionable flair of Mr. Dubois. The valet was right. She and Nicholas would be an embarrassment. She glanced out the window at two well-to-do misses in lace-edged walking dresses.

Master Reynard shook his head, a sharp gesture of impatience. "I suppose we'll have to make a detour. Bond Street is just ahead. Henri? No doubt you have a suggestion."

"Yes, of course." Anticipation lit the small man's face. "Weston's for Mr. Becker, to be sure."

"But..." Nicholas shifted uncomfortably beside her. "Isn't he the tailor to the *king*?"

"He is," Mr. Dubois said. "And now he will have the good fortune to be the tailor to the soon-to-be renowned composer, Mr. Nicholas Becker."

CHAPTER SIX

London sighs at the departure of Master Reynard. Lucky Brighton, to be the next stop on the maestro's tour of England. Come back to us soon, Darien Reynard!

-Tilly's Mayfair Tattler

Two hours later, they stepped out of the polished interior of Weston's. Nicholas wore a new suit of clothes that fit him better than anything he had ever owned before, and Clara thought he looked quite handsome. How clever of the tailor, to have a number of coats and trousers partially made up for customers who needed an immediate change of dress.

Of course, she imagined the king would brook very little delay for himself or his courtiers, should any of them desire a new outfit.

"You are entirely satisfactory, Mr. Becker." Mr. Dubois gave a sharp nod of approval.

Nicholas ran one hand down the dove-gray wool, his grin rather spoiling the impression of an effete young gentleman of the *ton*.

"I believe my two new suits will do very well," he said.

"They will have to suffice until the rest of your wardrobe catches up with the tour," Mr. Dubois said. "Certainly your trunks will arrive in time for the performance in Brighton."

"Speaking of which," Master Reynard said, "here's the coach now. We should be on our way."

Mr. Dubois cleared his throat and glanced pointedly at Clara. "We are not quite ready to depart, monsieur."

Annoyance flashed in the master's eyes. Clearly he had forgotten or ignored the fact that she, too, was in need of new clothing.

"What do you propose, Henri?" he asked. "We haven't much

time."

Clara folded her arms over her worn woolen gown. Half of her wanted to stubbornly insist they depart London immediately, that she would make do with her paltry handful of dresses and petticoats. But Mr. Dubois was correct. Her poor dress would reflect badly upon the tour, and thus upon Nicholas.

Darien Reynard's presence on the street was not going unremarked. As the genteel bustle of pedestrians caught sight of him, they slowed, their whispers buzzing like bees. The sun slid out from behind a cloud, and the rows of fashionable shops shone, their windows dazzlingly bright, the gilt lettering above their doors sparkling. Clara caught sight of herself reflected in the pane of Weston's: a pale-haired girl, unremarkable in her limp bonnet— despite the new ribbons.

The reflection also showed the crowd gathering as more people veered toward Master Reynard. The ladies were chirping with excitement, and the men swept off their hats and bowed to catch his attention.

"Mr. Reynard!"

"How fortunate that you have graced London with your inspiration."

"Oh, come see, it *is* him. No one else has a coach like that one."

Mr. Dubois leaned close to his employer. "Madame Lamond's is nearby. But perhaps we would be better off in the coach."

Master Reynard nodded, and tipped his hat to his admirers. "I agree," he said in a voice pitched only to their ears. "Into the coach. Now."

Mr. Dubois gestured for the footman to open the doors and set the steps. He took Clara by the elbow and assisted her into the vehicle, but the speculative voices of the crowd still reached her ears.

"Whoever might *that* be?"

"Surely Master Reynard would not escort a doxy so openly about the streets of Mayfair."

"He is far too refined to do so. And that… person… is certainly the opposite of refined!"

Titters of laughter accompanied the words. Face flaming, Clara scooted back on the seat until her shoulders met the padded cushions, letting the coach shield her from the sidelong glances and sharp tongues.

Nicholas sat beside her and covered her gloved hand with his own in silent sympathy. She could not help noticing how dingy her glove was, beneath the pristine whiteness of his new one.

Outside the coach, Master Reynard raised his voice. "I regret I must bid you farewell. We have an appointment to keep."

Disappointment riffled through the crowd, but he mounted the steps, lifted his hand, and ducked into the coach. The footman closed the door immediately, no doubt well used to such crowds and the master's need to extricate himself from them.

Clara kept her gaze fixed firmly on her knees, and the *unrefined* gown that covered them. Well then. She and Nicholas had known they were unprepared for the world Darien Reynard inhabited. The unkind words could not hurt her, and it was foolish to let them keep twisting and writhing in her stomach. Still, she could not venture a glance at the musician seated across from her. Had he heard the insinuations? Would he think even less of her, after hearing such things?

If so, he showed no indication of it. His long fingers drummed on the cushion, and he did not glance at her with either scorn or disdain. For all she could tell, she was invisible to him—a speck of dust or small, buzzing fly. Inconvenient, perhaps, but easily ignored.

The injustice stung her heart, and she turned her gaze out the window, pretending to admire the view.

Soon enough, the coach reached their destination. They alighted from the vehicle in front of a shop with *Madame Lamond* spelled out in curling golden script upon the dark blue door. When Master Reynard made no move to enter the modiste's, Mr. Dubois arched his eyebrows, his nostrils thinning with disapproval.

"It would be best if you attended, Monsieur Reynard," the valet said. "The results will be much more easily accomplished in your presence."

Master Reynard frowned, but stepped forward.

"Very well," he said, "but if I am trapped into going, Mr. Becker must come, too."

"Certainly," Nicholas said. "But please, call me Nicholas. Mr. Becker is my father. It feels beyond strange to hear that name addressed to me."

"You'll become accustomed to it," Master Reynard said.

Taking Clara by the arm, Mr. Dubois ushered her into Madame Lamond's. The shop smelled of roses and silk, and Clara blinked at the lustrous bolts of cloth displayed about the room. Once again the enormity of their change in station struck her, adding a tight hitch to her breath.

The bell over the door tinkled with their entrance, and a handful of stunningly dressed ladies turned to regard them. Their gazes slid dismissively over Clara and fastened on the gentlemen behind her. Most especially on Darien Reynard. They moved toward him in a cluster, a handsome blonde woman in the lead, who halted so close that her skirts crowded Clara's own drab gown. The woman laid her hand on his arm, her eyelashes fluttering.

"My dear Master Reynard! Such a delight to encounter you again, after our lovely interlude last year. I hope you will be in London long enough to..." She leaned forward, her voice dropping, "...repeat it."

"Lady Barlow." Master Reynard inclined his head. "Though nothing would give me greater pleasure than to take tea with you again, I'm sorry to say I am leaving town directly."

Clara did not think he sounded sorry in the least. The other ladies giggled behind their gloved hands, and Lady Barlow's smile veered into a pout. Her sharp blue eyes fastened on Clara.

"And who is this?" Her voice was sugary, but Clara heard the blade beneath. "What an *unusual* style of dress. Is she Irish?"

The watchers laughed again, though this time Clara was on the receiving end of that barbed mirth. She lifted her chin. Whether anyone knew it or not, s*he* wrote the music Darien Reynard used to dazzle the world. She would ignore the cuts and slights, and armor her soul with the secret of her talent.

"Excuse us." The master picked Lady Barlow's hand off his sleeve. "Is Madame Lamond available?"

"Master Reynard!" A curtain at the back opened, and a thin-faced woman emerged. She hurried forward and made him a brief curtsy. "I am at your service, sir."

"I do not doubt it," he said. "But I defer to Mr. Dubois to inform you of the particulars."

"Henri, my darling!" The modiste turned to Mr. Dubois, kissing the air to either side of his face. "How kind of you to visit my humble shop, though it is the best one can find outside Paris, you must agree. Now, who is this beauty you have brought to me?"

"Allow me to introduce Miss Clara Becker," Mr. Dubois said. "Sister to this gentleman here, the composer Nicholas Becker."

"Indeed," Master Reynard nodded. "Mr. Becker is a man of rare talent, whose works I will soon be featuring in all my performances."

The announcement sent a rush of whispers through the elegant ladies, and Lady Barlow's expression took on a decidedly acquisitive cast. Clara did not like the way the woman was eyeing Nicholas.

"Very nice to meet you both," the modiste said. "The whole town is talking of last night's concert, but I am sure you did not come here to discuss music. Now, what do you require?"

"Not much," Clara began.

"Everything," Mr. Dubois said.

"And when will you need this everything?" Madame Lamond asked.

"We depart London this afternoon," Master Reynard said. "I have every faith in your abilities, madame."

"This afternoon?" A wash of panic colored Madame Lamond's careful accent. "But... you ask much of me, maestro."

Clara sent Madame Lamond a sympathetic glance. The gentlemen obviously had no notion of the amount of work that went into making a dress—especially the complex and fashionable gowns the town ladies were wearing.

"Henri insists you are the very best modiste in all London," Master Reynard said. "I believe we must have a private word, madame. Excuse me, Miss Becker, gentlemen."

He took the modiste by the elbow and guided her past the full-length mirrors and books of the latest fashion plates. Once they had gained some distance, he bent and whispered in her ear. Whatever he said made Madame Lamond cover her mouth with her hand and laugh as though he had suggested something improper. Clara strained to make out what they were saying, but the two were speaking too softly.

Another exchange, then Madame Lamond nodded and they returned to where Clara waited with her brother and Mr. Dubois.

The modiste studied Clara for a long moment, tapped at her cheek with one finger, then gave a decisive nod.

"Yes," she said. "We can take in the waist and lengthen the hem. And the blue of the silk will complement her eyes."

"Not blue silk like you are using for my dress, I should hope," Lady Barlow said, clearly unashamed to admit to eavesdropping.

"Of course not," Master Reynard said, a glint of amusement in his eyes. "It will not be silk *like* your dress at all."

Mr. Dubois cleared his throat, covering what sounded suspiciously like a snort of laughter.

"You see, maestro," he said, "your presence is invaluable."

"Out, gentlemen!" Madame Lamond made a shooing motion. "Before you cause a riot in my store."

Master Reynard bowed. "We shall not encumber your genius any longer, but expect us to return within an hour and a quarter. Our journey to Brighton cannot be further delayed."

He, Nicholas, and Mr. Dubois made for the door. The shop quieted as the ladies, led by Lady Barlow, followed the gentlemen out. Clara watched them go, hoping Nicholas could hold his own in such company.

"Come, Miss Becker," Madame Lamond said. "We have not a moment to waste."

The modiste immediately set her seamstresses to altering a beautiful blue silk gown that looked ready to hang in someone else's wardrobe. Lady Barlow's, if Clara did not miss her guess. She was gratified, in a hot and unkind sort of way.

Madame Lamond produced new undergarments for Clara, then measured her and turned her about. Clara stood in nothing but her stockings and new silken chemise as partially made dresses went on and off her again with such smooth velocity she could scarcely keep count. The next hour was a blur of gorgeous fabrics, bloused sleeves, and necklines trimmed with lace. The modiste and two of her assistants were never still. One of the girls furiously ripped out seams while the other sewed new ones. Their scissors and needles darted, flashing like nimble fish in shimmering seas of fabric.

"Let us see how the fit is," Madame Lamond said at last, holding the blue silk dress for Clara to step into. The assistants buttoned her and adjusted the skirts while the modiste stood back to view their handiwork.

Another of her girls hurried over. "Madame, Master Reynard and his companions have returned."

"They may wait," Madame Lamond said. She turned her full attention back to Clara, and gave a satisfied nod. "Lovely. The dress suits you to perfection—as if it had been made for you from the first. Now, a touch of rouge, a little color for the lips. Hold still, yes, like that. And *voila!* Come, slip your dreadful boots on. Dear, dear, those need replacing as well. There is a mirror in the corner."

Clara followed, doing her best to manage the fuller skirts and sleeves. Madame Lamond positioned her before the full-length mirror in an ornate gilded frame.

"Look," the modiste said.

Clara did—and blinked at what she saw.

Someone she hardly recognized blinked back. Her reflection's eyes were wide and luminous, the hue of the dress a perfect complement to her fair coloring.

"I…" She set a hand to her cheek, and the elegant woman in the mirror mimicked the action. "Heavens."

It had never occurred to her that she could look so fashionable, as though she were ready to waltz around a grand ballroom or take tea with a duchess. The simple circlet of her braided hair seemed queenly rather than quaint. Her gold locket glowed serenely against the fine fabric, and the fashionable cut of the dress accentuated her curves. She had not realized quite how slender her waist could appear, or how full her hips.

She felt, in a word, beautiful. Breathless delight ran through her.

She, Clara Becker, looked beautiful. How shocking. How wonderful.

"It's splendid." She turned to Madame Lamond, her voice warm with gladness. "I cannot thank you enough."

"Well now." The woman smiled like a cat who had been in the cream. "You are made to wear such gowns, Miss Becker. I have a hundred clients who would pay a king's ransom to look as well as you do."

"Indeed!" Mr. Dubois approached, with the modiste's girl trailing behind. "She looks exquisite. Madame Lamond, you have worked a miracle. I, of course, expected no less."

Madame Lamond blushed. "Mr. Dubois, you are too kind. We had excellent material to work with. Please tell Master Reynard the rest of Miss Becker's wardrobe will be dispatched the moment everything is complete."

"Good, good. Come along, Miss Becker. The maestro and your brother await."

With a final, grateful smile at the modiste, Clara followed Mr. Dubois out of the fitting area. She kept her back very straight, as befitted her new gown. He led her to a side room equipped with a handful of chairs, where Nicholas and Master Reynard waited; Nicholas sitting patiently while the master paced.

"Gentlemen!" Mr. Dubois announced. "Allow me to present Miss Clara Becker."

"I say." Nicholas rose abruptly from his chair. "Clara, you look…"

"Magnificent!" The valet set his hands on his hips and nodded. "I knew Madame Lamond was the right choice. She is *always* the right choice."

Master Reynard strode up to her, then halted. Their gazes locked, and her pulse magnified to a heady, rushing rhythm. The surprise in his face turned to something more considering, as if he saw in her the woman she had glimpsed in the modiste's mirror. Lovely. Elegant. Desirable.

"Miss Becker." He slowly looked her up and down, and she felt a tingle in the wake of his gaze. "Quite a transformation."

"Turn, turn." Mr. Dubois made a twirling gesture with his hand.

Clara untangled her gaze from Darien Reynard's and spun, skirts and petticoats swishing about her. Then she spun again for the pure joy of being beautiful and admired and dressed in something that was gorgeously new.

"The rest of her wardrobe will follow, monsieur," Mr. Dubois said. "Everything is arranged."

"So it appears." Master Reynard's gaze drifted over her once more. "And now, with your permission, Henri, I think it's high time we departed London."

CHAPTER SEVEN

When they exited the modiste's Dare was relieved to find there was no gaggle of women waiting to pounce. At least there was some benefit to the drizzle spattering from the gray clouds overhead. His black coach waited; the driver, Samuel, hunched in his greatcoat, the luggage well-girded against the weather. At last, they were ready to set off.

Although—he slanted a look at Clara Becker—he could no longer begrudge the delay. She had turned out to be remarkably pretty, and he felt a twinge of remorse for overlooking it. Had he not, himself, been the victim of being judged by his appearance? When he was younger, passersby in the piazza had not even deigned to glance at him, until he'd begun to play. Then the ragged boy was suddenly valuable, although nothing inside him had changed.

His valet made to clamber up on the box with the driver, and Dare snagged his arm.

"No, Henri, you will not ride up front. It's five hours to Brighton, and it's raining."

"But, monsieur, your dignity—"

"Will suffer even more if you fall ill and are unable to dress me satisfactorily." Dare waved at the coach, gleaming blackly with a thin slick of moisture. "If you insist, you may clamber up with Samuel outside of Brighton. Now get in, before we are all soaked through."

Henri blew a breath from his nostrils but complied, taking a place in the far corner. Nicholas stepped into the coach after him, and Dare offered Miss Becker his hand. A blush colored her cheeks as she accepted his assistance into the vehicle.

Miss Clara Becker was lovely, and it complicated matters more than Dare would like. When he could simply think of her as the composer's drab sister, it was easy to relegate her to the fringe of his awareness. But now she was a luminous star rising on the horizon.

She settled her skirts, and Dare took the seat across from her. He couldn't ask Henri to switch, nor Nicholas—it would be too odd a request and he could not give them any good reason. The fact that he found Miss Becker attractive was something he could never breathe a hint of, especially to her brother.

Damnation. He'd known he should never have agreed to allow her to come along on the tour. The last time he'd traveled with a woman...

His throat tightened with loss. Francesca's face rose in his memory, dark-eyed and anguished. Swallowing, Dare banished the memories. That was the past, and the truth was he must travel with Miss Becker for the next few weeks. Surely he could manage that much without revealing his sudden attraction.

***

In the closeness of the coach Clara found it impossible to ignore Darien Reynard's presence. The force of his personality seemed to magnetize the air, filling it with invisible currents of attraction. He sat directly opposite her, one long leg stretched out so the tip of his boot nearly brushed the hem of her new gown. When she stole a glance at his face, she saw he was watching her, his green eyes brooding.

His lips were set in a firm line, and though there was no sign of displeasure in his expression, there was little of pleasure, either. Instead, he studied her as though she were an unexpected dissonance in the score of his life; different, possibly unpleasant, yet unmistakably interesting.

She craved and feared his notice in equal measure. Part of her yearned for him to see *her*, Clara the musician; dared him to look past his assumptions and impatience and recognize who she truly was.

Yet that way lay danger and ruin. Better to be the unwanted sister of the composer, no matter how the charade smoldered in her chest and charred the edges of her heart. It was only for a handful of weeks. She and Nicholas could bear up for that long, for Papa's sake.

The excitement and trepidation of leaving London mixed with the unsettling effect of Darien's observation, until Clara could scarcely draw a breath. Her ribs were tight, and dizzy confusion raced through her blood.

She dropped her gaze to his elegant hands, the fingers that coaxed such brilliance from his violin. They drummed softly against the seat. Was he hearing music even now, swirling in the air around them?

She was; a melody poignant with deep shadows and a high, breathless descant. Her fingers itched to write the music down, but she would make do by scribing the notes in her mind.

The coach bobbed over a rough patch of road, rustling the copy of the *Times* Mr. Dubois was reading. After Master Reynard had ordered him into the coach, the valet had taken his place and then, in silent rebuke, immersed himself in the newspaper.

Beside her, Nicholas leaned forward, his posture earnest. "Mr. Reynard, we—"

"No need to thank me further," the master said. "Tell me about what you are working on, your newest composition."

Clara felt her brother stiffen beside her.

"I, well…" Nicholas coughed into his fist. "As you recall, the *Air in E minor* was only just completed. As for what is next, it depends on where inspiration strikes." He grimaced, though she supposed he had meant it as a smile.

Ha. Inspiration was everywhere, and if it was shy, well, one had to take it by the elusive tail and haul it forth. She resisted the urge to kick her brother in the ankle. Master Reynard would think it odd.

The master raised one eyebrow. "I've no doubt you'll find ample inspiration in our travels."

"Of course." Nicholas turned to her with a strained expression. "Don't you agree, Clara?"

She pursed her lips and let doubt raise her brows. But at the look of panic in his eyes she relented.

"Yes," she said. "A new melody is waiting for you even now. I just know it."

When they arrived in Brighton she would smuggle her notebook out of her reticule and jot the tune down, somewhere unobserved.

"I would expect nothing less. I'll need a number of new pieces to premiere, after all." Master Reynard glanced at Clara. "As I recall, you were at my London performance."

It was not a question, and Clara wondered if he had actually seen her in the box, beside her brother. She nodded, the memory of the music that night striking her, so that the golden curtain of his celebrity fell once more between them.

"It was a splendid concert," she said, then fumbled to a halt.

"That last passage in the Beethoven especially," Nicholas added. "What about your accompanist, and Mr. Widmere… will they be joining us?"

"Peter has gone ahead to make arrangements. He'll meet us in Brighton and ensure all is satisfactory before proceeding again." A flicker of a smile brushed Master Reynard's lips. "You could say he is always one step ahead of me."

Nicholas smiled back. "As long as he is not one behind."

"No, he is far too skilled at his job for that. He also arranges for accompanists in the cities we pass through. Although *you* will accompany me on your own compositions, as we discussed previously. I would like to begin working on the *Air.*"

Clara felt a bitter twist at the words. She wished she could play her pieces with Darien Reynard, but it was not to be. And truly, Nicholas was an accomplished pianist. He would do well by her music.

"When is our first performance?" Nicholas asked. "It's not tonight, is it?"

His voice squeaked up at the end, and Clara shared his stab of fear. They were not ready!

"No," Master Reynard said. "I prefer to arrive the day before any performance, and Peter insists upon it, in case of delays in travel. We'll be playing one night in Brighton, then moving on for a concert in Southampton, then three nights in Bath, and farther north from there. Peter can provide you an exact itinerary, if you wish."

"Ah… certainly." Nicholas blinked.

Clara laced her gloved fingers together. Somehow, hearing the master's casual listing brought the enormity of their situation to the fore again. They were actually touring. With Darien Reynard.

"You'll grow accustomed to it, Nicholas." Master Reynard's voice was even, though a distant melancholy shadowed his eyes. "Soon you'll feel as though this coach is more home than anywhere else."

"How sad," Clara said, then bit her tongue. What an idiotic thing to say. Even if it were true. "That is… it's quite an elegant coach. Very lovely."

She glanced about the lavish interior; everywhere but at Darien Reynard. A snort of laughter issued from behind Mr. Dubois's paper. The pages rustled suspiciously, but his bright-eyed face did not appear.

"Clara." Her brother gave her an unobtrusive pinch on the arm. Painful, but well deserved.

"It's tragic, I know." Master Reynard sounded amused, though there was a shade of regret behind the words; the way a sprightly tune set in a minor key still carried the flavor of sorrow.

At this, Mr. Dubois set down his paper. He was smiling, as she had suspected. "Why then, monsieur, we must simply fit the coach up with a bed and washstand, and you will not have to stay in those beastly hotels any longer. Such a hardship, this life."

"When I was at the start of my career, I slept in far worse. You would have been horrified, Henri."

"I have no interest in hearing of it." Mr. Dubois winked at Clara, then snapped his paper up, leaving the conversation to them once more.

"I would like to hear of it," Nicholas said.

The time passed quickly as Darien Reynard told his stories, prompted by Nicholas. It was a clever way of keeping the maestro from asking further questions, and she admired her brother for thinking of it. Beyond that, it was fascinating to hear the master speak of the places he'd visited, his various adventures and misadventures. Occasionally he would catch himself, with a glance at her, and she suspected he was editing out his wilder exploits. Still, it was obvious Master Reynard had met with success in all aspects of his life.

Except, perhaps, those that included a home. And love.

Only once did he mention a woman: an Italian opera singer with whom he toured for some time. His voice had softened when he spoke of her, but then had grown hard again and he'd quickly passed on to other subjects. Had Signora Contini broken his heart? Clara could scarcely imagine it. Master Reynard seemed arrogantly invulnerable.

No, the only broken hearts were the ones he left strewn behind him as he toured the Continent.

Rain spattered against the coach windows, and Clara let out a silent sigh. She had seen little of the countryside, just glimpses of green fields and weathered stone walls between the squalls veiling the landscape. What was the point of being outside of London if she couldn't enjoy new sights?

As suddenly as it had started, the rain ceased. Ahead, she spotted the dark shapes of church spires, spearing the silver-lit clouds floating above.

"I see a town," she said, unable to suppress the catch of excitement in her voice.

"Brighton," Master Reynard said.

"High time." Mr. Dubois folded his paper away. "Fond as you are of the carriage, monsieur, can you bear to stay in the hovel that is the Royal York Hotel this evening?"

The master shot his valet a glance, but did not respond. Instead, he directed their attention out the window.

"The Royal Pavilion will be in view soon," he said. "Some call it a folly of the worst order, others declare it a masterwork of architecture."

"If one is drawn to vulgar excesses," Mr. Dubois added, though

Clara noticed his gaze, too, was fixed on the sights of Brighton.

She set her gloved fingertips to the rain-dappled glass. Outside, an exotic fantasia of domes and spires and latticework reached palely into the sky, surrounded by gardens that were lush even in such a bedraggled season. It was extravagant beyond words, this palace built by the late king when he served as regent for his mad father. She could not imagine what it would be like to set foot in that place. Like visiting fairyland, perhaps.

"We have a command performance there tomorrow afternoon for the king," Master Reynard said, as casually as if he were announcing a stroll in the park.

Clara whipped her head around to stare at him, her heartbeat stuttering, then racing forward in double time.

"The… the king?" Nicholas sounded as though he could barely breathe.

"Yes." The master smiled at Nicholas, no doubt in an attempt to be reassuring. "His youngest daughter is going to be married at the Pavilion. Most of the court has assembled in her honor, despite the fact she's a FitzClarence."

"The queen has been very kind to his illegitimate children," Mr. Dubois said. "She has a good heart, that one."

Clara blinked. They were speaking of the King and Queen of England as if—as if they were simply neighbors one gossiped about.

"Never fear, Nicholas," Master Reynard said. "There will be a piano at the hotel. Peter sees to such things. We'll have ample opportunity to practice."

"I'm not certain there are hours enough in my lifetime for me to feel ready to play before the king," Nicholas said, expression taut. "The *king*."

Clara mastered her own apprehension and gave his hand a reassuring squeeze. "Don't worry. Everyone will be watching Master Reynard."

"It will only be one piece, and you are a fine pianist," the master said. "But I'll do my best to perform with extra zeal and flamboyance."

"Perhaps you should wear a red velvet coat, as well," Mr. Dubois said, his large nostrils flaring with distaste.

"An excellent thought!" Mischief played about the corners of Master Reynard's lips. "Embroidered with peacock feathers. You *did* pack such a coat, didn't you Henri?"

Outrage lifted the valet's eyebrows, and Darien Reynard laughed, a warm, low laugh that invited them to join in. It was a laugh that resonated through Clara, a molasses-coated sound, slow and sweet and dark.

Mr. Dubois frowned at his employer as the carriage slowed. "Monsieur, I do wish you had allowed me to sit up front with the driver."

Master Reynard smiled slightly at his valet, then turned to the carriage door as the footman swung it open.

A gust of fresh, salted air blew inside, like nothing Clara had ever smelled before. She inhaled deeply, tasting the tang of adventure on the back of her tongue. Despite her worry for Nicholas and the upcoming performance, she felt something within her take wing.

The carriage was drawn up before a grand four-storied hotel. Gray and white gulls wheeled overhead, and a shining swath of rumpled water gleamed from between the buildings. The sea!

She longed to leap from the vehicle and run—most unladylike—past the hotel and down to the shore, where that great hushing expanse of water beckoned to her. Was it truly full of salt? Would she see fantastical creatures of the ocean leaping and dipping through the waves?

Already the sound of the sea was moving through her in the beginning of a counterpoint, the cries of the gulls transmuting to melody. For a moment she heard Darien Reynard playing his violin, soaring on the high notes while the piano murmured and sighed like the waves behind.

Inspiration indeed.

"Clara? Are you coming?" Nicholas had disembarked and was holding out his hand.

She blinked from her reverie. Gathering her skirts, she took her brother's hand and stepped out of the carriage. Immediately a liveried attendant held a large black umbrella over her, despite the fact the rain was down to a mere sprinkling. Each of them had their own attendant, though Mr. Dubois moved so quickly to the door of the hotel that his man was forced to sprint to keep pace.

"Come," Master Reynard said. "We'll get settled, and then rehearse."

He turned away from the carriage, where the luggage was already half unloaded by yet another set of servants, and Clara and her brother followed him into the hotel.

Thick carpet muffled their footsteps as they stepped into the quiet lobby. An enormous crystal and gold chandelier descended from the ceiling, and the scent of lemon oil and flowers infused the air. They were ushered by their attendants up a magnificent flight of stairs and along a short hallway, where Clara and Nicholas were directed to their suite of rooms.

"I'm just along the way, in the master suite," Darien Reynard said. "If Peter has done his job, which I've no doubt he has, there will be a piano. Come in half an hour, Mr. Becker."

Nicholas nodded, and they watched Master Reynard proceed down the hall. His stride was free and confident, as though he were the master of the hotel and the town of Brighton. Indeed, of England and the entire world.

"Your suite, sir, miss." The liveried servant held open the door and gestured them inside.

Lingering thoughts of Darien Reynard dispelled as Clara stepped into the sitting area. The room was decorated in shades of green and cream, a coal fire burned warmly on the hearth, and a bow window overlooked the park across the street. It was understated and elegant, and she was grateful all over again for her new blue dress. At least she *looked* as though she belonged here, even if she did not feel that way.

"Very good," she said, keeping her chin lifted.

"The water closet and bathing room are just there, and you will find a bedroom to either side of this sitting room. The footmen will be up with your luggage shortly. Will you be needing anything more?"

She exchanged a quick glance with Nicholas, then turned back to the hovering servant. "Ah. Perhaps you could send up some tea?"

"Immediately." The man bowed. "The bell pull is beside the door. Do not hesitate to ring if anything else is required."

"Thank you," Nicholas said. As soon as the man left, her brother turned to her. His voice held an undertone of mirth. "Clara—ordering tea as though you were a duchess! I think this life suits you."

"He seemed to expect *something* of us. It was the first thing I could think of."

"An excellent notion." Nicholas strode over to the window, flexing his hands. "It will help pass the time until I go rehearse with the maestro. Certainly it won't take a half hour to unpack our things."

As it transpired, they were not expected to do even that much. A maid arrived with the tea trolley, at the head of a parade of servants. The footman deposited their small bags, and two other maids bore the luggage off into their respective rooms. When Clara made to follow she was treated to a slightly shocked glance by the tea-trolley girl. So she and Nicholas sat in overstuffed chairs before the hearth, sipping tea from bone-china cups, nibbling the lemon cakes that accompanied the beverage, and trying to appear as though they were accustomed to such things. It was easier once the servants had taken themselves away, though her brother kept glancing at the ormolu clock on the mantle.

At length he set aside his tea and brushed a stray crumb from his trousers. "It's only been twenty-five minutes, but I can't wait any longer. Come and listen as soon as you have finished."

Clara wrapped both hands around her cup, savoring the warmth. She was not entirely certain how it would be, hearing her brother and Master Reynard practice the *Air*.

"I'll join you presently."

A welcome quiet slipped in as Nicholas shut the door behind

him. What a tremendously eventful day it had been. It felt like weeks since she had waved goodbye to Papa, not simply a morning and afternoon. She was hardly the same person who had followed Mr. Dubois to the carriage from her doorstep.

Clara took a last sip of tea and set down her cup. Finally she could investigate their suite without revealing her gauche curiosity to the servants.

She began with her room. The green and cream colors from the sitting room continued in the striped wallpaper—at least what she could see of it between the gilt-framed landscape paintings adorning the walls. Two brocade-upholstered chairs, a writing desk, a washstand, and the bed, which was twice the size of any she had ever slept in. She ran her palm over the richly patterned coverlet, the fabric more suited to a ball gown than bed linens. The carved headboard was nearly obscured by a pile of pillows. It would be a trick to fit herself in among them.

Despite the fact the room had been empty before their arrival, coals were banked in the fireplace, keeping the air at a comfortable temperature. Much as she appreciated it, Clara had to shake her head. How much coal must the Royal York consume in a day, heating unoccupied rooms? It hardly bore contemplating.

Nicholas's room was much the same, though darker greens dominated the color scheme and his bed was a four-poster. His suit hung in the wardrobe, but his shirts were missing. She recalled one of the maids taking them away to be pressed, along with Clara's spare chemise and nightgown.

Now for the bathing room. She pushed the white door open, and a sigh slipped from between her lips. A large copper tub sat beneath the single high window, the light gleaming on its graceful curves. A Turkish-style rug softened the tiled floor before it and an array of soaps and lotions graced the shelf to one side. It was the most elegant thing she'd ever seen. Though she had to admit, some of the appeal lay in the fact that should she desire a bath, *she* would not be the one to heat and carry the water. That was a luxury she could come to appreciate.

The clock in the sitting room gave a gentle chime, and Clara recalled herself. She ought to go hear how Nicholas and Master Reynard were progressing with the *Air*. But first...

Her reticule lay untouched where she had left it in the sitting room. Clara took it into her bedroom and locked the door. Graphite and notebook in hand, she notated the sweet, poignant melody that had swirled about her in the carriage. Darien Reynard's melody.

After a moment she turned the page and scribed the gull's song, and the sigh and rush of the waves. There. Those bits were down on paper now, and she needn't worry about losing them. She tucked her graphite away and glanced around the room. It wouldn't do to leave the evidence of her composing out in plain sight, or even in her reticule, where an inquisitive servant could discover it. She pressed her lips together. The bed. Heavens knew there were enough pillows to conceal almost anything.

The linens were wonderfully soft against her hand as she slipped her notebook deep into the pile of pillows. But she had delayed too long. It was time to go hear Darien Reynard play her newest work.

CHAPTER EIGHT

In recent years, critics have found Master Darien Reynard's playing, while still brilliant, lacking in spirit. However, his recent performance at King's Theatre showed a new, revitalized Reynard, at the top of his form in both technical virtuosity and musical heart. One can only hope this is a lasting change.

-Ariosa Reviews

The next evening, the black coach deposited Clara, Nicholas, and Master Reynard beneath the dome-topped portico of the Royal Pavilion. The white marble glowed translucent in the twilight, as if lit from within. Nicholas hesitated beside the familiar bulk of the coach, and Clara could not blame him. The exotic building before them seemed more like a prison than a palace.

Tonight, Nicholas would play before the king.

But it would do her brother no good to give in to her own anxiety. She gave him an encouraging smile and slipped her arm through his.

"Come," Master Reynard said, a slight furrow between his brows.

He strode forward, and liveried servants hurried to swing the tall double doors wide. The three of them were ushered into a large, octagonal foyer featuring floor-to-ceiling windows that let in the last reflection of silvery dusk.

Clara took a deep breath as she stepped over the threshold. She shivered, but the act of entering the Pavilion, however fantastical a place, had no transformative effect. She was not magically changed into a princess from a fairy tale.

Master Reynard marched ahead, violin case in one hand, his bearing supremely confident. She and Nicholas were carried along like flotsam in his wake.

"Look," her brother whispered, jerking his chin up.

She blinked up at the ceiling, which resembled the draperies of a huge, exotic tent. A curious, boxy chandelier glowed at the apex, and tassels hung down at the corners, nearly sweeping the floor.

"It's quite a spectacle," Master Reynard said, handing his greatcoat to the hovering servants. "The former king spared no expense to build his pleasure dome, as you'll see."

As the master drew her brother's attention to the fanciful brass fireplace, Clara slowly unfastened her pelisse. It had just arrived that morning, part of a posthaste delivery from Madame Lamond's. Clara's touch lingered on the silky fur trimming the edges before she gave it up to the servant. She would appear truly vulgar if she carried her overgarment about the pavilion, folded bulkily under one arm like some inanimate lapdog, but she found herself reluctant to let go of it.

Thank heavens for the modiste. Clara was only able to attend the performance that night because the delivery had included an evening gown. Her blue silk dress, no matter how lovely, would not have served for a function of this elegance, but the new teal and silver taffeta gown with gorgeous puffed sleeves was perfect. The lace at the neck was finer work than she had ever seen, and the wide, embroidered sash did not seem nearly as ostentatious as she had first thought; particularly not compared to their surroundings. She gave the room a wry glance.

For a moment she imagined entering the Pavilion dressed in her old Sunday best. They would have hurried her off to the servant's quarters. Shame curdled in her stomach; not for who she was, but for the foolish confidence her family had demonstrated when agreeing to this scheme. They'd had no notion, and now Nicholas was about to perform before the king!

A man garbed in the royal livery bowed to Darien Reynard. His gaze flickered over Clara and Nicholas, then returned to the master.

"We have been expecting you," the servant said. "This way, if you please."

Clara squeezed her brother's arm. They both needed the

reassurance that they were not completely lost here, adrift on a sea of courtly opulence.

It was difficult to keep from gawking as they trailed Master Reynard down a long gallery. The pink walls were riotous with Oriental motifs, the skylight overhead painted in a rich cobalt pattern. The servant led them between two staircases fashioned of iron to resemble some foreign wood, and along a short hallway.

"The Music Room." The man opened a red lacquered door painted with gold, and gestured them in. "His Majesty will appear shortly. Please, make ready."

Nicholas hung back for a moment, then surged forward, pulling Clara with him as he hastened after Master Reynard. There was no turning back.

The master checked his stride and nodded to Nicholas. "I've always thought playing in here was like performing inside an empress's jewelry box."

Glancing about, Clara agreed. Though the air was thick with heat and the smell of mingled perfumes, it was an extraordinary space. An enormous gas-lit crystal flower floated high in the center of the room, its soft colors glowing opalescent. Smaller gasoliers circled it, lilies of light depending from the domed ceiling where gilt dragons curled, their jeweled eyes winking. A large number of people gathered beneath the fanciful decorations, filling the space with a counterpoint of conversations.

A gentleman detached himself from a nearby group and made his way to where they stood.

"Master Reynard, what an honor. We are so fortunate you are here." He glanced over his shoulder to where a young woman watched, her expression eager. "My acquaintance is shy, but she wishes to communicate her ardent enthusiasm of your music."

"My pleasure," Darien said. He nodded to the young lady, who blushed and clasped her hands in delight.

As if an invisible signal passed through the room, heads turned toward them. Conversations hushed, then redoubled, and there was a general movement toward where Darien Reynard stood.

"Beg pardon," the liveried servant said, clearing a path in front of them. "Excuse us. Master Reynard must prepare."

Clara felt the weight of curious stares as they proceeded toward the shining piano at the far side of the room. Her feet sank into the plush carpet, and for a guilty moment she was relieved to be only the composer's sister. Nothing was expected of her but to turn pages for Nicholas.

In contrast, Master Reynard seemed completely at ease as he made his way to the back of the room, acknowledging greetings as he went. His dark coat was a welcome patch of calm amidst the excess, his serenity lending her strength. Clara kept her eyes fixed on his back, glad when they fetched up at the reassuring solidity of the grand piano. The keyboard was a bulwark between them and the crowd. She glanced at Nicholas, seeing near-panic in his expression.

Nothing could erase the terrifying fact that the king himself would soon grace them with his presence. *The king.* Her newest composition was about to be debuted for royalty. The thought held equal parts fright and elation.

Nicholas slid onto the piano bench, his shoulders stiff. Clara drew up a chair upholstered in Chinese silk and positioned it so she could easily stand and turn pages for her brother. The air was stifling, and she found it impossible to sit calmly. Her fingers twisted around and around, like the carved serpents twining about the nearby columns.

Master Reynard removed his violin from its case, tightened his bow, and shook his hair back from his face with a toss of his head.

"An *A*, please."

Nicholas played the note for the master to match, the ordinary act of tuning up lending a veneer of normalcy to the proceedings. Master Reynard played a run of notes, liquid and clear, and Clara closed her eyes, letting the sound briefly soothe her. Hopefully Nicholas felt the same effect. He was very pale, his lips pressed tightly together. She prayed he would not be ill.

At Darien Reynard's first notes, the crowd moved to the chairs facing the piano. A richly dressed fellow who seemed to be the master of ceremonies stepped forward and cleared his throat.

"Ladies and Gentlemen! His Royal Majesty, King William the

Fourth. Her Majesty, Queen Consort Adelaide."

Everyone rose and turned to the doors at the back of the room. Clara and her brother hastily stood, and Master Reynard tucked his violin under his elbow.

In the hush following the announcement, the king entered, his wife on his arm. He was stately looking, his white hair carefully styled, his features still strong above the collar of his heavily brocaded coat. The queen was rather younger, and reserved in her manner.

As the monarchs progressed into the room the lords bowed and the ladies sank into deep, reverent curtsies. Clara spread her skirts, the fabric rustling, and hoped her curtsy would not offer insult to the ruler of the British Empire. Gaze fixed on the figured carpet, she was certain the sound of her heart knocking in her throat must be audible to the entire room. At last, after an interminable length, the master of ceremonies spoke again.

"Please, be seated." After the rustles and whispers subsided, he continued. "It is with great pleasure that we present this evening's entertainment. Playing for your delight, the world-renowned violinist, Master Darien Reynard."

Vigorous applause followed his pronouncement, and the master stepped in front of the piano. They had decided yesterday he would begin with a solo piece, to give Nicholas a chance to hear the acoustics and ready himself.

Master Reynard swept another bow to the king, lifted his violin, and began. The Telemann *Fantasia No. 7* was a perfect choice, Clara thought as the ornate melody filled the room. It curled, notes swirling and opulent, the music perfectly fitting the surroundings.

From her place beside the piano she had an excellent view of the audience. And while Darien Reynard was compelling from any angle, she found herself watching the crowd as they watched him. Most of the ladies in attendance, and a fair number of the gentlemen, looked, in a word, smitten. Some regarded him avidly, as if he were a particularly appetizing dish; others gazed with dreamy expressions. She located the young man from earlier, sitting beside his sweetheart near the front. They were surreptitiously holding hands, the intimacy nearly concealed by her wide skirts.

The king nodded as he listened to the master play. The queen leaned forward, a wistful look on her face. A few scattered listeners had their eyes closed, but they did not sleep. All were enthralled by this single man playing a solo violin—so simple an act, and yet so stunningly complex. Darien Reynard held the king and the assembled court in the palm of his hand with an ease she found breathtaking.

The piece finished, too soon. The master waited for the applause to subside, then swept one hand toward the piano.

"Your Majesty, members of the court, it gives me great pleasure to introduce a tremendously talented new composer—Mr. Nicholas Becker."

Nicholas rose from the bench and made a stiff bow to the royal couple. His hands shook as he resumed his seat.

Master Reynard nodded at Nicholas, then turned back to the king. "We will play for you his newest work, the *Air in E minor*, never before performed. It is a true honor to premiere it in such company."

He brought his violin to his shoulder and waited for Nicholas to begin the first chord.

And waited.

The silence stretched while Nicholas sat, frozen, at the piano. Clara dug her nails into her palms, as the expectation centered on Nicholas grew more focused by the moment. *Oh, please, play.* Above, the glittering stares of the dragons turned malevolent. Her stomach tightened as if she had swallowed a stone. What would happen to them if Nicholas were unable to perform?

It simply did not bear thinking of. He would play. He must.

She leaned forward and set her hand on his shoulder, then spoke the word their father used when commanding them to play.

"Commence." She strove to imitate Papa's severe inflection.

The echo of the music master's voice penetrated Nicholas's fear. He let out a shaky breath, then spread his fingers over the keys. The first chord rang out, and Clara leaned back in her seat, her palms damp inside her gloves.

The first few measures were not as clear and confident as they had been in rehearsal, but at least he was playing. The violin joined in, the melody soaring and spiraling up to the gilded ceiling, and the tight line of Nicholas's shoulders eased. The *Air* was launched, and Clara could breathe again.

After the first page-turn she ventured a glance across the room. She could not say for certain, but it seemed the king was pleased. Yet even the King of England could not hold her attention long, not while Darien Reynard stood, splendid in his dark coat, and performed her music. He played all the yearning she had written into the *Air*, infusing it with depth and passion.

Last night he had played it ably, stopping to work out passages and discuss with Nicholas the phrasing and dynamics. She'd had to bite her tongue to keep from answering, but Nicholas had done well enough in her stead. That morning they'd spent two more hours shaping, polishing, and it was a revelation to Clara to hear Master Reynard take the notes and make them his.

He colored her music with his own hopes and hungers—invisible and unknown, but audible in the sing and pulse of his violin. It was enthralling. She barely remembered in time to turn the last page for Nicholas.

The piece finished, and there was silence. Clara held perfectly still, breath bottled up in her throat. Then the king rose, clapping loudly, and the rest of the court followed suit, their approval free and genuine. Clara exhaled, as Darien Reynard strode to the piano. Taking Nicholas by the elbow, the master drew him forward.

"Ladies and gentlemen, Nicholas Becker!"

The applause redoubled, and the tips of her brother's ears turned pink. Master Reynard clapped him on the back, then turned and met Clara's gaze. She'd proven her worth; he had to admit as much. He nodded to her, acknowledgement in his moss-green eyes, and she flushed with warmth.

They had done it. Their first successful premiere. She grinned at Nicholas as he returned to the piano.

"Oh, nicely done! You played the *Air* very well." No need to mention the uncertain start. "I've no doubt the king was pleased."

The residue of nervousness lingered in her brother's shaky smile.

"It was acceptable," he said in a low voice. "The next concert should be easier at any rate. No kings in the audience."

She patted the piano bench. "Master Reynard is commencing the finale."

He had decided to conclude the performance with a solo piece by Handel; something well known and sure to please, in the unlikely event the *Air* was not well received.

By the end of the Handel, Clara had to blink herself back to earth, the notes still ringing through her. She shot a glance at her brother. To her relief, he seemed quite recovered.

Master Reynard took several bows, and gestured again for Nicholas to join him. At last the applause faded, and the audience stood as the king and queen exited the room. The master tucked his violin away in its case, then tipped his head to Nicholas.

"Now we repair to the gallery, where you may continue to accept the praise that is your due."

Nicholas's eyes met Clara's in a quick, uneasy acknowledgement, then he nodded at the maestro. "Certainly."

Clara trailed behind them into the white and gilt gallery, the colors soothing after the saturated intensity of the Music Room. She found an unoccupied settee in one corner, and Nicholas fetched her a cup of lemonade before the crowd closed in around him. Master Reynard, too, was swept away, and she could not help but notice how obviously the ladies vied for his attention. There was nothing left for her to do but to perch on the cushion and sip her lemonade. Alone.

For a moment Clara indulged in imagining that *she* was acknowledged as the composer, receiving the admiration and accolades. But how quickly it would turn to shock and condemnation. Worst of all would be the look on Darien Reynard's face upon learning how they had lied to him. No. This was how it must be. Useless to try and imagine otherwise; their deception was too well begun.

She took another sip of lemonade, savoring the cool, tart sweetness, and looked about the room. The people were different even from the crowds in Mayfair. It was not every day she had the opportunity to observe the court at a close distance. Or any distance, for that matter.

They were dressed in the pinnacle of fashion, the men in proper long-tailed coats, the ladies in a bright array of puff-sleeved gowns and glittering jewelry. Queen Adelaide looked splendid, despite her sad eyes, in a blue velvet gown with gauzy lace sleeves. Diamond combs sparkled in her elaborately coiffed hair.

Clara's own chignon was far too simple, though she had added ostrich plumes dyed to match the teal of her dress—and blessed Madame Lamond again for including them. Still, her coiffure was noticeably lacking compared to the profusion of rolls and curls so popular with the ladies of the court.

Darien Reynard laughed—how quickly she had come to recognize that sound—and she glanced over at him. She could make out a bit of his black coat, a gleam of light on his dark hair as he bent his head to answer yet another gorgeously gowned lady. Clara sighed and turned her now-empty cup of lemonade between her gloved palms. The air in the gallery was close and sticky, and she longed for the sharp sea wind. At least on the beach her solitude had felt like part of the greater whole.

That morning she'd risen early, finally free to follow the call of the ocean. All night the waves had hushed through her dreams, beckoned her to the shore. In the early light the water lay pale and lucent. The strand behind the hotel had been quiet but for a few people: a boy prodding at the pebble-littered beach with a stick while his mother looked on, a white-capped girl hurrying head-down, her cloak wrapped about her thin figure.

Small stones had clattered softly under Clara's feet as she walked forward, directly to the water's edge. A constantly changing edge, a fascinating edge, where the sea pulled and sucked at the land. Heedless of the foam at her feet, she had bent and dabbled her fingers, then brought them to her mouth. Salt. But not a simple brine, for there had been a wildness, a rough tang to the flavor. Her first taste of the sea had not disappointed.

Clara sighed and took a shallow breath of the cloying air, so far removed from the freshness of the shore. She leaned back, simply another inanimate pillow lumped on the settee, and studied the pattern of the carpet. The cross-hatched red and gold was obscured by a variety of splendid footwear, but she had managed to count forty-four repetitions when a well-modulated voice broke her concentration.

"What have we here? 'Tis a neglected diamond, left to shine in brilliant solitude."

She glanced up to find a brown-haired gentleman beside her. His look was assessing, and for a moment she felt like a bird watched by a cat.

His companion, a fellow with a thin nose and richly brocaded waistcoat, nodded.

"Indeed, but her beauty has obviously blinded you. She is not so colorless as a diamond, not at all." He raised a quizzing glass and surveyed her through it. "I declare her a rare sapphire."

"Milady." The first speaker went on one knee before her, in a decidedly theatrical gesture. "You must forgive our poor manners—it is only that we are struck by your air and must make your acquaintance. I am Lord Rawley, and this stiff fool is my friend, Viscount Tilson."

"Not so foolish that I cannot spot a perfect jewel at twenty paces," the viscount replied. He tucked his glass away and made her a very precise bow. "But please, tell us who you are before my friend perishes of curiosity at your feet."

"I am Miss Clara Becker." She could not help smiling at them in turn.

"Indeed." Lord Rawley leaned closer and plucked the empty lemonade cup from her hands. "May I fetch you some more refreshment, Miss Becker? I declare, it would make my evening complete."

"No, thank you." Amusement bubbled through her, though she knew she ought not to encourage the fellow. Clearly he was a dandy.

"Say yes," the viscount urged, "for then Rawley will go away and we might share some pleasant conversation in his absence."

"Your conversation is as empty as this vessel." Lord Rawley waved the cup for emphasis. "No, what she needs is a bit of fresh air. I beg you, Miss Becker, allow me to escort you on a brief promenade.

There is no better sight than the Pavilion lit up at night. There are the most clever gaslights outside. Really, it's indescribable."

"Too true," Viscount Tilson said. "For a man with your limited vocabulary."

Clara blinked at the speed of their conversational volleys. "It is exceedingly kind of you," she began, "but I really don't think..."

"I must admit," the viscount said, tilting his head, "the air inside is warmer than one would like, although it is far worse in summer. We must be grateful the king chose to repair here for the winter holidays."

"And the marriage of his—" Lord Rawley checked himself, though Clara was certain he had meant to say *illegitimate*, "daughter." He exchanged a look with his friend that Clara could not decipher, then turned his brown eyes to her again. "Dear, dear Miss Becker. Do not say the thought of a breath of cool night air is disagreeable to you."

"I do not have my pelisse," she said.

The excuse sounded weak, even to her ears. Still, she did not think she should be stepping out with two newly met gentlemen. It did not seem quite the thing. She glanced toward the set of floor-to-ceiling doors—one standing open to the night. There were a few figures on the terrace, strolling slowly to and fro.

"You are among the court now." Lord Rawley stood and offered his hand. "No need to spend the evening perched here like a milkmaid on a stool. You will not be gone above two minutes. Why, your absence will scarcely be noticed."

That was true enough. Indeed, for the better part of an hour she had sat abandoned, her presence completely unremarked. Despite being acutely aware of every step Master Reynard took about the room, she was invisible to him. As for Nicholas... She shook her head. Let her brother enjoy his success.

"Very well," she said. "A *short* stroll."

It would break the monotony, and her new acquaintances were diverting.

"I shall recite a sonnet to your eyes." Lord Rawley took her hand and drew her to her feet, then tucked her arm firmly through his. "Or, no, to your hair, as fine and pale as moonlight. Or perhaps—"

"Pray, do not torture us with your verse," Viscount Tilson said. "Miss Becker has done nothing to merit such a terrible fate."

Lord Rawley ignored this comment as he led Clara out through the open door. "There now, you must admit this is better."

It was. The cold air bathed her face and soothed the sting of heat from her cheeks. Clara took a long breath, savoring the salt tang, though it was cool enough that she would not like to linger overlong.

Viscount Tilson stepped up to her other side. "The dome of the Saloon is quite impressive, but we need to walk out a bit farther to admire it properly."

He linked his arm through hers.

A frisson of alarm went through her. She was, to all effects, trapped between the two men. Clara tried to slow her steps as they maneuvered her toward the shadows.

"I think this is far enough," she said. It was difficult to sound at ease with her throat tight from apprehension.

"Ah no, my dear," Lord Rawley said. "It is not nearly far enough." Something in his tone made her skin prickle.

"Gentlemen, I must insist we return to the gallery at once." She forced her voice to be calm, though fear flavored her mouth.

"We will return you, in good time. But first there is so much we'd like to show you."

Lord Rawley held her arm fast and leaned uncomfortably close, the scent of his cologne thick about her. The look he gave her was predatory, the guise of the lighthearted dandy wiped from his expression.

Clara swallowed. It seemed she had rather dangerously misjudged her new acquaintances.

CHAPTER NINE

Clara thought furiously. Her escorts had cut her out of the fold quite neatly, and she was certain neither Nicholas nor Master Reynard had noticed her departure from the gallery.

The only thing she could do was scream. Surely she was close enough to the terrace that someone would hear. They must hear. She drew in a deep breath—but before she could cry out, a new voice cut through the night.

"Stop." The tone was one of absolute command, and her unwelcome escorts abruptly halted. "Return Miss Becker at once."

They pivoted to face the Pavilion, and Clara sagged with relief. Master Reynard stood facing them, fists on his hips, his expression forbidding in the dim light.

Lord Rawley released his hold on her as if scalded.

"Master Reynard, we beg your pardon." The menace she had heard in his voice was entirely gone. He looked like a cur cowering before a mastiff. "We didn't realize she was your—"

"Go."

Master Reynard jerked his head, and the man hurried past without another word, giving the maestro a wide berth.

"Viscount Tilson," Master Reynard said, stepping down onto the grass. "I would have thought better of you."

The viscount inclined his head stiffly and led Clara to within a pace of the gathering storm that was Darien Reynard. He held out his hand, and Viscount Tilson all but pushed her into his arms.

"We did no harm," the viscount said. "But I see we were mistaken in our assumptions. My apologies. Good evening, sir. Miss Becker."

He walked away, his gait suggesting he would have liked to run, but for his dignity. As soon as he was gone, Master Reynard took her by the shoulders.

"Miss Becker," he said, his voice hard. "I had thought you too sensible to be lured out by a pair of rakes intent upon your seduction."

Clara blinked up at him, the anger in his voice unmistakable. "I really don't think—"

"You must *start* thinking. This is nothing like your old life. There are dangers here you need to comprehend, men who will be attracted to your beauty and wish to take advantage."

He thought her beautiful? A rush of heat sped through her, dispelling some of the cold fear she had felt moments ago.

"We were only—"

"Another few paces and you'd have been out of the light altogether. Look."

He moved forward, still holding her, and she took two hasty steps back. She could feel the warmth of his body, smell the faint spice of his scent.

"We are completely out of sight," he said. "Anything could happen to you—would have, had I not seen you slip out the door with that pair of knaves."

"Surely someone… I was about to scream, I assure you."

"That would have been easily dealt with, too."

Clara narrowed her eyes. "I don't think so. I am not as helpless as you seem to believe, Master Reynard."

"Go ahead." He lowered his voice. "Cry out."

"It would not do for anyone to find us out here."

"*Now* you consider it. Come, Miss Becker. Try me." His fingers wrapped more firmly about her shoulders, his thumbs resting just at the edge of her bodice.

Oh dear. The way he said the words made a curious tingle brush over her. She tried not to notice how close his hands were to her bare skin.

"Very well."

She took a quick breath and opened her mouth to scream. In an instant, he pulled her smoothly against him. His warm lips descended, covering hers completely, and her cry dissipated into a gasp, a sigh exhaled into his open mouth.

Darien Reynard was kissing her, and it was the fiercest sensation.

His mouth moved possessively over hers, demanding and hungry, and Clara was caught up in a current of wild, passionate energy. She felt that same current when he played, but instead of his violin he had *her* beneath his hands. Oh, but his touch sent music vibrating through her, sweet and singing. The spaces beneath her skin rang with the notes of his kiss.

After a long, exhilarating moment, he made to lift his head, but she wove her fingers through his hair and moved her lips beneath his, mimicking his sure caress. He made a rough sound in the back of his throat and slid one arm around her, molding her against him. His other hand drifted to her neckline, the thumb stroking along her bare collarbone, and she was lost.

"What the devil!" Nicholas's voice sliced through the darkness. "Bloody hell, get away from my sister!"

Darien Reynard thrust Clara from him. Too late. The blaze inside her died instantly to ash. Their kiss had ended too soon—and far, far too late.

"Mr. Becker." Darien turned, keeping himself between Clara and her brother. "It's not what it seems."

Clara took a halting step forward. She swallowed, her throat tight with shame and fear.

"How could it be other than what it seems?" Nicholas's voice was hard, fury giving it a biting edge. "Prostituting my sister was not part of our agreement, sir. We will return to London immediately."

He brushed roughly past the master. Taking Clara by the arm, he began towing her back toward the terrace.

"Nicholas!" She yanked from his grasp. How could she explain? "We cannot leave the tour. Master Reynard was only demonstrating to me—"

"I could see what he was demonstrating, and I'll have none of it." Nicholas glared at Darien. "I'd foolishly discounted your wicked reputation. But you will not have another chance to lay hands on my sister. I should call you out, sir."

"No!" Clara stepped in front of her brother and laid a hand on his chest.

So quickly the most wonderful experience of her life had turned to disaster. The very idea of Nicholas dueling Darien Reynard made her blood turn to ice. She was not sure her brother had ever even held a pistol, let alone fired one.

"Listen to me, Nicholas," she said. "Think of Papa. Think of what we left back in London. We *cannot* return to that."

She would do anything to keep from slipping back into that gray, anxious existence.

Darien spoke, an undercurrent of tension beneath his words. "There is no excuse for my behavior. I offer my most sincere apologies, Miss Becker. And Nicholas, I swear to you I will not touch your sister again. Stay. We have just begun. Don't let this dreadful mistake be the end of things."

"It is the end," Nicholas said with a sharp shake of his head. "Clara and I will return to London at first light. And you, sir, are not welcome to perform the compositions of Nicholas Becker ever again."

"But—" Clara began.

"No." Her brother cut her off. "We will go immediately to the hotel and pack our belongings. The clothing, of course, belongs to Master Reynard and will remain behind."

Darien's face was set, unreadable in the dim light. He made them a bow—very correct, very formal. It was clear he knew that arguing with Nicholas would gain him nothing.

"I will summon the coach for you," he said. "The footmen will escort you from the Pavilion. Good night."

He moved past them without meeting Clara's eyes, strode across the terrace, and disappeared back into the Royal Pavilion. Silence, heavy with failure, filled the air between her and her brother.

"Nicholas." Clara stared into his eyes, beseeching. "I have been imprudent tonight, but truly, it was not Darien Reynard's fault. In fact, he saved me from worse trouble…"

She could not continue, could not risk seeing her brother storm back into the gallery, intent on confronting the knaves who had led her outside. Better that was left unsaid. She would not embroil Nicholas in a senseless duel to protect her honor.

He jammed his hands into his pockets, rumpling the elegant line of his coat. "Damn the money, anyway. Your virtue's worth far more."

"My virtue was not in danger."

She tried not to dwell on how she had felt in Darien's arms, the feel of his fingers moving over her bare skin as he tasted her lips. The kiss he had called a "dreadful mistake." She shivered.

"It's too cold out here." Nicholas pulled his hands from his pockets and took Clara's elbow, steering back toward the terrace. "High time we were quit of this blasted place."

***

Dare tossed an extra cravat into his traveling bag, and ignored the look on Henri's face.

"You will not accompany me," he said. "Don't argue."

"But, monsieur." Henri lifted his hands in dismay. "Your boots, your coat—"

"I'm perfectly capable of dressing myself. The only way to convince Nicholas Becker to continue on the tour is to remove myself from his immediate vicinity. I have faith in you, Henri. If anyone can talk Nicholas around, it's you."

Eyes dark with worry, Henri shook his head. "You place too much trust in me, monsieur. What shall I tell him?"

"Anything, so long as he agrees to stay on." Dare tucked his shaving kit into the bag and closed it firmly. "But I will also write a letter, if you wish."

"Please do so."

The writing desk in the suite held paper, pens, and ink. The force of Dare's impatience splattered the ink across the page, and he made himself slow, forming his angular words more legibly.

Nicholas,

Without you and your compositions, this tour is nothing. I entreat you to reconsider. Do not throw away your chance at greatness. Think of what you will be giving up. This door will not open again.

Take your sister back to London, but do not abandon the tour. Henri will accompany you in escorting your sister home, and then you can rejoin me in Southampton. I will increase your salary commensurately.

Again, my sincere apologies.

- Darien Reynard

Henri took the letter with a doubtful expression. "Monsieur. Were I Miss Becker's brother, I would not like to continue my association with the man who took such liberties with my sister."

"Damnation, Henri! It was just a kiss." Dare would never admit to anyone how quickly he had lost control of himself.

Anger—at Clara, at his own inattention, at the court that turned a blind eye—had made him act recklessly. He should never have kissed her. But, Christ, that kiss. He had meant it only as a warning.

A warning that turned to a conflagration between one breath and the next. Suddenly there had been nothing but the night, Clara's lips beneath his, and a blaze of desire, burning bright and hot.

He had behaved abominably. If Nicholas had not found them, Dare would have been as bad as any rogue of the *ton*. He'd been a heartbeat away from parting her lips and licking his tongue into the moist hollow of her mouth, an instant from slipping his fingers beneath her bodice and caressing the sweet curve of her breast.

A rap at the door proved a welcome distraction. Henri went to answer, but Dare knew it was the servant reporting that his horse was ready.

"You cannot ride out tonight, in the cold and dark," Henri said, for the fifth time.

"I must." And the miserable night ride would help cool the ache of unspent desire that rose every time he thought of Clara Becker.

She had no place in his thoughts, and no place on the tour. Henri would ensure she was escorted safely back to London. Then Dare could make his amends to Nicholas, and convince the composer to continue on to the Continent with him.

The grand competition was two months away, and Becker was his trump card.

That musical duel meant everything. No matter how tempting Clara Becker's lips and sweetly curved body, she could not compare to the permanent acclaim that winning the competition would bring. It would be the culmination of Darien's career; a lifetime spent honing his skill. He *would* claim the title of the greatest violinist of the era.

Nothing could be allowed to stand in his way.

CHAPTER TEN

Rumors Confirmed! We have it on utmost authority that Master Darien Reynard is touring with a new composer—the handsome young Mr. Nicholas Becker. Two gentlemen for the price of one, ladies!
-The Bath Gazetteer

Despite the luxurious bed, Clara slept fitfully. She woke frequently and peeked through the curtains to see if it was still safely dark, or if morning had broken, hard and unforgiving.

At length, the sky transformed from ink to paper. Exhaustion and sorrow weighing heavily on her shoulders, she pushed the rich coverlet back, and rose. The carpet was thick beneath her toes, and the well-banked coals in the hearth still sent out tendrils of heat. She shivered at the thought of returning to the cold, bare rooms of their house in London.

No. She must convince Nicholas to remain with Master Reynard.

Before the maids came to pack her few pitiful belongings, Clara dug her notebook from beneath the pile of pillows and slipped it into her reticule. She gave a longing look to the trunks that had arrived yesterday, full of resplendent gowns. Such expense and haste, to make clothing she would never wear.

With a low sigh, Clara opened her battered valise and donned her mended gray dress. It would help remind Nicholas of how very much they were giving up.

She heard him stirring in the sitting room—the thud of his door closing, the thump of his case hitting the carpet. When she pushed open her bedroom door, she saw him pacing beside the fireplace, his face tight, his blond hair mussed.

"Good morning," he said as she entered the sitting room. "Are you ready to depart? I have arranged our transportation back to London."

"No. Nicholas, we can't leave the tour."

"We cannot stay! Clara, if Papa knew, if he had seen, last night…" Nicholas bunched his hands into fists. "We must leave. It is the right thing, the only thing to do."

Swallowing back her impatience, she moved to her brother's side and set a hand on his arm.

"Don't you also remember what he said, when we agreed to this scheme? This is your chance to restore our family, Nicholas. You are the only one who can do so. Master Reynard's attentions…" Her voice trembled, and she drew in a steadying breath. "They meant nothing—to me, and most certainly not to him."

"He embraced you."

She forced a laugh. "Nicholas, do you truly think Darien Reynard finds *me* compelling, when he could have the pick of any lady in the country?"

The words scoured her soul as she uttered them, for of course she spoke the truth. Whatever had passed last night between herself and Darien, there had been nothing of verity in it. For either of them. She loved his musicality, was dazzled by his fame, but she knew very little of the man himself. And he knew even less of her. Their kiss had been a lie.

Nicholas frowned at her. "Then why?"

"Perhaps he had too much brandy. I assure you, had he been in possession of his senses, he would never have touched me."

"It does not change, nor excuse, what happened. And we are still leaving."

"I know you feel you must defend my honor. But are you truly willing to do so at the expense of our family's future? And speaking of honor, what of the deception we are perpetrating upon Master Reynard?"

His expression grew pained. "Clara, I—"

A rap at the door interrupted him.

"Who is it?" Nicholas strode to the door and yanked it open.

"Bonjour," Henri Dubois said. "I come with a message from Master Reynard."

"Then he can deliver it himself." Nicholas blocked the opening, keeping Mr. Dubois standing in the hallway.

"But he cannot deliver it himself, for last night he rode ahead to Southampton, leaving the coach at your disposal. Please, may I come in?"

"No."

"Oh, Nicholas." Clara took his arm, drawing him away from the threshold so that Mr. Dubois could enter. Once the valet was inside, Nicholas shut the door rather too loudly.

"What does your master wish us to know?" Nicholas demanded.

Mr. Dubois held out a letter, sealed with crimson wax and imprinted with the stamp of a violin.

Nicholas took it and broke the seal, the wax crumbling like bits of dried blood onto the carpet. Watching his expression, Clara saw the moment of hesitation, the turmoil of his emotions. Her brother wanted to do what was right, but the path was not so clear.

"What does it say?" she asked softly.

"He wants me to take you back to London, then continue on the tour."

"Of course." It made perfect sense, if one did not know that Clara was the true composer.

"For an additional salary," Mr. Dubois added. "Also, he tenders his sincerest apology."

She set her fingers to her mouth, resisting the urge to nibble at her fingernails. What a tangle this was. Darien had given Nicholas reason to continue on the tour. Remove the problem—herself—and pay him more. His solution did little to address the smirch to her honor, but that only strengthened her claim that the kiss had meant nothing.

Nicholas held the letter before him, long enough to re-read it several times over. She could feel him teetering on the decision point.

"Take me back to London and continue with Master Reynard," she said. "I will correspond with you regularly."

They could not speak openly, not with Mr. Dubois watching

with his bright, intelligent eyes. Clara pulled her worn shawl about her shoulders, and Nicholas looked at her for a fraught moment. The shadow of their poverty dimmed the lavish sitting room and her throat tightened with misery. She could not bear to return to that chilly, dark existence—but she would do it, as long as Nicholas went on.

"No." Nicholas lowered the letter.

"Mr. Becker," the valet said, "I must entreat you. Have you heard of the grand musical competition that is to be held in Milan this spring?"

"The London papers mentioned it," Nicholas said. "A duel between musicians, featuring Darien Reynard, yes?"

Clara had read the notice as well, but had not dwelt overmuch on it. Milan was worlds removed from their existence, and whatever transpired there had no bearing upon their lives.

Ah, how things had changed.

Mr. Dubois nodded. "The master would not say as much to you, but he believes he can only win the competition by playing one of your pieces, sir. To part company with him now, and in such a manner... I feel it would be a great blow to his genius. In fact, it might damage his career beyond repair."

Clara took a quick breath. Foolish as it was, if Darien believed he could not win without playing one of her compositions, it would be true.

"Master Reynard does not seem so fragile to me," Nicholas said. "There is a vast amount of music for him to perform."

"One can argue with the artistic temperament," Mr. Dubois said, "but the greater the talent, the more difficult the man. You must believe me that, should you abandon Master Reynard at this juncture, the consequences could be dire."

Clara caught her lower lip between her teeth, and glanced at her brother. If he destroyed the master's career, he would never be able to live with the burden. Already he carried too much melancholy inside his soul.

"Nicholas," she said. "Please. For all our sakes."

His mouth twisted. With a sharp gesture, he balled up the letter and threw it into the hearth. It blazed brightly for a single moment, before the flames consumed the fine paper.

"Very well," Nicholas said, in a voice as colorless as the ashes of the letter. "We shall not waste time in returning to London. Clara and I will remain with the tour."

Mr. Dubois's eyebrows lifted and he glanced from Nicholas to Clara. She met his gaze calmly, despite the sudden relief rushing through her.

"I have every confidence that nothing like last night's... episode will ever occur again," she said. "I will remain with the tour. With Nicholas."

"And keep out of Master Reynard's way," her brother said.

"Of a surety." She fingered the worn skirts of her gown. "Excuse me, gentlemen. I am going to change into a more suitable traveling dress."

She closed the bedroom door firmly behind her, shutting out her hopelessly romantic imaginings of Darien Reynard.

There could never be anything between them. If she were wise, she would erase the memory of that kiss from her mind; crush it like glass beneath the heel of reality until it was nothing but glittering dust, borne away by the wind.

***

Clara sat at the cherry-wood writing desk and gazed out the window of her enormous suite in Carlton Towers; the grand country home of the Earl of Surrey, where Master Reynard and his party were being housed prior to their performances in Leeds and York. The earl and his countess were not currently in residence, for which Clara was grateful. She did not think she would ever feel at ease among the nobility.

The misty landscape outside provided no inspiration. It was too soft, too undefined. She returned her attention to the paper before her and, compressing her lips together, crossed out the lines she had written moments before. The discarded page took its place with a dozen other failed attempts on the desk beside her.

It was a shocking waste of paper, but Darien Reynard could afford it. What he could not afford, however, was to have no more compositions by Becker. She tugged at a loose strand of hair and closed her eyes, her mind chasing after any elusive hint of melody. She would not fail in this.

"Clara?" Nicholas rapped at her door, then opened it without waiting for her response. "How's the newest piece coming?"

She fixed a smile on her lips. "A bit slowly, but well enough."

She closed her hand around her stick of graphite.

"Inspiration is everywhere, or so you've told me." Nicholas tilted his head at her, concern shading his eyes. "Your two sea pieces turned out admirably."

"Yes."

She'd been able to complete the melodies that had come to her in Brighton. But she had finished those compositions ten days ago, and nothing since had inspired. Rather the opposite. Everything was difficult now, and the joy and excitement she had felt on the early days of the tour had quickly soured.

"How did your rehearsal go?" she asked, attempting to deflect her brother's attention.

She had paused in the hall earlier, listening, but relations between Nicholas and Darien were strained enough without her presence adding to the tension.

Somehow, while performing, both men were able to lay aside their differences and work together in service to the music. The rest of the time, however, Darien Reynard avoided them, continuing his habit of taking a horse ahead to the next town at the end of each series of concerts.

Nicholas shrugged. "Adequately. He's asking for the new composition. I'm glad it's going well, as I can't put him off much longer. It's hard enough working with him as it is." A note of resentment entered his voice. "I still wish I could have—"

"What, fought with him like two brawlers in the alley? Let it go, Nicholas. Nursing your anger at Darien Reynard won't make things easier."

Though perhaps it did make things simpler for her brother. He hid behind that screen of emotion, used it to deflect the maestro's curiosity. She wished she had something, anything, to distract herself from thoughts of Darien.

Despite her resolution not to think of him, every night behind her closed lids she remembered the intensity of his expression, the light in his mossy green eyes as he lowered his face to hers. The sensation of being in Darien's arms was printed on her skin, pressed into her body so clearly that she could not forget.

Even as she wanted to. Even as he had so obviously put that kiss, and her, from his mind.

Her fingers tightened so firmly about the graphite that it snapped.

"Clara!" Nicholas gave her a startled look. "I thought the composition was going well. What's troubling you?"

"What's troubling me?" She opened her hand and let the broken lead drop to the table. "What could possibly be marring the happiness of my days? Hm, let us think on that a moment. Could it be that I'm trapped with two impossible men, dragged the length of England like a useless puppet—"

"If anyone ought to complain of being a puppet, it's me." Nicholas crossed his arms, his voice sharp and unhappy. "At least *you* have a talent. I'm only pretending. It's not easy for me either. And add to that the fact I have to work with that reprehensible man..." He flung himself down in a nearby chair.

"Darien Reynard is not reprehensible." She hated how prim her voice sounded. "How many times do I have to tell you? He has not looked at me once since that night, and not spoken above seven words to me, either." She had been counting.

"He might simply be biding his time. Be careful, Clara."

Oh, if only she thought that were true. But it was clear she was completely forgotten.

"I am careful. Now go away. I have music to compose."

Nicholas shoved back his chair. "Best you finish it soon."

"I shall."

Although how she was to finish something she could not even start... Clara shook her head and took up the longer half of the graphite.

As soon as Nicholas closed the door behind him, she set her lead down again. Blast. She picked up the page sporting her last effort and stared at the handful of notes she had sketched there. Aimless. Useless. She crumpled the paper into a tight ball. Then the next. The next, until she had a row of expensive rubbish lining the desk.

The fire burned sweetly on the hearth, the coals sending out a shimmering warmth that did not match Clara's mood at all. She stood, swept up the balls of paper, and dropped them into the fire.

Flames leapt up, the paper uncurling and dancing like souls consumed, hot and bright and angry. Like a spurned woman, like a deceitful man, like stubborn pride and fury and desperation. Dancing in the flames, while the devil watched.

Yes. Yes! At last she heard it—the quick staccato beat of the piano, rapping notes out while the violin played with the fury of a fallen angel. Fire and passion and wickedness all coiled together in a mad rush of melody.

She rushed back to the desk, grabbed a new sheet of paper, and began to write furiously.

***

From her vantage point in the hallway outside the half-open door to the music room, Clara could see Darien Reynard's lifted brow as he accepted the pages from Nicholas. She rested her fingertips on the elaborate gilt doorframe and leaned closer, straining her ears to catch their conversation.

"*Il Diavolo?*" Darien asked. "Do I dare ask what inspired this piece?"

Nicholas tapped his fingers nervously against his trouser leg.

"It's a composite," he finally said. "Drawn from a number of experiences."

"I see." Darien flipped to the second page and studied the notes scribed there. "This is a bit more... technically ambitious than your previous works. You plan to put me through my paces."

Oh, yes. Wait until he attempted the cadenza. Clara swallowed back a sharp, bitter laugh. Her composition served him right enough; served them both. She might be invisible, but there was no denying her presence. Not when *she* was the one quite literally calling the tune.

CHAPTER ELEVEN

Anton Varga Takes Roma by Storm…

The musician's recent concerts have proven his unmatched genius on the violin, and there is no doubt he will dethrone Darien Reynard in Milan this spring. Audiences shall be in for a spectacle as the two men clash in competition, and a new master is crowned!

-La Forza

"**D**amn." Dare pulled his horse up and peered through the sheeting rain at the bridge spanning the river ahead.

Or what was left of the bridge. The torrential downpour had swollen the river, and part of the wooden structure had been torn away. The far bank was unreachable, the remains of the bridge sticking only partway into the grey, turbulent water. There would be no crossing here.

No one would be out to make repairs, not this afternoon. Indeed, the rain-filled sky was dim enough to presage an early twilight, and it was a long, muddy road behind him. At least the coach would not have to backtrack quite as far. The heavy vehicle was slow and unwieldy, the driver hard-pressed to keep them from foundering.

Shaking his head at the impassable river, Dare wheeled his mount back the way he had come. His greatcoat was sodden, his hat wet through and no obstacle to the cold droplets sliding off the brim. Since reaching Northumberland, the weather had been miserable. It had nearly been enough to drive him back into the coach. Nearly, but not quite. Even riding in the insidious rain was better than spending time with the Beckers.

Nicholas was as prickly as ever—and blast him for his latest composition. *Il Diavolo* was an incredibly demanding work. Dare had spent hours working out the fingering for the difficult passages, cursing Becker with every other breath. And praising him with the rest, though Nicholas seldom took his words of approbation well.

To be fair, the composer had written an equally challenging piano part for himself. In rehearsal, they stumbled and swore and halted every few measures, but Dare could hear the infernal brilliance of the piece. The music would be stunning, if both of them survived the task of making the impossible thing come together.

It was good to have the distraction, something to keep his thoughts from Clara Becker. Not that he was always successful. Christ, not that he was successful at all, with her luminously pretty face watching him every time he turned around.

It had been a surprise to find that Nicholas had not deposited Clara in London before catching up with Dare in Southampton. He supposed the composer needed his sister's support to buoy him up before performances. In truth, her presence in Brighton had been essential.

Still, Dare had never before been in the position of trying to *ignore* a woman with whom he was in daily contact. In a rather ironic twist, it made him even more aware of her.

There was something disturbingly arousing in that careful dance of proximity; the spaces between them charged with meaning. Dare found himself measuring how far he stood from her slender figure. An arm's length from brushing the tips of his fingers across the nape of her neck. Three steps from touching her shoulder in passing. Even when she was behind him, he could tell her presence by the faint perfume of her lavender scent.

He rarely let their gazes cross, and tried not to wonder what secrets flickered in Clara's silvery-blue eyes. Every woman harbored mysteries, yet he suspected hers ran deeper than most.

And so, he restrained himself. Like a man too long from drink, who, when poured a glass of the finest French brandy, begins with savoring the aroma. Rich, intoxicating, filling his senses with the promise of more. Perhaps a drop spills over the edge, and the aficionado places his mouth there, against the cool glass, and licks that single droplet, letting the liquor burn against his tongue. Then, nearly trembling with effort, sets the glass down where the firelight can flicker through it, his self-control coiling the desire within him until it is sharp and poignant.

Dare could not sip the liquor that was Miss Clara Becker—but that did not stop him from thirsting.

His horse pricked its ears and Dare squinted through the downpour, making out the dark blur of the coach ahead.

"Ho!" he called, riding up to his driver.

Poor Samuel sat huddled on the bench. He lifted a pale face and pulled the weary horses to a halt.

"What news, master?"

"Bridge is out. We'll have to turn back to… what was that last town we passed?"

"Milfield, 'twas. More a village than a town, sir."

"There was an inn."

And not many travelers in this weather, Dare would wager. They would find accommodation for the night, even if he had to pay extra to convince earlier patrons to give up their beds and sleep in the common room.

"Monsieur!" Henri stuck his head from one of the coach windows. "Come inside, I beg of you. This weather is horrible."

"I would only get the rest of you wet. We're turning around, at any rate."

"What? We are not continuing on?"

"No, we'll have to wait for bridge repairs on the morrow." From the corner of his eye he caught the pale blur of Clara's face behind the rain-streaked glass.

"But," his valet sounded shocked, "you do not expect us to sleep on the road? In this nasty rain?" He batted his hand at the drops flying past the opened window.

"We will be at an inn, Henri. Don't look so horrified. Now close the window. I'll see you in the village." Dare could not help feel a thin trickle of amusement as his valet complied, muttering about fleas and straw-covered floors.

The Green Man Inn proved Henri's dire predictions wrong, and

Dare was glad of it. The innkeeper's wife hastily took his coat, exclaiming at the rivulets streaming off it, and seemingly unconcerned that her gleaming wooden floors sported new puddles.

"Ale, sir, or will ye be wanting something warmer?" The innkeeper hurried to the bar.

"A pint now," Dare could use the rough fortification of country ale, "and supper when my companions arrive. You do have rooms for the night?"

"Aye. How many?"

Dare settled the details, glad to find they were the only custom for the evening, though the innkeeper advised him a few of the regulars liked to drop in for their jar and a bite of stew. The common room was comfortable, warmed by a large hearth at one end. Oil lamps shed a cheery light, an antidote to the endless pewter drizzle outside.

By the time the coach arrived, Dare was mostly dry, though his boots were still damp, and his hair. Likely it was curling, too, in that irritating way it had. He'd let it get too long—mostly to annoy Henri, but now it was beginning to annoy him as well.

The bustle in the yard outside transferred to the doorway. Clara entered first, and Dare gave her a curt nod. He looked to the others, trying not to see the shadow of hurt in her eyes.

"Monsieur, you are drenched!" Henri beckoned to the innkeeper's wife. "Madame, a towel if you please."

The stout woman pursed her lips, her bright eyes assessing the newcomers. "I'll bring several. Wet enough, the lot of you."

Half an hour later, after getting settled into his room and letting Henri fuss over him, Dare descended to the common room for supper. Both Nicholas and Clara were there, at a table near the peat fire.

Nicholas slid over on the worn bench to make a place for him. "I think our meal's nearly ready. Is Mr. Dubois coming down?"

"He'll join us as soon as he has finished pressing my coat to his satisfaction."

"That may be another hour, then," Nicholas said, and actually smiled.

Dare hid his surprise. Perhaps the smell of fresh-baked bread—and the half-empty pints of ale sitting before Nicholas and his sister—had mellowed the man's usual animosity. Or perhaps it was the simple surroundings, so unlike their usual run of fine hotels and estates, that put the Beckers at ease, for Clara seemed more relaxed as well. Her expression was not taut with unhappiness as he had so often seen it, and the damp had coaxed her fine, straight hair to loosen in its braid.

That braid. So practical, so unfashionable. Dare's fingers ached to unplait it, to free that fall of moonlight. He could imagine her, standing naked with her glorious hair down about her. It would part at her shoulders, showing her upper arm, the curve of—

"…tomorrow night?" Nicholas turned to him, expectation of an answer writ upon his face.

"Ah." Dare tried to order his scattered thoughts. Damn. Clearly he needed to find some female companionship, and soon.

Across the table, Clara sent him a reproachful look. "My brother is concerned we will not make Edinburgh in time."

"We're very near the border," Dare said. "Peter arranges the tour with just these types of delays in mind. It shouldn't be a problem, though we'll be short on rehearsal time."

"Rehearsal, is it?" The landlady bustled to their table, carrying a tray laden with bowls of stew and fragrant loaves. "Do you play? Why, we've a fortepiano in the private parlor. After supper you're welcome to it, though it hasn't been played in…" She paused, a bowl of stew in one hand. "Nigh on five years, I'd say. Elsie Simmons used to nip over and give us a tune, but she married a Yorkshire man and has gone since. More ale?"

Nicholas nodded, and the woman fetched an extra glass as Mr. Dubois joined them.

"Monsieur, you are well?" The valet took the place beside Clara and peered over at Dare. "It is not healthy, riding about in the rain. I cannot recommend it. An ague may take you."

"Henri, I keep you on as my valet, not my nursemaid. I assure you, I am in excellent health."

"Mr. Dubois has a point," Clara said, giving him a direct look.

"What would we do if you were to fall ill? Has that ever happened?"

"As a matter of fact, it has." Dare took a bite of stew.

"Really? What did you do?" Nicholas leaned forward, a light of interest in his eyes that Dare had missed seeing the past few weeks.

"It was in Sweden, last winter. I had agreed to play for the queen's birthday celebrations. The day before there was a huge feast, and, well, I don't suppose you have ever tried aquavit?"

Both Nicholas and his sister shook their heads, and Henri rolled his eyes. "Vile stuff, monsieur. You learned your lesson there."

"Were you poisoned?" Clara asked.

"Only in my judgment. Do you know, the Swedes have a curious custom. They go naked into an overheated box until they can stand it no more, then run out and roll in the snow." He darted a quick look across the table, to see Clara's cheeks flush with embarrassment at the topic.

"It sounds most unpleasant," Nicholas said.

"Not at all. It's quite invigorating."

Henri gave a snort. "Until you caught the terrible chill. Not so invigorating then."

"No. And when I was shaking so hard I could barely hold my violin, it was horrible. Still, I was determined to perform."

"What happened?" Nicholas asked.

"I could not disappoint the queen—though that is the only time in my life I expect to play reclining on a chair. I managed the piece, and then had to be carried out."

Clara clasped her hands tightly together. "How dreadful for you!"

"Ah," Henri said. "That was not the worst of it. No, the worst was that... that *weasel* continued the concert and claimed your place of honor."

"He saw his chance, and he took it." Dare lifted his glass and let the ale soothe the sour taste from his mouth.

"Who?" Nicholas asked.

"Anton Varga." Henri spat the words. "The most ungrateful, slime-dwelling—"

"Enough. We don't need to descend to his level." Tempting

though it might be.

"Varga?" Nicholas tilted his head. "He's a famous violinist in his own right, isn't he?"

The valet made a face. "Upstart. He wants to be *the* most famous, and takes every chance to try and unseat Master Reynard. And after all you taught him!"

Nicholas set down his spoon and looked at Dare. "He was your student?"

"Briefly." And what a mistake that had been. The arrogant young man had arrived at Dare's lodgings in Vienna, demanding that the maestro teach him everything. "A very difficult student. Most of our short time together was spent with Varga trying to prove he was the better player."

Henri pushed his empty stew bowl away. "That has not changed. But this spring you will settle the matter once and for all."

"You are speaking of the competition?" Clara asked.

Dare allowed himself to look fully at her. The question echoed in her expressive eyes, and her soft lips were slightly parted. He recalled too well the feel of that softness under his mouth, the way her tongue had tentatively met his. It had been her first kiss, surely.

He cleared his throat.

"Yes, the musical duel between us in Milan this coming April. The winner will be celebrated as the foremost violinist of the day." And the loser would slink off, a mere footnote to history. Dare glanced at Nicholas—his trump card, his talisman. "It's a beautiful city. You will enjoy it."

The composer opened his mouth, no doubt to issue a protest, but Dare overrode him. "In fact, I think *Il Diavolo* will be just the thing to ensure my victory."

"You do?" Clara said. "But, I have heard you practicing and..."

She twisted an errant strand of her pale hair between her fingers, clearly reluctant to finish her thought.

Dare laughed. He couldn't help it. "And it sounds dreadful, yes. Your brother is a fiendish composer, there is no arguing the fact. But April is months away."

Once they returned to London he would press Nicholas into

continuing with him to the Continent. And Clara? He could not envision her staying behind. Her support and company seemed vital to her brother.

More months of travel with Clara Becker. More months of sublimating his desire for her into his playing. It would be difficult, but not impossible. He need only keep the competition in his thoughts. And the dire specter of losing his composer, should he lose control. It was sufficient motivation.

"More ale?" The innkeeper's wife bustled up to their table and began clearing the remains of their supper.

Dare nodded. It was a relief to spend time with Nicholas without the man glaring at him at every turn. And even better to have Clara speak to him without that brittle edge in her voice, that scrim of ice that had encased her since the night of their kiss. The thaw was a pleasant change.

Might he ensure it was a permanent one? At the very least, he could apologize once more for his actions. She was a sensible young woman. Surely she would understand, though he did not expect her forgiveness.

Still, if Clara looked upon him a bit more kindly, that would help her brother's regard as well, which could only help the music. So far they had struggled through, but Dare missed those first, early rehearsals, when things had been far easier between himself and the composer.

"Now that supper's done, would you care to repair to the parlor?" the innkeeper's wife asked. "I'd dearly love to hear some music again, and that I would."

CHAPTER TWELVE

Clara tried—how she tried!—to keep from watching Darien Reynard during supper. But when he laughed, that sweet, dark sound settled low in her stomach, warm and disconcerting. It was a relief to repair to the inn's small parlor, where she would not have to sit facing him.

"Clara." Her brother grinned at her. "Let's play the Beethoven four-hands."

She glanced at the small fortepiano, an instrument built before the turn of the century, if she was not mistaken. "I don't think it's big enough. There can't be more than five octaves."

"We'll make do." Nicholas folded back the keyboard cover and played a run of notes. "Reasonably in tune, too. Come, Clara."

Her brother had not been in such high spirits for weeks, and she credited their humble surroundings. They'd eaten together at a table not set with linens and fine china, with no obsequious servants hovering to satisfy the least demand, no stilted, uncomfortable conversations between bites of lobster bisque. The parlor was cozy, not elegant in the least, and Clara released an inaudible sigh. The rain outside enclosed them, and it was as if they were removed, set apart from the cares of the world for the space of a country evening.

"You play?" Darien gave her a penetrating glance. "I should have guessed it."

"There was no escaping Papa," Nicholas said. "He was the sternest music master in London, and proud of it. Indeed, Clara was much more disciplined about practicing than I."

"That's because I didn't have friends calling me to play hoops in the street." She gave him an arch look.

"Don't think I didn't notice you escaped your chores by playing.

Papa always valued practicing over household work." Her brother slid over on the bench and patted the space beside him.

"A wise man," Darien said.

He looked serious, but Clara caught the spark of humor in his expression. Their eyes met, then held for a heartbeat too long before she glanced away, a shiver tingling through her.

"Bah." Henri perched himself on one of the chintz-covered chairs. "One cannot eat or wear music, no matter how beautiful."

"And you, Henri!" Darien settled on the sofa facing the piano. "The evening will not be complete without a song from you. It has been far too long."

The valet frowned, but the quirk of his brow indicated pleasure at the request. "Perhaps."

Nicholas shot her a quick look. "Ready?"

She felt ridiculously nervous playing before Darien Reynard, though surely not as terrified as Nicholas had been before the king. The thought gave her no comfort.

"I'm not certain I remember the second movement."

"You will." Her brother set his hands on the keys. "Commence!"

He played the opening theme, barely giving her time to catch up. The music bloomed around them, the cheerful runs, the interplay between melody and counter-melody drawing her in despite the lighter, unfamiliar keyboard, the fact of Darien watching them perform.

How curious. So many times she had seen him play, but had never imagined their positions reversed.

His regard became more pronounced when she and Nicholas began the *rondo* movement. She could feel the delicious weight of his gaze upon her. How good it was to at last be *seen* by him, to be known, at least in some small measure, for who she truly was: an accomplished musician. The relief of it was physical, as though a part of herself, tightly wound for weeks, was uncoiling, her shoulders loosening, her lungs able to breathe more deeply.

As the melody ascended, she shot Darien a quick, sideways glance, and was rewarded with a genuine smile. In that moment, she felt as though they were equal. Not a man and a woman, not a maestro and his admirer, but two musical souls, recognizing one another.

Then Nicholas nudged her with his elbow, his signal to speed up. Attention drawn back to the music, she gave him a nod, and together they increased the pace, matching note for note until the piece raced, tumbling headlong to a breathless, laughter-filled conclusion.

"Up to your old tricks, brother mine." She leaned against Nicholas's shoulder, mirth still bubbling through her as Darien and Henri applauded wildly.

"Ah, that was lovely." The innkeeper's wife hovered just inside the door. Her husband stood behind her, one hand resting on her shoulder. "To be sure, I have never heard anything so fine."

"Well, Beethoven," Nicholas said, his eyes shining.

Darien nodded, the warmth in his expression unmistakable. "One of the most memorable performances of the *Opus 6* I've heard. But come, Henri, give us a song."

The valet cleared his throat, then stood. "I give you *Amis, la matinee est belle* from *La Muette de Portici*."

"French opera?" Clara swiveled on the bench to face Henri.

She never would have thought it. But then, it did make sense that the valet of the most celebrated violinist in the world would have a musical bent, himself.

Henri took a moment to gather himself, then began. He had a strong, clear tenor that, while it would not earn him a place on the grand stages of Europe, was very pleasant to listen to.

When he reached the choral portions, Nicholas turned and began picking out a delicate accompaniment on the piano. The melody familiar, Clara hummed along, taking the soprano part and blending her notes to Henri's. It was a happy song, addressed to the fishermen of a village, and the lighthearted theme perfectly suited the evening.

Upon finishing, Henri swept them a bow full of flourishes. Clara's hands stung from her applause, but the valet certainly deserved it. The innkeeper's wife hastened to bring him a new mug of ale, then handed it over like a blushing maiden.

"'Tis as good as being in London. Or Paris at that!" She glanced at her husband. "Who'd have thought, John? Our very own parlor, turned into a concert hall. But you, sir." She directed her crescent smile at Darien. "Do you sing as well? I saw you carry in a case of some kind."

"I do not sing—"

"And thank heaven for that," Henri said, rolling his eyes.

"—but I will play. In fact," Darien looked at Nicholas, "what do you think of attempting *Il Diavolo*?"

Clara saw the convulsive movement as Nicholas swallowed, and then her brother straightened his shoulders. "Very well. I will forgive your mistakes, if you will forgive mine."

"Agreed." Darien rose. "Let me fetch my violin and the music. We shall master this piece yet."

"Come, come," Henri said, gesturing to their hosts as Darien exited the room. "No need to stand in your own doorway like unwelcome guests. Be seated, and you will hear something marvelous."

"Or hopefully something not too dreadful," Nicholas said under his breath. "I owe you a particularly evil turn for this, Clara."

Giving him a bright smile, she stood and stepped away from the piano bench. "You hardly need me at your elbow, then. I'll just make myself comfortable. Good luck!"

He narrowed his eyes at her, but before he could say anything more, Darien had returned, case in one hand and his mahogany music stand tucked under his arm. After unpacking his violin, Darien arranged his music, then glanced at Clara.

"There's a particularly tricky page turn midway through, Miss Becker. If you would be so kind? I will signal you."

"Certainly." She knew the exact place. It had either been cramp another line at the bottom of an already over-full page, or put in an awkward turn. Perhaps someday she would re-transcribe the piece to avoid it, but not just yet.

The maestro took his time tuning his instrument, although with the keyboard slightly out of true it was more a question of finding the least egregious notes. At last he seemed satisfied. He nodded to Nicholas, and Clara settled back into her overstuffed chair. The little parlor was the perfect setting to perform such a difficult piece for the first time, and she was glad of it for her brother's sake. The peat fire gave off a comforting, smoky smell and the oil-fed lamps shed a warmer, more inviting light than the harsher gaslights used at their performances.

Nicholas raised his hands and brought them down in the first crashing, delicious chord. The violin shot off into the melody, an arrow's volley of sharp-tipped notes that flew up, and up, and up. Darien Reynard had his eyes closed, of all things. Had he memorized the piece? Certainly his fingers danced unerringly, despite being perched so high up on the fingerboard. To Clara's relief, he opened his eyes as the music moved into the *spiccato* section. She was not certain she would be able to forgive him if he had already learned the whole of *Il Diavolo* by heart.

This was the part she had heard him working on, over and over. The bow flew on and off the strings in a percussive dance, while the left hand had to stretch and reach for intervals no sane composer would demand. An eleventh. A thirteenth; surely courting the devil into the piece with that one. Clara bit her lip as Darien missed one note, then another. But it was not mirth she was holding back, to her surprise, but a fierce desire that he succeed.

Dark hair fell over one eye as he strove with the music, concentration etched in the set of his lips, the line of his jaw. Then he lifted his head and met her gaze, and the intensity in his eyes seared her. Good lord. It was a wonder the sheets of paper had not ignited under that look. *Il Diavolo* indeed.

But that was the signal for the page turn. She had been waiting; indeed, she'd had to keep herself from jumping up too early. It would not do to let the maestro know how very familiar she was with the music.

She came to stand beside him, careful to give his bow enough room, and felt the heat rising off his body. She had not been so close since their kiss, and her skin tingled with the memory of it, sudden sparks coursing all through her.

With a deft touch, she turned the page. The paper did not betray the trembling of memory. Would anyone else's kiss have swept her with such a tumult of sensation? Somehow she did not think so. Her body was attuned to Darien Reynard, no matter how she might deny it. He was the bow, she the string, set in motion by his proximity. The anger she had polished like a shield fell away, leaving her exposed to the raw fact of her own yearning. It was hopeless, disastrous, and there was nothing she could do.

Swallowing, she moved back into the cooler spaces of air that did not hold his warmth. Back to her chair, back to listening to the tangle of melody he and Nicholas strove to unravel. The innkeeper and his wife sat, eyes wide, as the music soared, stumbled, soared again—but Henri, to Clara's discomfort, was watching her, a flicker of sympathy in his bright gaze.

Surely he had seen dozens of women react thus to Darien Reynard. She clasped her hands in her lap and pointedly turned her attention to Nicholas, who did all he could with the piano part. But that was harder still. Her fingers twitched when he missed a series of chords, and the muscles in her legs were tense, as though they would leap up and propel her to the keyboard.

Better to watch Darien and let him weave his dark spell around her than to let her body betray her deep knowledge of the music. At least her fascination with him was nothing out of the ordinary, though her brother would not be pleased if he noted it. Happily, both he and Darien were absorbed in wrestling with the devil.

By the time they reached the *cadenza*, Clara was lost in the piece, too. Would she never tire of hearing Darien play her music? Another secret thrill went through her as she watched him. The notes sparked off his instrument, the bow zigging and zagging in a wild stitchery of melody. It was exultant, and primal, and she caught her breath as he and Nicholas came careening into the very last chord.

"Bravo!" She was on her feet in an instant, applauding so fiercely her wrists ached from it. She was not sorry she had written so difficult a piece; not when it spurred the performers to such heights.

Henri and their hosts stood as well, and between the four of them they made a satisfying enough noise. The innkeeper even essayed a rough "ho!" of approval, while his wife dabbed at her eyes with a corner of her apron between bouts of applause.

Darien, a wide grin on his face, clapped Nicholas on the shoulder. "Well done! *Il Diavolo* shall be vanquished yet."

"Yes." Nicholas actually returned the maestro's smile. "Though you nearly left me behind in the *scherzo* section. I hadn't anticipated such... velocity."

"Very good," Henri said, nodding. "Very good indeed. This calls for something celebratory, and I have just the thing." He turned to the innkeeper. "Sir, if you would fetch some small glasses. I don't suppose you keep any snifters about?"

The innkeeper shook his head, and Darien raised his brows.

"You are breaking out *La Compte*?" he asked. "Henri, we are honored."

The valet gave a sniff. "This is an occasion that warrants it. I shall return in a moment." He followed the innkeeper out of the room.

"Isn't that a rather expensive cognac?" Nicholas turned to Darien. "You travel with your own supply?"

"No, it is Henri's. Saved for only special circumstances. It's a rare privilege that he's bringing it out now." Darien tucked his violin away. "But then, abandoning all humbleness, I do think we deserve it."

Nicholas gave a muffled snort of laughter. "You are not known for your humility, sir."

A barb, though leavened with humor. Clara shot her brother a glance. She had heard enough from Nicholas these past weeks about Darien Reynard's failings.

Henri hastened back into the parlor, a greenish-black bottle cradled in his arms.

"The greatest violinist in all Europe should not be humble," he declared, clearly having caught Nicholas's comment. "Indeed, false modesty sits well on no one. But now, let us have a toast."

The innkeeper set out six glasses, and Henri deftly poured two inches of cognac into each. Not a single drop was lost, and the valet re-corked his bottle with a look of satisfaction.

"To greatness." Henri raised his glass.

Clara followed the gesture with the others, then lifted the glass to her mouth. The intense fumes served as a warning, and she took a careful swallow, the alcohol tingling against her lips with a pleasant heat.

"Ah." Darien held his cognac to the light. "This never ceases to surprise me. Thank you, Henri."

"It is very good," Nicholas said. "I haven't much of a taste for cognac, but still…"

Henri looked pleased, though his nostrils flared for a moment. "This is not any cognac, you understand, but a bottle of '11, recognized by connoisseurs to be the very finest vintage."

"Aye." The innkeeper nodded. "I had a bottle of '08 once, but 'twas not nearly so smooth."

"Did you?" Henri turned to the man, a light of appreciation in his eyes, and they wandered over to the bar to discuss obscure vineyards.

The wife shook her head. "Ah, and now they'll go on like that for hours, if I know my man. But thank you, all. 'Twas a fine evening, indeed. I'll not soon forget it."

"It truly was our pleasure," Darien said, and Clara heard the sincerity in his tone.

"Indeed." Nicholas nodded.

Clara tried not to comment on his agreement. Perhaps the two men could finally reconcile during this last week of the tour. A pity it could not have happened earlier. She took another sip of cognac, the liquid burning a spicy trail down her throat. She turned to her brother just as he took a step forward, and collided with his arm.

"Blast." Nicholas glanced at his waistcoat, now splashed with the remainder of his cognac.

"Oh dear. I *am* sorry," she said.

"Don't let Henri see you waste his liqueur so carelessly." There was a note of laughter in Darien's voice.

"Perhaps I can wring it out, back into the glass." Her brother's tone was dry. "Though I doubt it would improve the flavor. If you will excuse me."

The innkeeper's wife took his empty glass. "I'll just wash this out, then. A pity, it is."

Clara couldn't decide if she meant the damage to Nicholas's clothing, or the loss of fine cognac.

"Miss Becker, a moment." Darien set one hand on her arm as she turned to follow her brother.

Her pulse leaped at his touch.

"Yes?" The word came out rather breathless.

He took a step closer, which did not help matters. Clara felt as though she were a moon, pulled helplessly into his orbit. Too close— perilously close.

"I wanted to commend your musicianship. You are very talented."

More than he would ever guess. "I grew up in a musical household, as you know."

"That does not always confer depth of musicality. You've an innate gift."

"Thank you."

Knowledge of her deception twisted in her, hard-edged and uncomfortable. She tried to move away, but his hand was still on her, firm and compelling.

"Wait." His mossy green eyes caught hers, a curious vulnerability in their depths. "I owe you a sincere apology. Long overdue, in fact."

"You owe me nothing." Must he be so contrite, and rob her of her last defenses?

His fingers rubbed up and down her arm, the touch shocking, even through the fine wool of her dress. He seemed unaware of the motion, of what his touch did to her. Her senses skewed crazily, and she fought not to lean toward him.

"Clara, I was wrong to kiss you, we both know that. But you must understand that afterward, I acted as I felt I must. I am sorry if I have seemed... cold." He pressed his lips together, his gaze searching her face.

She closed her eyes a moment and took a deep breath, flavored with cognac and Darien's cologne.

"Master Reynard." Formality would have to serve her now, since her anger at him had fled completely. "There can be nothing between us. Please, don't pretend otherwise."

Dear heaven, how she wished it could be different. But too many obstacles lay between them; the enormity of her lie the tallest mountain of all.

"Nothing?" His voice was low now, smoky and persuasive. "Not even... friendship?"

Friendship? With Darien Reynard? It would be like befriending a fire, or a feral wolf, and she did not think she was capable of it. Indeed, she was already half in love with the man—a truth she could no longer avoid. It was a state that precluded something as simple as friendship.

"I don't— "

"Consider it." He slid his hand down and closed his fingers over hers, then lifted her hand to his mouth.

The press of his lips against the back of her hand nearly made her knees give way. Damn him, she was in enough turmoil as it was. She could not afford to plunge back into those early daydreams she had nurtured. Not with the tensions between him and her brother, not with the memory of their disastrous kiss still flaring brightly through her.

"I would be pleased if we could be friends, Miss Becker."

There was no answer she could make that would not sear her. She dropped him a mute curtsey and retreated, the back of her hand burning. She glanced down at it, surprised he had not left a mark on her pale skin.

Instead he had only burned a kiss into her soul—invisible, and inescapable.

CHAPTER THIRTEEN

A Musical Evening Beyond Compare~
The night after their well-received performance in the city, Master Darien Reynard on violin and Mr. Nicholas Becker on piano delighted listeners at the Duke of Hamilton's estate. Their Mozart was delightful, but the duo's rendering of Mr. Becker's composition, Seascape, *was truly sublime. A rare musical genius has moved through our midst, and we are the richer for it.*
-Edinburgh Edict

"Master Reynard?" Clara tapped on the dressing room door, still buoyed by the notes of the concert he had finished. The music swirled through her, lending her joy, and hope.

The door opened and Darien gestured her inside. "Miss Becker. An unexpected pleasure."

He smiled at her, and she tried to ignore the fact he'd removed his dark coat and undone his cravat. The white fabric of his shirt made his skin seem darker, his hair soft midnight. Did he have Mediterranean blood? She had not thought to wonder before. He was simply Darien Reynard. But even the greatest violinist of the day had to come from *somewhere.*

She was not here, however, to ask about his origins.

"Master Reynard…" Oh, this should not be so difficult. She lifted her gaze to his and put all her sincerity behind the next words. "I wanted to thank you. Your generosity, you've done so much for us—"

"I need no thanks, though I'm happy I could provide some assistance to your family. Still, with Nicholas's talent, it was more than an even trade."

Nicholas's talent. Clara swallowed and half turned from the

maestro. She was not sure he understood how very dire their circumstances had been, or that he'd saved them from a life of certain destitution.

The small room was crowded with flowers, the smell of orange blossoms permeating the air with sweetness. Orchids and anemones embraced and tangled in a wanton display. She followed one meandering vine of ivy and tried to collect her thoughts. It seemed her thanks were unnecessary, but she'd had to offer them.

"It was an excellent concert," she said at last. "Cambridge likes you very well. I don't know when I've seen so many bouquets. They must have plundered their hothouses."

He laughed. "When we play on the Continent, then you'll see bouquets to exclaim over. Sometimes there's hardly room for me in the dressing room. Luckily, I've never been prone to sneezing fits."

"The Continent?" She swung back to face him. "But we return to London tomorrow. The tour is over."

"*This* tour, yes. I have every intention of bringing your brother, and yourself, if you wish it, along with me on the next one. We need not depart immediately, but—"

"We cannot come." She hugged her arms about herself. "Nicholas could not…"

She made herself stop before she blurted out too much. Her brother was immeasurably relieved to be returning home. He had told her at great length how good it would be to set aside the mask of Nicholas Becker, composer. The deception had been exhausting him; she could see it every time he took his bow before a standing ovation, every time he accepted praise for something that was none of his doing. They could not continue touring with Darien. How soon until her brother faltered? She feared the black melancholy even now hovered over him, waiting to descend.

Yet as Nicholas's smiles began to come more freely, her own had begun to fade. What did she have to return to? Certainly, she would be glad to have the burden lifted from Nicholas, relieved to shed the constant worry her notebooks would be discovered. She would be free to compose without having to lock herself in her room.

It had used to be enough.

She glanced at Darien. He watched her, a frown creased between his dark brows. "Of course you will come," he said. "The competition in Italy is only two months away. Nicholas must be there."

"I don't think you will be able to convince him of that."

The frown moved down to Darien's mouth. "Does he still hate me so much, then? I had thought he'd forgiven me at last. Our rehearsals and performances are going so well, I would not have guessed it."

How could she possibly explain? "It is not that he dislikes you—"

"Clara." Darien stepped forward and took her by the shoulders. "Be honest. What can I do about Nicholas? You know your brother well. You must tell me."

Shadows hovered in his eyes. Under his intent gaze, her secrets trembled close to the surface.

The impulse to reveal everything rushed through her, hot and immediate. Oh, how she yearned for him to know she was the composer! There was a unique and wordless bond between them, if only he could see it. See *her* for who she truly was: the woman who wrote the music he loved.

"Yes," she whispered. The edge of truth burned, but it was a welcome fire. Her pulse pounded, each beat striking through her, like a clock telling the hours. It was time. Time. "Darien, I—"

"Master Reynard?" a too-familiar voice called from the hallway.

Oh, God. Nicholas, knocking at the door. Darien standing too close, his hands on her shoulders.

"In here." With one swift move he pivoted and thrust her into the wardrobe.

She caught her balance, then crouched between his coats. The wool rasped softly against her cheek as she fought to contain her breathing, the scent of him all around her. Her fingers trembled and she laced them tightly together. Darien pushed the wardrobe door closed, but the latch did not catch and she could see a slice of the room beyond.

"Nicholas. Come in."

She heard her brother step into the dressing room. He cleared his throat.

"I wanted to thank you before we returned to London," he said. "You've been exceedingly generous, not only to myself but to my family. It means a great deal to us."

"You are very welcome." There was a quiet note in Darien's voice, as though he knew how important these thanks were. Perhaps, with Nicholas giving him almost the same words she had, he did understand. "It has been my pleasure. These last concerts have been excellent."

"Yes." Nicholas sounded glad. "I'll always remember them."

"You know…" The maestro moved into her line of sight and began unbuttoning his gold-embroidered waistcoat. "My agent informs me that audiences on the Continent are clamoring to hear your music. When I play your compositions to best Varga, the world will be at our feet. It would be good if you were there."

"Ah. But I don't have to be, for you to win. Do I?"

Darien hesitated a moment, then shrugged out of his waistcoat. "No. But it might help. Certainly, if you performed with me, your fame would be assured. As would a slew of publishing contracts."

"Well, those could be sent to me in London." There was a stubborn note in her brother's voice that Clara knew all too well. Nothing would entice him to continue touring.

Darien nodded, as if he recognized pushing would only make Nicholas balk further. He turned his attention to his cuffs. "So. Home to London it is. Are you ready to return to the hotel?"

"Almost. I must go find Clara."

"I'll meet you at the carriage in fifteen minutes," Darien said. He sounded remarkably calm at the thought of Nicholas looking for her.

She did not hear her brother leave, but a few moments later Darien swung open the wardrobe door. "It's safe."

Trying not to think of how rumpled her plum-colored gown must be, Clara took his hand and let him assist her out.

"You see," she said. "I don't think Nicholas can be convinced."

"Perhaps."

Darien looked thoughtful, and she suspected he would not let them go so easily. The thought worried and elated her all at once.

His expression cleared and he focused on her again. "But tell me. What were you about to say, earlier?"

Realization scratched against her heart, a sharp-edged knowledge she could not escape. She had been so close to ruining everything, to destroying Darien's career with her selfish, unconsidered words. His entire future rested on the deception she and Nicholas had foisted upon him. The recognition the master deserved could only be his if she let the lie stand, and let the world continue to believe for all time that Nicholas Becker was the composer.

Her silence was the greatest gift she could give Darien. The only repayment she could ever make.

"It doesn't matter," she said.

"Of course it does." He drew her forward. "Clara—"

"No."

She stepped into him, her skirts brushing his trouser legs, and slipped her hands up to his shoulder. No more questions. Tomorrow she must bid him farewell, but tonight she would kiss him. One final kiss, to remember. She tilted her face up and brushed her lips over his. He closed his eyes, his body suddenly taut, but he did not push her away, or even command her to stop.

Heat sparked through her, and a curious excitement born of her own boldness. She pressed closer, re-learning the shape of his lips, sipping the warmth of his breath. Her breasts, her whole body, tingled where she touched him, and she wanted to lean into him, push herself hard against his strength. But wanting and action were so often separated by caution, and so she continued the feather-light kiss, praying he would not move away.

"Clara." Her name, whispered into her own mouth. As Darien finished the word, whatever spell bound him motionless broke.

With a sudden, nearly violent move, he brought his arms around her and pulled her against him. His lips opened over hers, hot and demanding. Her yearning spilled over, like a goblet of liqueur, sweet and fierce and obeying only the rule of gravity.

It was a kiss filled with near chances, hopes and regrets distilled into a single moment of desire. Clara closed her eyes against the prickle of tears. This kiss would be a bright, burning star for her to chart her life by, the only thing in a dark sea full of night. She would look up and navigate her future by its light, by the memory of Darien's kiss. His body printed on hers, the heat of him enveloping her through the thin silk of her gown. His tongue delving into her willing, open mouth. His strong arms around her, inescapable, secure, the both of them leaning into one another, as though their hearts might—if only they pressed close enough—touch.

And then it was over, leaving her aching with unspoken words, unspent tears. The kiss was over, the tour was over, and tomorrow she would watch him go forward into his own life, while she stayed behind in hers. Holding the knowledge inside her, fragile as a fallen leaf, she stepped back and offered him a small curtsey.

"Farewell, Darien. And thank you."

She could not meet his moss-green eyes, could not wait for a reply. She was breaking. The door was smooth under her hand as she left his dressing room, and he did not call her back.

CHAPTER FOURTEEN

The merry pranksters of Cambridge were out in full force at Maestro Reynard's recent concert. A number of young gentlemen appeared dressed in unrelieved black—down to the dying of their hair! Each one proceeded to court every nearby female with claims that they were the true Master. Darien Reynard took the jest with good grace, going so far as to insist that his imitators stand and take a bow at the end of his performance…

-The Courier

It was raining; a gray, dreary drizzle that shrouded the buildings of London like a widow's veil. For once, Darien shared the coach with them. But then, he would have it to himself soon.

Clara could feel him watching her. Darting a look across the carriage, she found his expression brooding, a thin line etched between his dark brows. Their gazes met, then held as yearning trembled wildly inside her.

She was only grateful Nicholas did not notice. Her brother was in the grip of unusually high spirits, though as they penetrated deeper into London, his expression turned pensive.

"This looks rather like our old neighborhood," he said with a glance out the window. "I thought we were going to Papa's new house."

Nicholas had directed Darien's agent to send his pay directly to their father, and Clara had written Papa, urging him to find newer, better lodgings at once. Certainly they had sent enough for him to do so. There was no reason he should stay a minute more in that hovel they had once called their home.

Darien shifted. "We are going to the address Peter gave me—the place he has been delivering your money."

"But..." The coach slowed and Nicholas leaned forward, shaking his head. "It *is* our old neighborhood. Our old house, in fact." His voice rose. "Darien! Are you certain my pay has been delivered as instructed?"

The footman opened the door, letting the cold, wet air seep in. Nicholas was right. There was the cracked walkway, the peeling front door, and waiting on the stoop—

"Papa!" Clara flew out of the carriage and dashed up the walk, into the quick comfort of his embrace. She would not cry. She would not.

"Clara," he said. "It is so good to have you home. And Nicholas. Come, let me see you. Such the gentleman you look." He nodded to Darien. "Master Reynard, we have much to thank you for."

"What are you saying?" Nicholas pivoted, waving at the house. "Nothing has changed! Where is the money I sent?"

"Yes, Papa." Clara kept a hand on her father's shoulder. "Why are you still here? I thought you'd removed to better lodgings."

The only thing that had prevented her emotions from crumbling during the return to London had been imagining Papa's bright new home. She'd never anticipated coming back to this dreary place. Tears pricked the back of her throat. She and Nicholas had struggled so, and to what end?

Papa sighed. "Come in. Come in, all of you, and I will explain."

The walls were closer together, the carpet dingier than she remembered, and Clara felt her spirits sink a bit more with each step. The same threadbare furniture in the parlor, the inescapably familiar smell of must and old cabbage. The taste of hopelessness. She tried not to breathe it in, but there was no other choice.

Her father sat, as though his bones pained him, and gave them a sober look.

"Well. I had hoped..." He cleared his throat and began again. "Your money came regularly, Nicholas. But it was not enough."

"Not enough?" Nicholas began pacing. "How can a small fortune be not enough? Do you know what I had to—"

"Papa," Clara cut in. "Please explain."

She did not want Nicholas to spill his litany of grievances, his unhappiness with Darien, who stood silently just inside the doorway. The air was heavy enough without those words.

"We are too deeply in debt." Her father bent over his cane, his voice rough. "When your mother was ill, we spent everything, and more, and more, and it was still not enough. I did not want you burdened with the knowledge, but if not for Master Reynard, it would have been debtor's prison for me. Servitude for you both."

"You should have told us!" Clara hurried to him and placed her hands over his gnarled ones where they gripped his cane. "We should have known."

"It would have changed nothing."

Darien stepped forward. "Now, however, I think it changes everything."

It did. Clara's thoughts whirled in a storm of implications, but one thing was as clear and sharp as lightning. They could not stop touring with Darien Reynard. She was no longer safe savoring the memory of his kisses. Not when they would still be together, when every day she would be close enough to touch him. Taste his scent on her tongue. Feel the heat of his leanly muscled body as she passed him in the hallway. She swallowed.

"No." A note of disbelief rang in her brother's denial. Nicholas's pacing grew sharp and awkward. "We will remain in London. We must. You said there will be new publishing contracts for the compositions." He halted in front of Darien.

"And there will be." Darien's voice was calm, though she detected an undercurrent of tension. "But not right away, and certainly not before I perform in Europe."

He did not add *with you*. He did not need to.

"Surely there will be advances," she said, her heart twisting for Nicholas.

He had managed, barely, to hold up under the strain of the last few weeks. Knowing the deception was coming to an end had strengthened her brother, even as it had sapped her.

"No," Darien said. "Even for the most famous composers, publishers will only pay once they have the manuscript in hand."

"We could borrow," Nicholas said.

"No borrowing." Papa shook his cane. "No debt, ever again. Nicholas, you and your sister fared well enough on this tour. You could do another."

Clara glanced about the room, chilly despite the extra coals heaped on the grate. Cold winter air pressed inexorably through the thin walls, seeped through the rickety window frames. Soot sifted down onto her soul. She could not bear to live here again.

She could not bear to see her brother's misery eat away at his soul.

"Nicholas…" She did not know what to say.

He ignored her outstretched hand and went to stand at the window, arms crossed. Papa only shook his head. His face was lined with cares and he looked older now. Though perhaps it was only their absence, and this new knowledge, that allowed Clara to see the struggle etched on his face.

"I will leave you to discuss your options," Darien said. "And I remind you that my offer to tour the Continent stands. In fact, considering the extra distances and performances the tour will entail, I shall increase your salary. I'll call again later this afternoon."

He inclined his head and strode out, not waiting for a reply. The door closed hollowly behind him, and this time Clara did not watch as the black coach pulled away.

"Well." Papa did not move from his seat, his gaze fixed on Nicholas. "It seems clear enough what you must do."

It was eerily like the last time Darien had been here, but now there was no celebratory sense, no vast relief that their fortunes had changed. Things had become infinitely more tangled.

"Papa," Clara said. "It has not been easy for Nicholas, you must understand that."

"And returning to this would be?" He thumped his cane on the floor. "Look at you both, with your fine clothing, your cheeks no longer hollow from hunger. That is what I want for my children, not this life of poverty!"

"I could resume teaching." Nicholas turned from the window and jammed his hands in his pockets. "My students would return, or

I could find new ones. Touring with Master Reynard must surely have lent me enough prestige."

"Perhaps," their father said. "And perhaps not. You could try, yes. But what if it were not so? What if you gained only a meager number of students, or none at all? We would be as badly off as before. And it would be too late to mend, with Master Reynard long gone to the Continent."

"If we went with him," Clara said, "the money would be enough—"

"You said that last time!" Nicholas glared at her. "But it has not proven to be the case."

"I did not make such promises," she said. It had been Papa. But Nicholas would not turn on their father with such anger, and so Clara bore the brunt of it.

Papa heaved himself up from the chair and went to stand beside Nicholas at the window.

"Do not blame your sister," he said. "If you go with the maestro to the Continent, it will be different. There will be greater exposure, more publishing contracts. Enough to build a secure foundation for our family."

"I cannot." Nicholas drew his shoulders in toward his chest.

"You have been," Papa said. "The secret is still safe, yes? Our debts are nearly erased."

Clara wrapped her arms about her waist. It was plain that she and Nicholas must continue on with Darien. And Darien needed them, as well, needed his "composer" with him to best Anton Varga. That was nearly as important as keeping their family from the hard London streets.

"I'm going upstairs," her brother said.

Without meeting her eyes, without looking at Papa, he left the parlor. His footsteps sounded slow and heavy as he climbed the stairs.

"Ach." Papa let out a sigh, melancholy as the wind that crept in through the chinks in the sill. "He will see the sense of it."

Clara could only hope. And despair.

***

"This will do," Dare said. "I'll direct my agent to send a deposit immediately."

He glanced with satisfaction about the airy, marble-floored foyer of the town house. Not so grand as to be overwhelming, not in the very tip-top of neighborhoods, but with an easy gentility the Beckers would appreciate.

"And the furniture?" the hovering landlord asked.

"Leave it all for now. It's suitable enough." Far better than anything the family currently owned, with the exception of their piano.

Regardless of whether or not Nicholas and Clara agreed to come to the Continent, he would see the Beckers out of that hovel and into a better neighborhood. Common decency demanded as much. He could not leave his composer in such penury. Nor Clara, he had to admit. The expression on her face had been pinched and unhappy from the moment she'd set foot in the door of her old home, and it pleased him that he had the power to improve things for her and her family.

"A full year, sir?"

"Yes." By that time, the Beckers' situation should be stable, no matter what choice they made.

"Very good. Let me draw up the paperwork and give you the keys." The man hurried off.

Dare turned, glancing down the hallway and into the spacious drawing room. The house would do quite well, indeed. Now he had the pleasurable task of informing the Beckers they had a new home.

Less than an hour later, his carriage drew up in front of the Beckers' current dwelling. It looked even more pitiful in comparison to the comfortable town house. Dare stepped down from the carriage and hurried to the front door.

Clara answered his knock. "Master Reynard. We did not look for you quite so soon."

Despite the reluctance in her words, her smile was genuine.

"I have news," Dare said. "I've let a house for you."

"I beg your pardon?" Her smile slowly faded. "We need no charity from you, sir."

"It's not charity." Damn it, she wasn't taking this the right way at all. Her expression, instead of glowing with gratitude, was guarded.

"Is it not?" she asked. "You have not spoken to us much of your own path out of poverty. Did you gladly take handouts along the way?"

"That's different."

It wasn't, though. He had made his fortune by trusting only himself, accepting assistance from no one. Dare shifted on the step, an unaccustomed feeling heating the back of his neck. Shame.

Half of him wanted to apologize, but the other half was sparking with anger. He did not like being made to feel ashamed. Especially when there was a grain of truth in it.

"If you did not mean it as charity," Clara said, "then it's outright bribery. Your kindness overburdens our family."

"Then let the blasted house stand empty. I'm sorry I even thought of it."

"Clara?" Her father came up to the door and gave her a stern look. "Why do you keep the maestro standing outside? Come in, Master Reynard."

Lips set in a tight line, Clara took a step back, allowing Dare to enter.

Mr. Becker called up the stairs for his son, then led them into the parlor. He settled into one of the tattered armchairs and leaned his cane against the side. Clara perched nearby, and a moment later, Nicholas hurried into the chilly room.

"Mary, please fetch us tea," Clara said to the brown-haired girl who hovered outside the parlor.

"A moment." Dare held out his hand to the maid, whom he had learned was a distant relation with even worse prospects than the Beckers' own. "I have news that concerns everyone in this household."

"What is this news of yours?" Mr. Becker leaned forward, a shrewd glint in his eyes.

Nicholas looked anxious, and again Dare wished things could

have been simpler between them. But even if he had not been so damnably drawn to Clara, he admitted that the perfect meeting of creative minds he'd dreamed of would not have come to fruition. Nicholas did not seem to have the desire, nor the temperament, for such a collaboration. Dare tried not to let it disappoint. After all, the man was still an incredibly talented composer.

"Here." Dare held out the keys he had received from the landlord.

"What are they?" Nicholas eyed him suspiciously, as though Dare cradled a handful of poisonous spiders.

"The keys to 44 Chester Court. Your new lodgings, if you'll have them."

"Ah," Mr. Becker said, while Clara's eyes widened. It was a neighborhood that held some prestige.

"You can't bribe us into coming with you," Nicholas said. "Don't take the keys, Papa."

Despite his son's words, the elder Mr. Becker held out one hand, palm up. Dare gently deposited the key ring in his seamed hand.

"The place is paid for," Dare said. "If the house stands empty for the next year, it's your choice. And it's not a bribe, it's a thank-you. Dispose of the place as you please."

"It is greatly appreciated," Mr. Becker said. He cleared his throat and gave his children a meaningful look.

"It was a kind thought," Clara said at last, though her tone belied her words.

"Yes." Nicholas jammed his hands into his pockets.

"I apologize if I acted hastily," Dare said, with a glance at Clara. "I wanted to see you provided for, no matter what choice you make. It was, perhaps, presumptuous of me. But the lease is only for one year, and then you may move where you please. Or simply stay here."

Clara pulled her shawl tighter around her shoulders. "It would be a waste for the house to stand empty for that time. Papa, you deserve better surroundings than this."

"You all do," Dare said.

Mr. Becker glanced at his son, and there was a wealth of

unspoken words in that look: duty and provision and family, if Dare were to guess. He tried not to hold his breath, but damnation, he wished the composer would simply choose to come with him.

"Papa," Nicholas said, then tightened his lips and began to pace.

An awkward silence descended, marred by the sound of Nicholas's footsteps. The edges of more words tried to pierce through, but the quiet was too thick, impenetrable.

Dare folded his arms and watched the others. Both the serving girl and Clara focused on Nicholas, their heads turning together as he tromped from one end of the room to the other. The father, mouth pursed, glanced at his son, then to the floor. Clearly this was Nicholas's choice to make.

At last the composer halted and brushed the hair out of his eyes with a weary gesture.

"Very well." His voice was quiet, weighted like that of a man accepting a sentence of deportation. "We will move Papa into the town house you have so generously provided, and Clara and I will continue to the Continent."

A flare of triumph went through Dare, but he tamped it down. It was not a straightforward victory. But then, he was learning that nothing with the Beckers was ever simple.

CHAPTER FIFTEEN

Maestro Reynard Returns to the Continent!

After touring England and Scotland, the virtuoso violinist returns to grace the rest of Europe—this time with his new composer, Mr. Nicholas Becker. Word of Mr. Becker's talent has spread, and audiences are eager to hear the offerings of this newest musical star in the firmament.

-l'Assemblee, February 1831

The wind of the English Channel tangled Clara's hair, teasing long strands from her usual coiled braid as the boat to Calais bore them across the water. Rain spattered her cloak, but it could not dampen her spirits. London was behind them.

Over the winter holidays they had settled Papa into the new house, and she had to admit it was a lovely place. Even Henri had agreed it was acceptable. Seeing the genteel elegance, coupled with the look of relief on Papa's face, had seemed to help Nicholas, too. At any rate, he was smiling more frequently. It went far to ease her fears. As long as her brother could picture Papa content and cared for, she hoped Nicholas could carry the burden of their secret a short while longer.

Now they were headed for the Continent, the future. The dark mass of France rose before them above the ruffled waters. Salt and adventure flavored the air, quickening Clara's breath. The clouds were beginning to break and tentative fingers of light reached down, sparking silver off the sea and touching the coastline with color.

Inside her, a melody unfurled; a dove winging eastward in the clear air. Clara closed her eyes and followed that bright strand, the music that would resonate in Darien's strings and fly to freedom.

"Are you glad?"

She would know that voice anywhere, among a thousand voices. Clara opened her eyes and turned to see Darien leaning against the railing beside her. His dark hair blew across one cheek, soft as feathers against the line of his jaw. She wanted to lay her hand there, feel his breath touch her skin.

"Yes." Gladder than she could ever say. She feared her expression would give her away, and dropped her gaze to her gloves. "How soon until we reach Paris?"

"Three days, but the roads are not so bad, even this time of year. We'll stop tonight in Boulogne, the next in Amiens, and reach the city two days before our concert at the *Conservatoire*."

"Henri seems pleased to be returning to France." Indeed, the valet had begun strutting about as soon as they departed Dover, clearly anticipating being back on his home soil. "He is from Paris? Does he have family there? He has not mentioned it."

One corner of Darien's mouth curved up in a wry smile. "My valet feels keenly the sacrifices he must make to travel with me. Speaking of Paris only makes him unhappy, and so he does not. But once we are there, he will talk of nothing else. Don't be surprised if he insists on remaking your brother's wardrobe, and yours as well."

"But…" Clara smoothed a hand down the fine, pale wool of her walking dress. "These clothes are barely two months old. I hardly think we warrant new ones. And the expense!"

Darien shook his head. "I'd rather pay for a dozen wardrobes than have to endure Henri's wounded disapproval. You will be in Paris, the styles are *a la mode*, and it would be criminal if you didn't reflect the very best. Or so Henri sees it. I'll have to endure it myself, no doubt."

"Well then." She caught the self-deprecating glint in Darien's eyes. "I suppose if the great maestro can suffer a new wardrobe, I can as well."

"How superior you make me sound."

"It's fortunate I know how terribly human you are. Imagine, you even slurp your soup with a spoon."

She was rewarded by his warm, dark laughter, and could not help smiling back. It was a novel sensation, teasing Darien Reynard.

Two weeks ago she never would have imagined it, but somehow she did not see the most celebrated musician in the world standing beside her. Or, she did, but it was only a part of who Darien was, not the whole of this complex, driven man.

"Darien…" It seemed a good time to broach a question she had been worrying over. "Do you think, now that we'll be on the Continent, you might return to the carriage? It doesn't seem right, your riding ahead."

There. She had said it. And though it might make things more difficult, she had never liked knowing he was out riding in the rain and wind, suffering the worst of winter because of their illicit kiss.

"Ah." He sobered. "I don't think your brother is any more genially inclined toward me than before."

"Nicholas can…"—*go to the devil*—"keep his feelings to himself. Both Henri and I think you should return to the carriage, and we outnumber him. It's hardly fair to make you ride the breadth of Europe because Nicholas is being unreasonable. If he's so blessed unhappy, let *him* take a horse."

Darien's expression tightened. "I don't think his reaction was unreasonable, given the circumstances." He glanced over his shoulder, then returned his gaze to her. "As to what more has passed between us, Clara—let us agree that it's better forgotten."

Sudden grief blazed through her. "Am I so easy to forget, then? Simply dismiss me from your mind?"

He closed his eyes, some strong emotion etched across his features—fear or regret, she could not name it. When he opened his eyes again his face was shuttered, and she castigated herself for ruining the easy camaraderie they had shared.

"Miss Becker. If you must know, you are not forgettable. In the least. But you must *also* know how infinitely foolish it is to act upon any attraction we may feel. It could ruin everything."

He was right. She turned to face the waves, her grip hard on the railing, and tried to blink away her stupid, stupid tears. And yet… he had all but admitted he was attracted to her. It was a grain of sand she would polish into a pearl, a secret treasure against her heart.

"I know." Her voice came out a whisper.

He moved to stand closer, and she forced herself not to lean toward his heat. The backs of his fingers brushed, feather-light, against her cheek.

"I am sorry," he said.

She did not look at him. She could only stare at the pewter waves churning all about the boat. After a long moment he left, and the wind bit through her cloak, a chilly reminder of her own solitude.

***

Paris, at least, did not disappoint. There was something in the air, some refined yet zestful quality that made Clara feel as though she were sipping champagne. She let Henri shepherd her off to the modiste's with no protest, glad to have something to occupy her mind other than Darien. Every time she looked at him, her heart hurt. Yet she could not keep from looking.

"*Bien*," Henri said, clapping his hands together as Clara paraded about the dressmaker's salon in an opulent dress with hastily basted seams. "You look delicious. The lace heightens your fairness to perfection. *C'est magnifique.*"

Here in Paris the little valet seemed to sparkle, his high spirits impossible to resist. Even Nicholas laughed as Henri squired them around the town, insisting they sample pastries and watch street performers and admire the paintings in the Louvre.

Her brother had accompanied them on this particular outing, but spying a nearby bookseller's had begged leave to browse while Clara took her fittings. She was happy to see the spring in his step as he entered the little shop. With a wave, he'd left them to the tender mercies of the seamstresses of Paris.

"Now, *cherie*," Henri said once the fitting was concluded, "we will gather up Nicholas and visit the milliner's. No ensemble is complete without a hat! You must be garbed to perfection for the Marquise le Vayer's salon this evening. Everyone of musical consequence will be there."

Yes, the salon. A shiver of nerves went through her. Both she and her brother had the impression that the gathering tonight was more important than the concert billed for tomorrow. Even now, she knew Darien was rehearsing *La Colomba*, the dove—her newest piece.

And a troubling piece it had turned out to be, too.

When she'd handed the completed composition to Nicholas, he'd scanned it with lifted brows.

"Clara, I can't give Darien this. It's too…" He glanced at the ceiling, as if the words he needed were printed there.

"I know, it's a bit short, but the melody—"

"Is too joyful! Look." He shook the pages at her. "This first passage is nearly delirious. I never would write something like that. Never."

She swallowed. "It darkens, later on. The third page."

The dove, flying away under storm clouds, until it becomes lost to sight. An apt metaphor for the state of her heart.

"It had better," he said in an undertone, flipping through to the end. "You could make this easier, you know."

"Indeed." She set her hands on her hips. "By writing only gloomy music? You know I can't do that—I don't write to *suit* anyone. I must write what I hear. What I feel."

"Then I pray you will not feel quite so *giddy* for some time." He gave her a sharp look, but the subdued ending seemed to appease him. Frowning, he had taken *La Colomba* away.

Darien demanded new pieces to premiere in each capital city, so there was little her brother could do, short of writing his own blasted compositions. What Nicholas said made sense, however. She supposed it was fortunate her own mood had taken a turn toward melancholy. It would not do to engage suspicions, either her brother's or Darien's, by being too lighthearted.

She shook herself free of her thoughts while Henri left strict instructions with the seamstresses. The valet whirled Clara back into the scintillating bustle of the Parisian streets.

"Your brother has a taste for poetry, *non*?" he asked.

"Any books, but yes, poetry especially." Books had been an impossible luxury, but no longer. "I fear we may need to buy an extra trunk to carry his purchases. We've left him in the shop far too long."

Henri quirked an eyebrow at her. "Then we will leave some of your old, dowdy clothes behind to make room."

She laughed. "Our new wardrobe is good enough for London, but not the Continent?"

He made no reply—obviously he thought it unnecessary—only opened the door to the bookseller's and gestured her inside.

Stepping into the shop was stepping into another world, tranquil and ink-scented. Light from the transoms caught in dusty motes, and the sound of a page turning only underscored the quiet. Clara felt as though an answering silence opened within her, a promise of solace and solitude that only a book could answer. She moved down one of the rows, trailing her fingers along the spines: some ridged, some with gold lettering, some tautly bound with cloth. Each book a possible adventure, waiting. She would like to have a story in which to immerse herself, some distraction during the long journeys in the coach.

Darien had returned to riding with them, and Nicholas had said nothing. Still, the trip from Calais had been full of odd silences. She had tried not to watch Darien, tried to erase the memory of those sensuous lips on hers, but it was no use. Their kisses were etched into her soul. He met her gaze too often, something hungry in his eyes—a hunger that, when she glimpsed it, made her breath quicken.

Henri consulted his pocket watch. "Miss Becker, I regret we do not have time to linger. Books are very well in their place, but you cannot wear one this evening to the salon, even if we trimmed it with lace and faux fruits."

The notion of making her entrance with a book perched on top of her head made her smile. "Perhaps we might return tomorrow, before the concert? It may be the only way we can tempt Nicholas away, you know."

Indeed, only the promise they would come again persuaded her brother to leave. He gently set a copy of Blake's poems on the already-impressive stack he had amassed, then asked the proprietor to please send them to the hotel.

"Come, come." Henri made shooing motions. There was a decisive French accent in his hands now, as well—an extra flip of the wrist that lent an amused impatience to the gesture. "The Galerie

Vivienne awaits."

"I thought we were going to the milliner's," Clara said, obediently leading the way out of the quiet shop.

"Ah." The valet smiled at her, one brow faintly lifted. "You have not heard of the Galerie? It is one of the grand sights of Paris, not to be missed."

Nicholas caught up to them with two long strides. "According to you, none of the sights of Paris should be missed. The whole city seems nothing but an endless buffet of amusements."

"Not the whole city." Henri's smile folded in on itself and was gone. "There are quarters... But," he gave a sharp shake of his head, "those are not of concern at present. Look, ahead is the entrance to the Galerie."

The street led up to a tall arched passageway where plaster nymphs and goddesses posed on the pilasters. *GALERIE VIVIENNE* was spelled out in large letters above the arch, and through it Clara glimpsed more archways, and a soaring glass-and-iron-fretted ceiling. As they entered the passage, cobblestones gave way to serpentine mosaics. The clatter of the street smoothed away as they emerged into a long, spacious loggia lined with genteel shops.

Clara studied the crosshatched shadows on the floor, then glanced at the transparent ceiling two stories overhead. "How very clever. One of the most vexing things about shopping in the rain is having to dash from place to place, unfolding and folding one's umbrella. This is quite refined."

Henri smiled modestly, though his tone was proud. "We French have had an idea or two. To be fair, there is your Burlington Arcade in London, though it is not quite on par with la Galerie. But come, the milliner's is a little farther, and then perhaps we shall meet Monsieur Reynard at the café."

In the Parisian fashion, there was a restaurant with tables spilling out into the—well, "street" was clearly not the proper word. The walkway. Bright chatter floated from the patrons, and as they passed the café the scent of coffee and perfumes mingled pleasantly.

"Darien intends to meet us?" Nicholas asked. "I thought he was spending the afternoon practicing."

The valet raised his brows. "One must eat sometime. I told him we would be at the café here at two. Perhaps he will join us. Or perhaps he will not."

Clara resolved not to dwell on the possibility. She had done remarkably well to avoid thinking of Darien all morning. Now, however, even the row of tinctures displayed in green glass bottles in an apothecary's window made her consider the color of his eyes. She sighed.

"Are you fretting about the salon, Clara?" Nicholas asked.

She rather thought he revealed his own worry with the question.

"I'm certain it will be a perfectly pleasant gathering," she said. "There is nothing to worry about."

"Aha!" Henri said. "Then you do not know much of our salons. Revolution is bred behind those doors, poetry is born, grand symphonies conceived. Not at all pleasant, but the very essence of life itself."

"Is there to be revolution tonight?" Nicholas swallowed. "I thought it was a musical gathering."

Henri cocked his head. "And who is to say that musicians are not, in their own way, as world-changing as revolutionaries? Look at you. Your music is forming the sensibilities of Europe, even today. We are in your hands, yours and Monsieur Reynard's. Where will you lead us?"

It was a thrilling, uncomfortable notion. Nicholas looked startled for a moment, then answered with a shrug. Unsatisfactory, perhaps, but what other response could he make? Clara could not look at her brother, but from the corner of her eye, she saw him jam his hands in his coat pockets. If they were, as Henri claimed, "forming the sensibilities of Europe," then deception was at the core.

She shuddered. No one, no one, must ever discover that secret.

They walked without further conversation, their steps echoing faintly as they passed through a great domed room and down another graciously ceilinged passageway. Here the shops sold trifles and novelties, and soon they fetched up at the milliner's.

"*Voila,*" Henri said, holding open the door. "Let us proceed to the hats. That particular violet one in the window, with such a dip—

très elegante. It will look very well on you, and for the trimmings…"

Clara stepped inside and gave herself over to the consolation of ribbons and feathers, the sweeping concoctions of headwear. Certainly, they did not have hats quite so lavish in England—but, as Henri stressed, they were in Paris now, and must look the part. It did not take long, to Nicholas's evident relief, to settle on appropriate trimmings for the violet hat. The thing was extravagant, but she knew better than to argue with the valet once he had made up his mind.

As it happened, Darien did not join them at the café, though Clara could not help watching every tall, dark-haired, broad-shouldered man who passed. Paris was astonishingly full of such specimens, a few of whom returned her gaze with frank approval.

But none of them were Darien Reynard.

CHAPTER SIXTEEN

*"**C**her ami!"* The Marquise le Vayer, a petite lady wearing sapphires, kissed Darien Reynard's cheeks and drew him forward, leaving Clara and Nicholas to trail behind him into her well-appointed salon. "How splendid that you grace us with your presence again. Come, come, introduce your companions. Is this the composer I have heard so much of?" The marquise sent Nicholas a significant glance, one dark brow arched.

Once again, Clara was invisible. She stifled her stab of irritation. Their hostess had not meant to slight her, and to his credit, Darien had become scrupulous about presenting her.

Behind the marquise, the room was a bright swirl of faces and movement. The sound of a piano drifted through the conversation, playing a piece Clara did not recognize. She dipped a curtsey to the marquise as Darien introduced first herself, then Nicholas.

"Enchanteé." The marquise's bright eyes lit on Nicholas again. "A new composer among us. There are many people here you must meet, though it is a pity that wretch Berlioz is off in Italy." She gave a theatrical sigh. "He has deserted us."

"Yes, winning the Prix de Rome must be a severe hardship," Darien said dryly.

"For us! Believe me, that man will be quite famous some day. Well, perhaps his travels will inspire him." She smiled at Nicholas. "As I hope your travels have inspired you. Come with me. Tell me all about yourself, and I will make all the introductions."

"I really... That is..." A touch of panic in his blue eyes, Nicholas glanced at Clara.

She gave a half shrug. What could she do? Whisper in his ear about the details of composing as he circulated the room? He would have to fend for himself.

"You English." The marquise slipped her arm through Nicholas's. "Don't worry, I have some fine cognac. We will have you comfortable in no time."

"Go," Darien said. "You're in excellent hands. I'll find you when it's time to play."

Clara pressed her lips together and watched as the marquise led her brother away.

"Don't look so anxious," Darien said in a low voice. "Everyone here is perfectly friendly. The marquise hires burly footmen, too—a helpful reminder for those inclined to misbehave. Now, let's go hear the music."

The marquise's townhouse was divided into a series of rooms. Darien led her through the first, and for once he was not accosted at every turn. Of course he was recognized, greeted—but a certain awestruck quality was missing from the assembly. Clara guessed he found it refreshing. Though he was always gracious, even after a long day's travel, she knew the constant press of fame wore on him. The deepening of the crease beside his mouth, his eyes narrowing slightly as he dealt with yet another gushing female. Clara had seen it often enough.

But tonight he looked relaxed and at ease; and far too handsome.

She glanced about, hoping for distraction. It would not do for her to spend the evening uselessly sighing over Darien Reynard. Luckily, distraction was simple enough to find in the marquise's salon.

A pale, dark-haired woman stood in animated conversation with a haughty-looking gentleman. Ordinary enough, until one realized the woman was wearing an evening coat and trousers! Scandalously peculiar, yet no one else seemed to remark on it. Trousers. How would it feel, to be shed of skirts? She would have to borrow a pair from Nicholas—and why had she never thought of it before?

"Ah." Darien noticed the object of her attention. Not surprising, though Clara was doing her best not to gape. "Baroness Dudevant. If she lights up a cigar, try not to emulate her."

"A cigar?" Clara blinked at the notion. What an odd, mannish woman this baroness was. "Trousers are one thing, but I've no desire to try *that*. Is she a musician?"

"A writer, though she only pens little pieces for magazines as far as I know. But she appreciates good music, and has some interesting ideas about spirituality."

A jolt of jealousy went through Clara, sharp and hot and completely unexpected. "Does she? Do they include women picking up the dubious and unsavory habits of men?"

"You find men dubious and unsavory?" Laughter laced his voice, and she felt her cheeks flame.

"I said their *habits*. Which not all men share."

"If I ever take up smoking cigars, I shall endeavor not to do it in your presence. But what is wrong with wearing trousers? I think gentlemen would look quite odd in skirts."

She laughed at the image he invoked, and let the last shreds of jealously dissolve. "But think how grand you would be in performance, your skirts swishing to and fro as you played."

"Unkind." He leaned closer. "Though I wouldn't mind seeing you in trousers, Miss Becker."

His voice sent a shiver through her. Unfair of him to smile at her so, his eyes glinting with humor. To flirt with her in the crowded anonymity of a Paris salon. She stared back at him and his expression shifted, an intensity tightening his features while their gazes held. Held. The memory of reckless kisses burned in the air between them.

At last Clara remembered how to breathe, and Darien looked away.

"The piano is in the next room," he said.

She swallowed and attempted to make her tone light. "Then by all means, let us visit it."

An unremarkable melody filled the awkward silence between them as Darien led her to a settee near the piano. He settled beside her at a scrupulously correct distance, and Clara tried not to wish that he were nearer. She was too aware of the heat of him, his scent, the way his elegant, long-fingered hands were clasped loosely together.

"Master Reynard." A sandy-haired man sitting near them leaned forward. "Will you be playing this evening?"

"Of course," Darien said. "How can one come to la marquise's and not play? I would be outcast in Paris forever."

The fellow pursed his lips and glanced at the young man at the piano. "Let us pray our lugubrious Hungarian friend finishes soon. I would like to hear some real music."

A woman seated behind Darien giggled. "Ah, Liszt is not so bad. If he would only apply himself, he could be great."

"Yes, madame, we all know where you would like him to apply himself," the gentleman said.

She swatted him on the shoulder with her fan. "You are only jealous because *you* have no talents that interest me. Now hush. I am trying to enjoy the concert."

The man rolled his eyes in mock disgust, but subsided.

Clara listened, and found she was in agreement with the woman. Mr. Liszt played passably, with the sloppy technique of someone whose natural talent had taken them a certain distance, then left them there. Hard work would move him forward, if he were ever inspired to it. And she heard a hint of something interesting in the melody he played, like a silver glimmer of trout in deep water. If the man were patient and skilled, some day he might be able to fish up something wild and dancing and lovely.

Perhaps she could say as much to him, without revealing herself as a composer. She glanced at Darien, and found he was watching her, his eyes unreadable as dark agates. No, it was too risky. The fellow at the piano would have to find his own way.

Soon enough, Mr. Liszt brought his playing to a close. Clara made a point of clapping loudly, though her gloves muffled the effect. It seemed as though the dour-looking young man could use the encouragement.

"Lovely!" the marquise said, sweeping up to the piano and gifting the assembled listeners with a glorious smile. "It is a pleasure to hear everyone, of course, but tonight we are particularly lucky to have Darien Reynard with us. And his talented new composer, Nicholas Becker. Please, take your seats, and do move closer together so that others may join us when they hear the maestro begin."

She watched, nodding her head as the empty seats filled.

Darien rose, and Clara caught his sleeve. "Play well."

Oh, what a silly thing to say. As if he needed her good wishes.

"I will, thank you." His eyes smiled at her. "Your brother has composed another fine piece. The beginning is especially glorious."

A ripple of joy expanded outward from her heart, quietly circling her entire body. She'd written that part for him—the bright and breathless melody that the thought of his kiss had evoked. And he had felt it.

"Yes," she managed. "I think so, too."

His smile moved down to his lips, and she suddenly couldn't bear to look at him, couldn't bear the fierce longing that slipped free. She laced her fingers tightly together in her lap. If she met his gaze, she was certain her secrets would be laid bare, and he would recognize her as the composer.

Foolish, but he *had* heard the echo of their kiss in the music, and she was afraid.

After a heartbeat he moved away, and she let out a long breath. Her fears were only fancies of the imagination. Darien had no cause to suspect anything. She would do well to remember that, and not behave in a way that raised his curiosity. Ah, but she was torn. She was no longer invisible to him, he'd made that clear enough on the ferry to Calais. Yet she could not become known to him either, no matter how she might wish it. It was as if she balanced on the edge of a cliff and felt the pull of the air, the promise that just once, she could fly. Take one step into the sky, and become airborne.

But the gravity of her deception was inescapable. The only flight possible was in secret, in her compositions. *La Colomba* would have to be wings enough.

With that thought, the music began. The room immediately hushed as Darien Reynard danced with the notes, his bow sweeping smoothly over the strings, his expression holding an intensity that any woman would yearn to have trained on them. Clara squeezed her hands together and leaned forward. As he traveled the melody, she was beside him, the notes etched in her soul even as he etched them in the air, matching perfectly.

A part of her noticed that Nicholas was playing very well, but only Darien could hold her attention. Her heartbeat matched the pulse of the music, the high notes pinpricks of tears at the back of her eyes. When the mood of the piece changed it was a relief to let go of the glory. The notes tumbled and spun away from the memories of stolen kisses and back onto safer ground, where winter rain filled the skies of France and dreams belonged only in the dark, solitary hours of night.

The last chord sounded, and the silence was a vast held breath. Clara could hear the diminishing echoes of the strings inside the piano. Darien stood motionless, the tip of his bow barely touching the instrument, and Nicholas's head remained bowed over the keyboard.

Then the room erupted. People sprang to their feet, the vigorous applause nearly drowned out with cries of praise. Several chairs were knocked over, and one woman spilled wine on her skirts, but did not seem to care overmuch. Clara moved backward, against the general surge toward Nicholas and Darien. She did not need to hear the approbations. *La Colomba* had flown well.

She fetched up against a wall papered in an elegant gilt and violet pattern, and watched the room swirl with excitement.

"Ah, another one who feels no need to scramble for Reynard's notice. I honor you for that, mademoiselle."

Clara turned to see a tall, auburn-haired man leaning against the wall next to her. His nose was large and somewhat curved, giving him a feral, hawk-like appearance. The glint in his eyes made her feel oddly vulnerable. He looked at her the way a raptor might view a hare.

"I don't believe we have been introduced, sir." She kept her tone frosty. No more luring out onto the terrace for her—she had learned that lesson well.

"Who cares for such formality? We are at the marquise's salon," he said. "Everyone here has something to recommend them. And again, I approve of your excellent taste. I, too, see no need to fawn at the *master's* feet."

"Didn't you enjoy the music?" What a boor this fellow was.

He waved one hand. "Oh, the piece was pretty enough, I suppose. Too mawkish for my tastes, but look at the composer. A pretty, sheltered young man. Give him a few more years, some hard lessons, a mistress or two—"

"Sir!"

He trained that assessing gaze on her once more, then gave a sharp nod. "Ah, I should have noticed the resemblance at once. I understand he is traveling with his sister. So you see, I have no need of an introduction after all, Miss Becker. And what was at first intriguing behavior on your part is now, sadly, explained away."

"I can only count myself grateful to be English, if *your* behavior is the regular thing at Paris salons. Good evening." She turned pointedly from him, looking across the room for Darien or her brother. Surely they must be finished by now.

"Aha, she has claws." The fellow had the audacity to come around and stand directly before her. His gaze dipped to the bodice of her low-cut gown, then traveled slowly back up to her face. "And a lovely figure as well. Tell me more of yourself, Miss Becker. How do you like traveling with Reynard? Does he treat you... *well?*"

Clara felt her eyes widen. Was he insinuating she was Darien's mistress? The nerve! "That is absolutely none of your concern. Now go away, whoever you are."

"I think I shall stay," he said, his eyes bright with malicious interest. "In fact—"

"Gracious!" The marquise's voice cut through the swirls of conversation filling the room. Clara glanced up to see their hostess hurrying forward, a look of mild alarm on her face. "I did not expect you to be in town yet, monsieur. Not that I am unhappy you are here." She laid one crimson-gloved hand on the man's arm. "Come, let me fetch you something to drink."

He gave a slow shake of his head. "No. I am quite entertained here, thank you."

"But..." The marquise now had two hands on his arm, and it looked to Clara as though she were trying to discreetly drag him away. Their hostess lowered her voice. "Monsieur Reynard is coming this way. Please."

"Never fear." The man gave the marquise a smile edged with spite. "I left my pistols behind. At any rate, we are engaged in another type of duel." As if sensing Darien's approach, the man turned, his nostrils flaring in a sneer. "Good evening. *Master.*"

Darien seemed calm, but Clara caught the furious gleam in his eyes, the way his shoulders bunched under the perfect tailoring of his coat.

"You, of all people," Darien said, "are absolved of calling me 'master.' Unless you still consider yourself my pupil,and a tiresome one, at that."

Understanding washed over Clara. This was Varga. Anton Varga—Darien's rival and nemesis. The man's animosity made perfect sense now.

A dull red flush crept up from Varga's collar. "We'll see who's worthy of the title soon enough. I hope you have not grown too attached to it."

His attention shifted, and Clara saw that Nicholas had come up beside Darien. Her brother's gaze went first to Darien then to Varga, and his fingers wove restlessly together. Clearly he was as uncomfortable as she with the antagonism surging between the two musicians.

"Oh, look. It's your pet composer," Varga said. "I can't say I had any taste for that piece of his. The beginning was remarkably… cloying."

"See here." Nicholas stepped forward, and Clara stifled a groan.

Her brother had no business trying to interfere. He was nothing but a mouse caught between two feral cats. Darien pulled Nicholas back, giving him a cautioning look, but it was too late.

Varga obviously knew weakness when he saw it, and he did not hesitate. "Yes, that style is far too romantic, though I'm sure it plays well here in Paris. The French have a weakness for the effeminate."

Clara slanted a glance at Nicholas, concern squeezing her breath when she saw how pale he was. They were only words but, crafted to wound, they had hit uncomfortably near the mark.

Darien lifted a brow, though she could tell he was seething. "As usual, you have no ability to discern real talent. Your loss, as they say."

"Ha!" There was no mirth in Varga's voice. "*Your* loss, when we meet in Milan. Especially if you are pinning your hopes on this mollycoddle. Personally, I'm more intrigued with his sister. There's a pretty piece for you, far better than the boy. But if you prefer the brother, there is no accounting—yaah!"

Varga's hand flew up to guard his face, but he was not in time to stop Darien's blow. He reeled back and the room pulsed with excitement, a crowd quickly forming about the two men.

"Monsieurs, no, no, I beg of you!" the marquise cried, interposing herself between the two men, her arms outspread. "We must not have violence."

"Or if we do, let's keep it away from the instruments," someone called.

"Reynard." Varga was breathing heavily, a red welt forming on his cheek. "You will answer for this."

"But not tonight," pleaded the marquise.

The muscled footmen Darien had spoken of earlier appeared. One clamped a meaty hand over Varga's shoulder, obviously preventing him from attacking Darien.

Darien shook his cuffs down and gave a scathing look at the watchdog hovering at his own side. When he spoke his voice was cold.

"Keep your base thoughts to yourself, Varga. No one cares to hear them." He pointedly turned away from his rival and bowed to their hostess. "Marquise, thank you for the memorable evening. I'm sorry it had to end on such a note. We will be taking our leave now."

Her expression a touch wild around the eyes, the marquise nodded in return. "*Bonsoir*, and thank you."

As Clara turned to follow Darien out the door, she could not help glancing at Anton Varga. He was watching his former master, the hatred in his expression so plain it made her skin prickle with dread.

CHAPTER SEVENTEEN

Rivals Come to Blows!

Witnesses report that Maestro Darien Reynard and Monsieur Anton Varga exchanged hostilities at the Marquise le Vayer's salon last evening over the charming sister of composer Nicholas Becker. Such delicious troubles are sure to multiply as the men prepare for their grand duel in Milan!
-Le Salon Extraordinaire

Clara watched out the coach window as the French countryside rolled past, a stitchery of fields and stone walls. It was not so different from England, though the landscape was drier, the church steeples more ornate.

Sadly, she had already finished the novel she'd purchased in Paris. Perhaps Nicholas would lend her one of his volumes of poetry, though she feared she would not be able to immerse herself quite so satisfactorily in verse as she had in Mary Shelley's latest tale.

In the corner across from her, Henri settled back against the leather cushions of the coach and heaved a sigh.

"Today we leave the soil of France, and I bid my country *adieu.*" He glanced at Darien. "I think, monsieur, the concerts were very well received. You will not find better audiences anywhere in Europe."

"I agree that the French are without parallel," Darien said. "The attitude of *listening* in the Conservatoire was remarkable—I could not have asked for better."

Clara would find out if audiences differed soon enough—they were bound for Prussia and Austria before swinging south to Italy for the duel. She pulled her cashmere shawl closer around her shoulders. The thought of meeting Anton Varga again made her shiver.

"I'm glad we're leaving," Nicholas said. "I don't want to stay in any country that has Varga within its borders."

Unhappiness was clear in his expression, the way he hunched his shoulders forward. He had taken Varga's insults quite badly, and the handbills printed by the man's supporters, repeating his barbed words, served to wound Nicholas afresh. *Girlishly Romantic!* the headlines had shrieked. *Stupefyingly Sweet, the ramblings of a mediocre mollycoddle.* The harsh words seemed impossible for Nicholas to ignore.

Clara set her hand over her brother's. She was worried, but every time she tried to voice her concerns he shrugged her away. The other night, after the concert in Reims, he'd locked himself in his room with a bottle of cheap cognac. In the morning he'd emerged hollow-eyed and wincing. She had said nothing, but fear for him wrapped cold tendrils about her heart.

"We will see Varga in Milan," Darien said. "There's no help for that. But hopefully not before."

Henri folded his arms. "I think he will follow and make trouble for you wherever he can. Do not let down your guard."

These words made Nicholas look even more miserable. He pulled his hand from beneath hers and turned to stare out the rain-smeared window.

Clara sighed. Only a small breath escaped her lips, but Darien glanced at her, sympathy clear in his deep green eyes. Ah, but she did not want his sympathy.

Emulating her brother, she turned her head to once again look out at the countryside. At least she was writing suitably gloomy pieces now. Her next one would be titled *Ombra*. Shadow.

***

"... and now, my favorite part of every performance..." Darien's voice drifted to the wings as he began the introduction that would bring Nicholas on stage.

Clara hurried behind the curtains, panic beginning to spin in her chest. It was too dim to run, but her heart beat as quickly as if she were sprinting. Where was Nicholas? Why wasn't he waiting backstage, as he always was by now? In less than a minute, Darien would announce his name—*Nicholas Becker!* It was the cue for her brother to step into the lights, take his place at the piano, and perform her newest composition with Darien Reynard.

Except that Nicholas was missing.

She stumbled as she entered the hallway leading to the dressing rooms. "Nicholas!" she hissed, but only dark silence greeted her.

No—not fully dark. A thin line of light shone from beneath his dressing-room door. Praying her brother was within, she ran to it and wrenched it open.

"Hurry!" she cried. "You must…"

Nicholas was there. She drew in a ragged breath, but panic welled again as she took in his state. His eyes were closed and he sprawled in the single armchair, a glass in his hand. An emptied cognac bottle lay on one side on the floor, and she kicked it away as she hurried to her brother.

"Nicholas—wake up!" She grasped his shoulder and shook, gently at first, then more roughly as he did not respond. "You must play. Get up, get up!"

At last his lids opened a fraction. He blinked, then closed his eyes again, mumbling inaudibly. His head sank back down to his chest, and further shaking could not rouse him.

Dear God. He had drunk himself insensible. There was no way he could perform.

The floor tipped beneath her, the inevitable slide into ruin just underfoot. How quickly everything was lost.

Through the open door, Clara heard the wash of applause, sharp with expectancy. And—her stomach tightened at the thought—the King of Prussia was in the audience. Darien needed the noble's support in Milan. A misstep here would spell failure.

No. She would not allow it.

She stepped into the hall and closed the door, then smoothed her hair back with both hands. If Nicholas could not play…

Then she must.

Fear clamped about her ribs, but she forced herself to hurry back toward the wings. She felt light-headed, as if she'd stumbled into a dream—a dream rapidly becoming nightmare.

The audience's applause died completely away as they waited for Nicholas to appear. In that moment before the hushed murmurs of speculation could begin, Clara walked on stage. The footlights were blessedly bright, shielding the watching crowd from view. She gave Darien a wide-eyed glance, hoping desperately he could read her intent.

He locked gazes with her, his expression surprised. When it was clear Nicholas was not going to appear, Darien raised one eyebrow in question, and she gave him a nearly imperceptible nod. With a poise she could only admire, he settled his features and turned back to the audience.

"Our composer is unfortunately indisposed," he said. "Please welcome his sister, Miss Clara Becker—a talented pianist in her own right—who will instead accompany me this evening!"

The response was polite, but she barely heard it. The first disaster had been averted. Now she merely had to play beautifully for Darien, without any preparation or rehearsal; and in front of the highest nobility of Prussia. At last she understood precisely how Nicholas had felt that evening at the Royal Pavilion, and her heart stretched in sympathy. And pain. But she could not think of her brother now. Only the music, only this moment.

Throat dry, she seated herself at the piano.

Her pulse was hammering so loudly she was not sure she could find the beat. She glanced at Darien once more, and he brought his violin up under his chin. His gaze met hers, nothing but confidence in his green eyes. Darien believed she could do this, and the knowledge lent her courage.

Leaning toward the keyboard, she began the introduction.

Ombra. The piece was full of shadows and silvery silences, the beginning a subtle interplay of long-held tones exchanged between the piano and violin. Her every sense was attuned to Darien as the music reached the first abyss—two beats of stillness they must hold for an identical interval before ascending again into the dark melodic waters. Clara held her breath, sensed that Darien held his... and the release was perfect, her hands on the keys matching note for note as Darien drew his bow across the strings.

She breathed a silent prayer of thanks.

Despite the complete lack of rehearsal, despite the fact she had not played often during their travels, this was *her* music. And Darien played beside her, strong and steady. Awareness shimmered in the air between them. Darien tossed long skeins of notes from his violin into the welcoming waves pouring beneath her fingers. The audience breathed softly as the spell of music wrapped them in mystery.

Something inside her soul broke open then, something Darien had begun with his kisses. Here, performing with him, it could not be denied. It was sweet and poignant, and suffused every note.

It was love.

Despite the secrets that must remain locked in her heart, this one had flown free.

She loved Darien Reynard. This was no naïve, star-struck emotion, but something complex and nuanced, something balanced between light and shadow, the way the music balanced between sound and silence.

She played then, her heart fixed on Darien as together they wove magic. More intimate even than their kisses, this musical passion was as close as they would ever come to physical passion. Every note joined with his, every beat echoed in her, and she gave herself up to it.

He watched her as they played, his dark hair falling across his forehead, a wild light in his eyes. Despite the simplicity of the piece, she had never heard him play better, the notes from his violin deep and yearning and vibrant. Tears rose in her throat when they reached the last stanza, the end of the music waiting and inevitable.

And then it was over. The crowd applauded, with a few cheers for punctuation. It was a warm enough reception, even though the audience had not received the Becker they'd been expecting.

Clara rose and took Darien's offered hand.

"Well done," he murmured. "Very well done."

Together, they bowed, his bare palm warm against hers, his clasp solid. She tried to let go, to make him take a solo bow, but he would not release her, and so she received the acclaim with him in equal measure. It felt astonishingly good, as though she were basking in the warmth of a full summer sun. And though the audience might think they were clapping for Nicholas, she accepted her due, for the performance *and* for the composition.

Darien took her arm and led her from the stage.

"What of Nicholas?" he asked, as soon as they reached the wings

"He will be fine." She felt her cheeks flame at her brother's mortifying condition. "By morning, I expect."

"You played wonderfully," he said.

Hidden by the shadows, heedless of the applause surging behind them, he pulled her into his arms.

She went willingly, their joined music still echoing through her. His lips touching hers was simply the next movement—an inevitable extension of the intimacy they had experienced onstage. Clara set her hands on his shoulders and lifted herself onto her toes, pressing more deeply into the kiss. She could not help it, any more than she could help the music scribed in her soul. The feel of his arms around her was fierce and exhilarating, and she opened her mouth to his, taking his breath and giving hers in return.

"Reynard! Reynard!" It was clear the audience would not be denied an encore.

He lifted his head. "I must—"

"Yes," she said. "Go back onstage."

Still, neither of them seemed able to let go, their bodies melded tightly together in the dim light, shielded from view by the folds of curtains. Heat flared between them, and Clara wanted nothing more than to slip her hands under his coat, to get as close to this amazing, talented man as she could. This man who had partnered her perfectly in the music, as though their souls converged.

The rhythmic thud of feet on the floorboards added to the din, and Darien slowly opened his arms.

"Don't go far," he said, as if afraid of losing her.

"I'll be with Nicholas."

"Good. Your brother has some explaining to do."

Darien gave her a smoldering look, full of promises and questions, then turned and strode back into the lights. A full-throated cheer went up as he retrieved his instrument, pacifying the beast of the crowd.

She watched him a moment more, hands cupping her elbows as desire tangled with fear. Would Nicholas be all right? Did Darien suspect? And most of all, would he kiss her again?

When Clara entered her brother's dressing room, he was still unconscious. His gold hair was disarrayed, his cheeks flushed, and suddenly she saw the little boy her brother used to be, not the troubled man he had become.

"Dear Nicholas," she whispered. "I'm so sorry."

She should not have pushed so hard for them to come to the Continent—but she had wanted it, the way a beggar craves a fire in midwinter. Even with all the reasons to go, there had been one compelling reason to remain in London. Her brother's sanity. Seeing him sprawled and rumpled in his chair, lost in drink, reminded her how fragile he was. There had been almost no sign of his melancholy while they toured England, so she had convinced herself that he was well. That he was, indeed, cured—because she wanted it to be so.

Her throat tight with worry, Clara went to the washbasin and dampened a cloth, then gently washed Nicholas's face. The notes of Darien's encore drifted down the hall. Would the maestro demand they leave the tour? Wouldn't it be best if they did? Questions spun like whirlwinds through her, moving so quickly she could not grasp them, or even begin to answer.

She must wake Nicholas and get him back to the hotel. She smoothed her brother's hair back and pulled his jacket into place. Applause sounded, like waves on a distant beach.

"Nicholas, please wake up. The concert is over." She set a hand on his shoulder. "We need to go. Wake up."

"Hnh," he said, his eyelids flickering.

"I see." Darien stood at the door. His voice was cold. "And what excuse does my composer have for drinking himself insensible and placing all of us in an impossible situation?"

Clara took a step toward him. "I—"

"Don't bother. It was a rhetorical question." Disapproval flashed in his eyes. "I'll fetch the footmen to help with your brother. And I will have some explanations. From both of you."

CHAPTER EIGHTEEN

Dare managed to hold his temper during the short coach ride back to the hotel—though he wanted to shake Nicholas until he came to his senses. And kiss Clara until she lost hers.

Damnation. *This* was why he did not tour with others. He had no control over Nicholas, and yet the man had far too much power over the outcome of the concerts.

So much for the master's influence. Bitter laughter dried in Dare's mouth.

He could not manage his composer. Worse yet, he couldn't manage his own emotions where Clara was concerned. His doomed affair with Francesca Contini had taught him never to mix passion with music. It had been a painful lesson, indeed.

Why was he unable to remember it when Clara was in his arms?

A fortnight. That was all Dare needed, and the musical duel would be over and he would send the impossible Becker siblings back to England.

He clenched and unclenched his fists in rhythm with the horses' hooves. Across from him, Clara was nearly invisible in the dimness. But though he could not see her, he was far too aware of her: the scent of lavender, the faint rustle of her skirts, the sheen of a stray bit of lamplight caught in her fair hair. The hot memory of his lips over hers.

When the footmen swung open the coach door, Dare leapt down and took a deep breath of the cool night air.

"Remove Mr. Becker from the coach and carry him to his room," he directed. "Clara, you will come with me."

He held out his hand and assisted her down, then tucked her arm through his. There would be no escaping.

"But…" She glanced to the footmen, hefting Nicholas from the vehicle. "I need to—"

"I'll send Henri to tend him."

Dare burned—with anger, with desire. With the aftermath of the performance he and Clara had, so unexpectedly, so brilliantly wrought.

It had been a horrible moment, when he announced Nicholas and the man had failed to appear. Dare had kept his bearing confident, but tension spun taut in his gut, the sick fear of failure he hadn't felt for years. The future had flashed before him—King Ludvig's disapproval, Dare's defeat at the upcoming duel, Varga strutting and crowing while Dare was stripped of his dreams. Then what?

A gaping hole beneath his feet.

He had nearly plunged into it right there, an abyss of failure, full of misery and the poverty he had spent his life escaping. Then Clara had stepped onstage and given him one look from her luminous eyes, and the world had righted again. The floor was solid, his violin steady in his grasp, the pulse of the music true and sure.

More than sure. The music had flown then, the way he had always dreamed it could. The magic he had felt waiting in Becker's compositions had at last fully opened, and he had played straight into its heart. With Clara.

They reached his suite and he ushered her inside.

"Monsieur." Henri greeted him, then turned to Clara. "And mademoiselle. Is everything well?"

Dare handed his coat to his valet. "It is not. Would you please go tend to Nicholas? He's in need of assistance."

"Of course! He is ill?"

"He was reckless with a bottle of cognac," Dare said. "Take him a tincture."

"Oh, would you?" Clara's expression was anxious, her cheeks pale. "I know he'll feel simply dreadful in the morning."

"In many ways, no doubt," Dare said. The man's aching head was the least of his concerns. "His remorse had best be enough to keep him from such behavior again. I won't have it."

"Darien," Clara said, "I promise you—"

"Don't make promises on your brother's behalf."

Dare forced his shoulders to relax. It wasn't her fault Nicholas had shown such bad judgment.

"Good evening, then," Henri said. He sent Clara a thoughtful glance, then returned his attention to Dare. "I will stay with Mr. Becker to ensure all is well."

Dare did not miss the speculative light in Henri's eye as he left. Certainly the valet was aware of the impropriety of leaving Clara alone with him. She seemed too distressed to notice, however.

"Please, forgive Nicholas." Her silver-blue eyes were stricken. "He is fragile, and I should have known... If you must blame someone, then blame me."

"And how is it your fault?" He took her hands. "Did you purchase that bottle for him? Open it and pour it and make him drink to the dregs?"

She pressed her lips together and shook her head. "No, but I ought to have seen how troubled he has become."

"You possess a mirror that reveals your brother's thoughts? A crystal ball that shows his every state of mind? Clara, I cannot blame you. Nicholas is responsible for his own choices."

"No." Her voice was small and miserable. "He wouldn't have come to the Continent... and Varga's horrible insults... You don't know."

It was impossible to cling to his anger in the face of such unhappiness. He led her to the settee and sat beside her, keeping a firm grip on her hand.

"Then tell me," he said.

She looked at him and took a deep breath. "Nicholas is more sensitive than you realize. When our mother died, he fell into a terrible melancholy, and I fear it is returning."

Genius always had its price. She shivered, and Dare slipped an arm around her shoulders. He would have to take care not to push Nicholas to the breaking point, but it was difficult to excuse his behavior that evening.

"Your family did mention his troubles," Dare said. "Is drinking heavily one of the signs?"

"No." Her brows drew together. "But that may only be because we could not afford spirits before. I don't know."

"I will try not to be too hard on him, though I must take him to task."

Nicholas was the key to victory in the duel. It was yet more proof that a man's success should rest squarely upon his own shoulders, owing nothing to anyone. And needing nothing in return. That way only led to bitter disappointment, as first his unreliable father and then Francesca had taught him.

"Thank you," Clara said. The hope in her eyes stabbed him.

"You thought I'd dismiss him from the tour? Send you both back home to London, words of shame ringing in your ears? No."

At least, not yet. Despite the problems each sibling presented him, the thought of Nicholas and Clara leaving the tour made a strange, discontented hollowness settle behind Dare's ribs.

Dare took a breath, and banished it.

"Two weeks until Milan." Her voice was subdued, as if she feared it was an endless expanse of time.

"There can be no more incidents," he said. "Tonight almost ended in disaster. I'm only glad you had the presence of mind to take the stage with me. You performed remarkably—on a piece I thought would be unfamiliar to you."

She set one hand to her throat and did not meet his eyes. "Nicholas likes me to play the compositions for him, so he may sit back and hear how the music is going."

"Still, you played superbly." The echo of the music rang through him, his heart pulsing again at the sheer exhilaration of performing with her. "I'm curious. Tell me how—"

"Darien." She lifted her head, something like panic fluttering through her eyes. "I should go. See to Nicholas."

"Henri is there. No need to leave."

They were sitting very close together, their legs touching, his arm still about her. Heat spread through him as he felt awareness filter through her. Her expression changed, softened. She wet her lips with the tip of her tongue, and his whole body tightened. How quickly comfort transformed to desire.

"But..." There was no protest in her voice, despite the word.

"The performance tonight, the way you played." He searched her face, looking for answers to a question he did not even know how to ask. "I wonder—"

"Kiss me," she said, her voice low.

Before he could think, he *was* kissing her—kissing her as he had ached to do since their stolen embrace in the wings. His lips were over hers, pressing them apart so he could taste her, his tongue entering the warm, moist hollow of her mouth. She let out a little sigh and slid her hands up his shirt, her fingertips resting on his collarbone. Points of heat tingled through the fine fabric where she touched him.

More. He needed her closer, her curves against him. The feel of her was intoxicating. Every time he kissed her, his blood burned hotter.

Riding that wave of fire, he gathered her tightly to him. One hand cradled the back of her head, his fingers unerringly finding her hairpins and pulling them out. At last he would see the soft, pale light of her hair falling free. Mouth still commanding hers, guiding her with his kiss, he laid her back against the settee's cushions.

She was pliant and warm, her dress a silvery silk that hushed as he ran a hand over it. His palm cupped one rounded breast, the thumb moving over the material, coaxing, seeking. There, the hardened peak of her nipple. He brought his fingers up and lightly gripped her through the silk.

"Ah." She gasped into his mouth and arched up beneath him. The sound sent another jolt of need through him.

The dress was ridiculously easy to slip off one shoulder. Dare bared the upper curve of her breast, then the rosy nipple. He plucked her gently, like a harp string, and felt the vibration thrum through her. He dipped his head and drew his tongue over the taut peak, then fastened his lips there, drawing more breathy sighs from her.

Her leg moved restlessly against him, her silk-clad thigh slipping against his leg, back and forth. The movement was artlessly sensual, pure fire to his blood. His hands roved over her, hungry to touch every curve and hollow, craving more. He wanted her naked underneath him, her pale skin softer than the silvery fabric of her gown, her hair spread out over his pillows.

Clara Becker in his bed, and the consequences be damned.

No. He must halt this, while he still could. With a guttural murmur, he leaned back. She opened her eyes, those extraordinary light blue eyes, now bright with passion.

"Don't stop," she said, curving her hands over his shoulders and pulling him toward her.

No matter what Clara thought she wanted, no matter what her brother had done, he could not ravish her, much as he wanted to. She deserved more consideration than that.

But he would taste her mouth again. One more kiss, and then he would stop.

He bent and covered her lips with his, his hand over the softness of her breast. Desire scorched him, eddies of heat hazing his mind.

Dare straightened, bracing himself above her. She blinked at him, lips moist from their kisses, her glorious hair tumbled down about her bared shoulder and breast.

"You should return to your rooms," he said. Even to his own ears, he sounded unconvincing.

"Not yet." Her voice was husky and low. "Please."

Damnation—she undid him utterly, and seemed oblivious of the fact.

Clara wound her arms about his neck and pulled him back down, and the fire inside him turned to an inferno. He plundered her mouth, caressed her breasts, then slid his hand down between her legs. The smooth silk of her dress moved back and forth beneath his fingers as he stroked her there. She moaned into his mouth, a sound that made his cock strain even harder at the front of his trousers.

He would not take her, but he *would* pleasure her. Indeed, she seemed almost to the sweet, jagged edge already. So beautiful, so responsive. She filled his senses. The scent of lavender water mingled with the musk of arousal, her breaths coming faster as he stroked between her legs.

He nudged her thighs wider and pressed harder with his fingers through the fabric of her dress. Her head fell back and he laid a line of kisses on her neck, across her cheek. Faster. She moaned again, and he dipped his head, his mouth fastening again over the taut peak of her breast. His fingers moved even more urgently at her center.

"Ahh," she gasped, arching up against him.

Pleasure shuddered through her. He could feel it surge, then slowly ebb. Dare stilled his hand and lifted his head, watching her. Clara's face was flushed with passion, and he did not know how he had ever thought her plain. She was beautiful.

She was his.

The thought came, unbidden, and he was afraid to examine it too closely. He thrust it to the back of his mind, then brushed a kiss over her lips.

Her eyes slowly opened. For a moment she simply looked at him. Then she smiled, sweet and tentative, and his heart thudded into place, finding a stronger, newer rhythm.

"That was..." She shook her head.

He cupped her face with one hand and drew his thumb across her lips.

"Come," he said, "I'll see you back to your rooms."

Though desire still pounded through him, Dare helped her sit. He did not glance at the open bedroom door as she drew her dress back over her shoulder and knotted up her glorious hair.

Together, they slipped through the hall to her rooms. Forcing himself to a proper distance, Dare took her hand and brushed a kiss over it.

"I'll go check on Nicholas," he said. "Sleep well."

"Good night." The word was ripe with gratitude.

"Indeed," he murmured. Sleepless night was more likely.

Before he could behave any more rashly, he turned back down the darkened hallway. It was a long moment before he heard the click of the latch as her door closed.

Dare rounded the corner, then halted with his back to the wall. He leaned his head against the mahogany paneling, closed his eyes, and drew in a ragged breath. Bloody hell—he had come very close to taking Clara's virginity. Had he so little control?

There was something about her he could not resist, something pulled forth by the music. Tonight, onstage with her, he had felt the most intense musical connection of his life. Even in the midst of his passion for Francesca Contini, they had never performed together so perfectly.

"Darien?"

He jerked upright and opened his eyes. Clara stood before him, her expression concerned.

"Are you well?" she asked.

Far from it.

"Well enough," he said. "I thought you had retired for the evening."

"I left my reticule in your rooms." Her cheeks flushed.

"I'll bring it to you, or have Henri deliver it tomorrow at breakfast."

"No. Please, I'll just fetch it now."

The last thing he needed was Clara in his rooms again. He could not keep his gaze from her lips, from the pale skin of her décolletage. Arousal hummed through his body.

"If you insist." He turned and led her the few doors down to his rooms.

When they reached his small parlor, she spun, concern bright in her eyes. "I don't see it."

"Are you carrying diamonds and sapphires about?" he asked, trying to lighten her mood. "I'm sure your reticule is here, unharmed."

She didn't reply, only hastened toward the settee and started lifting the pillows. A lock of her pale hair slipped free from the loose knot on the back of her head, and Dare flexed his fingers, remembering that silken softness. A flash of satin beneath the furniture caught his eye.

"Here," he said, scooping up her bag from the floor. It was surprisingly heavy. "You *do* store jewels in here, don't you?"

"It's just my notebook." She snatched the reticule from his hands.

"You keep your secrets close at hand." He supposed many women kept diaries, but he hadn't expected Clara to carry hers with her. "Do you write about me, I wonder?"

He gave her a teasing smile, but the look on her face remained serious.

"When you touched me tonight..." She stepped up to him and laid one hand on his chest. "Is there an answering pleasure a gentleman might feel?"

His whole body tightened at the question. If she was trying to distract him, her ploy was working.

"Yes." The word came out almost a growl.

"Teach me."

Bloody hell. "No."

She set her reticule on the settee, then twined her arms about his neck. Pulling his head down, she kissed him, her mouth sweet and demanding on his. The feel of her soft curves made the banked fires of his desire flare into nearly unbearable brightness. Clara.

He gathered her tightly against him and kissed her as though he were a drowning man and she was air. The memory of their music crashed over him again, bringing a wave of need so intense he could not withstand the force of it.

There was only Clara, and a fierce wanting he could not name, wound so tightly about him he was blind. He swept her into his arms and carried her to his bed. It was the work of moments to unpin her loose coiffure.

With deft fingers she unbuttoned his shirt and pulled it off, while he undid the fastenings of her gown. He looked down at her, her mouth full from his kisses, her moonlit hair spread out across his pillows, and forced himself to speak.

"Clara," he said, voice rough with desire. "Either I stop now, or not at all. Do you understand?"

She stared up at him, her lips softly parted. His groin tightened, but he held himself immobile above her, waiting for her answer.

"Yes," she said, her voice sure and strong. "I want this. I want *you*, Darien—all of you. Now. Tonight."

The words were alcohol to his flame. He all but ripped the rest of her clothing off, and then his own, until they were both naked upon the sheets. The rosy tips of her breasts beckoned his mouth and hands. As he caressed and sucked them, she breathed little sighs, spurring his arousal even higher.

He slipped his hand down between her legs, this time with no gown in the way, only naked skin to naked skin. His fingers played in her springy curls and she parted her thighs. He pressed deeper, feeling her moisture. Slowly, he slid one finger inside, her hot slickness enclosing him. Then another finger, stroking, teasing. She gasped and arched against him.

Dare pulled his hand away, and she made a disappointed moan.

"A moment," he said, forcing himself to lean away from her.

It was his habit to keep a packet of French letters on the bedside table. Deftly, he drew one on and fastened the tie at the base of his cock.

Stop, the voice of responsibility cried.

But it was far too late. He suspected it had been too late the moment he'd agreed to allow Clara to come on the tour. He had tried to keep his distance, had ridden alone the entire length of England, the coach behind him, but it had not been enough. He'd forced himself to keep his distance, though memories of their kisses had branded his bones.

Tonight, the dry tinder of his soul had caught fire, and there was no extinguishing that blaze.

***

A wild sonata clamored in Clara's blood—music so sweet and fierce it consumed all other thoughts. The feel of Darien's hands on her made wild sensations rush through her. She wanted to press herself against him, feel his body against every inch of hers. She was so unexpectedly wanton. Or perhaps not so unexpected. Hadn't she spent endless nights replaying their kisses, yearning for his arms around her?

It had been a wishful dream, yet here she was, naked in his bed.

A brief whisper of propriety insisted she should leave now. It was not too late. She could rise and pull her gown back on. She could leave and close the door behind her, shutting out the possibility of what might have been.

If she stayed, if she let Darien make love to her... what would her family, and society, think?

Her fingers tightened over his shoulders. Blast respectability. She was done with denial, finished with self-sacrifice. Why should she constrain herself when that very evening Nicholas had indulged himself without a care for her, and put the entire tour in jeopardy?

What she was doing now only endangered her heart. No, not even that, for she had lost it to Darien Reynard long since. This would be another secret to carry, but one that filled her with light instead of shadow.

He watched her, hunger in his eyes. Clara pulled in a deep, shivery breath. This night was hers to choose.

"Are you ready?" he asked.

"Yes." She pulled him down over her.

The tip of him pressed at her center. Slowly he moved forward, his maleness against her soft feminine parts, opening, parting her.

She had to remember to breathe through the awkward mystery of it. There was a brief, tearing pain, and then he filled her. Filled her and kept pressing in, so large, so long that she did not know how she could possibly take any more of him. Yet somehow they fit. Their hips touched and he held himself still above her. His face was set with concentration and a fierce self-control.

His gaze met hers, full of warmth, and she released her breath. Her body relaxed, too, the tightness easing, though the wonder remained. This was how it felt to be joined, man to woman. She tilted her hips, exploring the sensation. It was a bit uncomfortable, though her body seemed to be adjusting quickly.

Then he began to move, slowly, carefully, the slickness of desire mounting as he slid out. In. Out.

The fullness of every stroke made her catch her breath, but not in pain or even discomfort. No, this was something different, something uncharted and elusive. She felt as though they were on a river cloaked in mist, traveling together toward a destination she only half understood. Still, he knew the way.

It was evident in his assured touches. She was under the hand of the master, her body an instrument made of breath and skin and passion. A sweet, subtle tension curled inside her, echoes of the delight he had induced when he'd touched her with his fingers.

The feeling rose and rose, up from where he entered her. She teetered on the brink of a vast, thundering mystery. The boat of their bodies had come to an endless plunge of waterfall.

She clung to his shoulders, eyes fixed on his, and fell over the edge.

The current seized her, thrust her headlong into sensation, a glittering sheet of water and air and pure noise. It was like standing in the center of a cacophony of drums, the rhythm shaking her apart until she hardly knew where her body ended and Darien's began.

She cried out in pleasure that was nearly pain, and he arched over her. A shiver gripped him and he let out a deep moan. The skin beneath her hands was pricked with gooseflesh as she smoothed the plane of his back with her palms.

At last his shuddering ceased, and Clara breathed out a sigh. They had reached the still, quiet pool at the end of the river, though she would not emerge unscathed from that journey.

She was changed, forever.

CHAPTER NINETEEN

A Shocking Substitution!

Listeners were surprised last evening when, instead of composer Nicholas Becker, his sister took the stage to accompany Master Darien Reynard. Consternation turned to contentment as Miss Becker proved herself of sufficient musical skill. Still, one wonders what befell her brother to prompt such an unexpected replacement…

-Der Frankfurter Korrespondent

Clara woke with her usual moment of disorientation, blinking at the unfamiliar drapes and framed paintings on the wall. Another hotel, yes… in Prussia. She stretched, savoring the softness of fine linens against her bare feet.

Then the knowledge of what she had done last night burst inside her, brilliant and blinding.

She and Darien had made love. The physical memory of passion washed over her, leaving her senses tingling. She'd traded her virtue for a taste of paradise, and she was not sorry.

Although she was afraid.

Everything was irrevocably changed. Secrets webbed her in every direction, binding her in a tangle she could not see how to unravel.

How could she possibly face Darien across the breakfast table? Worse yet, how could she face Nicholas?

She wanted to pull the brocade coverlet over her head and spend the rest of the morning there, hiding in the dark cave of her bed, replaying the glorious night and grappling with her conscience. But she could not leave Nicholas to deal with Darien alone.

Exhaling deeply, she flung off the covers and rang for the

hotel's maid to come assist her in dressing. She'd had ample opportunity during the course of the last few months to perfect the art of concealing her thoughts and emotions, though the events of last night would put her façade sorely to the test.

When she entered the private dining parlor, Nicholas jumped to his feet. In the cold morning light he looked weary beyond words, and so young. The two years between them suddenly felt like twenty.

"Nicholas," she said, his name catching in her throat.

He twisted his napkin violently, then dropped his gaze to the blue figured carpet beneath their feet.

"I am sorry," he said. "And so ashamed."

She went to his side and touched his arm. "I forgive you."

It was that simple—and that fraught.

"What do we do now?" he asked.

Clara darted a glance at the yellow-liveried servant standing by the door. His face was impassive, but she would never make the mistake of thinking he was so much furniture, the way the nobility and upper classes seemed to do.

"We enjoy our breakfast," she said firmly, although enjoyment was not a likely state for either of them.

At least Darien had not yet come down to eat.

The servant brought her a plate of coddled eggs and toast, though she had no appetite. Across the table from her, Nicholas buttered his toast, then set it down, untouched. The clink of silver on china was their only conversation. She took a bite of toast, the crunch too loud in the silence, while Nicholas chased bits of egg about his plate with his fork. The egg always escaped.

Clara knew she ought to say something, but no words came. Her tea was warm, and she wrapped her chilled fingers around the cup, little caring that the brew was too weak.

"Clara." At last Nicholas leaned forward, his voice low. "Do you think... Is Master Reynard going to dispatch us back to England?"

"He told me he will not." She kept her voice steady, though her cheeks were warm—no doubt stained with color. "The musical duel is so near, he could not send us home even if he wished to. No one else could perfect *Il Diavolo* in time."

Her brother pushed his uneaten breakfast away. "I cannot—"

"You will." Darien strode into the room, his voice stern.

The servant flurried into motion, pulling out a chair then pouring the maestro's customary cup of coffee and setting it at the head of the table. Within moments, a plate filled with eggs and sausage from the chafing dishes followed.

Darien sat and fixed Nicholas with an implacable look. "Whatever your failings, Nicholas Becker, we have no choice but to go forward. You will continue touring with me. You will play every performance, to the absolute best of your musical abilities. And," with a violent movement he speared a bit of sausage, "you will *never* have a repetition of last night's inexcusable behavior. Is that clear?"

Nicholas dipped his head. "Yes, Master Reynard. I am very sorry."

"You're fortunate your sister was there to save the evening from disaster." Darien's tone was chilly. "She deserves your apology in full measure."

Her brother looked at her, his expression so drenched in misery that Clara could not keep from rising. She circled the table and set a hand on his shoulder.

"I've forgiven him," she said to Darien. How could she not, when she was guilty of even worse?

"We depart in one hour," Darien said. "Be ready."

He did not glance at either of them as he set about consuming his breakfast. Clearly it would take time before he forgave Nicholas. If ever.

"Excuse me, Clara. Master Reynard." Nicholas covered her hand briefly with his cold fingers, then pushed his chair back and stood. Shoulders bowed, he left the room.

Clara curled her fingers over the back of his empty chair and looked at Darien. His green eyes snared hers, his words to Nicholas echoing between them.

Last night's inexcusable behavior. Did he think the same of her?

After their passion was sated he had taken her silently back through the halls to her suite. She had made sure to collect her reticule from his settee, trusting he had forgotten his curiosity about its contents. In the dark hallway outside her door he pressed a lingering kiss to her lips, then slipped away. They had exchanged no promises, no whispered words of *yes* and *tomorrow* and *more.*

She was teetering on the edge of calamity; her brother's mistakes, and her own, sharp as knives within her. What had she done? She had traded her innocence—gladly, thoughtlessly—for a night of perfect pleasure in the master's arms. What was left to her?

"Clara." He uttered her name like a caress. "Thank you for last night. You were wonderful."

The servant might think he meant her piano playing, but she heard the deeper currents behind Darien's words. The heat in his eyes lured her, a moth to his flame. How could what she had felt last night be wrong? She smoothed her palms across the mahogany chair back.

"You were, as well." She held his gaze, though her body flushed with memory.

His sensuous mouth tilted into a half smile. "We will play again."

"I look forward to it."

"Perhaps this evening, then." His eyes were full of desire, and promises.

Clara's heart flew into a giddy spiral of joy, her earlier fear obliterated. No matter what else transpired, she would have this passion with Darien.

It was all she had that was truly *hers.* It was enough.

***

Dare and Nicholas performed in Leipzig that night. The concert went well enough, despite Nicholas's subdued demeanor, though the music did not come close to matching the glory of the previous evening.

Thoughts of Clara burned in Dare's pulse. When they returned to the hotel, he bade his composer good night, then paced impatiently in his suite. As soon as Nicholas had safely retired, Dare slipped to Clara's rooms and tapped lightly on her door.

She opened it at once and he stepped in, locking the door behind him. The soft pink and green of her gown set off her coloring, the rich fabrics underscoring the cream of her skin, the silk of her hair.

"You look beautiful," he said, taking her in his arms. "Delectable."

She smiled and laced her fingers about his neck. Lowering his lips to hers, he plundered her mouth, while his fingers plucked hairpins from her hair. Tonight, he intended to take his time, and show her far more of what could pass between a man and a woman.

Hair loosened from her coiffure, she took a step back and glanced at her half-open bedroom door.

"I'm... not sure how to go about this," she said.

"Then I will teach you. Come."

Taking her hand, he led her into the bedroom. Banked coals in the hearth warmed the room, and a lamp shone beside the turned-down bed, burnishing the pale sheets to gold. He set her on the linens and bent to loosen the buttons on her elegant boots.

"Darien." There was laughter in her voice. "I can take off my own shoes."

"Let me."

He wanted to open her like a precious gift, slowly peel back the coverings until she was revealed. The urgency that drove him still burned, though he banked it to a smolder. Time enough to build it into a raging fever. He intended them both to enjoy every step of that journey.

Her feet were cased in silk stockings. Dare took a foot in each hand, fingers wrapping around her arches. Her skirts and petticoats were disheveled, showing trim ankles and a glimpse of her calves.

She half sat, bracing herself up on her elbows, and tilted her head at him. The quizzical expression on her face made him smile.

"What, you're expecting me to throw myself on you and devour you whole?" An untamed part of him leapt up at the thought, like a wild wolf, but he forced it back down.

"I..." Her cheeks flushed.

"When a starving man sits at a lavish banquet, he does not gorge himself. No. He samples."

He moved his hands to her ankles, slowly sliding his palms over the warm silk. Farther up, to her knees. The soft fabric of her skirts folded, giving way before his advancing hands. She watched him, her lips parted with arousal, as he reached her garters. They were tied with pale green ribbons. He let his fingertips skim, just grazing the naked skin of her thigh. It was a delightful boundary, the edge between covered and uncovered. He would let it stand a bit longer.

"He savors," Dare said, bending to place a kiss on her ankle.

Then the side of her knee. Just below her garters, on the softness of her stocking. No lips against her bare, warm skin—not yet.

She drew in a breath and her thighs parted slightly, inviting. The sweet, musky scent of her arousal drifted to him, and his cock tightened against his trousers. Under the pretext of stroking her stockings, he opened her legs, each pass of his hands pressing her wider.

"He tastes."

Now he let himself put his mouth on her naked skin, his tongue licking above the garters. She fell back against the pillows with a gasp. Pushing her skirts even higher, he explored the delicious softness of her thigh, trailing kisses up to the lace-edged line of her drawers. Another boundary that would soon fall. Anticipation wound tight inside him at the thought of all the ways he wanted to savor her.

He stepped back just to look at her—her glorious hair unbound, her legs exposed and wanton, the shoulder of her dress still slipped down, the enticing edge of her nipple revealed. She was beautiful and sensual, moonlight and starlight. And she was his.

"Turn over," he said.

"Why?"

So many possibilities, but one perfect reason. "So I can unbutton your dress."

She turned and pillowed her head on her arms. Her skirts bunched beneath her, her hair a sweep of palest gold across her back.

He kicked off his shoes, then lay down on the bed beside her.

Her hair was fine and silken, reaching nearly to her waist. A wealth of softness. He caressed it, spread his hands and let the locks slip between his fingers. The fragrance of lavender-water mingled with the secret scent of her, and he found himself breathing in heavily, as if he could absorb her with every sense.

Brushing her hair aside, he began to undo the row of pearl buttons running down her back. There were over two dozen, but he took his time, watching the rise and fall of her ribs as she breathed, letting the hungry fire inside him simmer.

"Aren't you finished yet?" She looked back over her shoulder.

"So impatient." He gave her a smile. "All in good time. The banquet, remember?"

She made a little pout, an expression he had never seen on her before. He knew her face when she was serene, or anxious, or sometimes smiling. But this endearing, half-teasing look nearly brought him to his knees.

"When is it my turn at the table?" She made as if to rise, and he set his hand on her back.

"When mine is over." He anticipated it would take hours. "Lie still."

She tossed her head, but obeyed, and another thrill of desire went through him. He opened her gown, pushing it past her shoulders and midway down her arms. The fine material of her chemise followed, bunching at the edges of the corset, revealing more of her exquisite skin. Her corset concealed her lower back, but he bent and pressed kisses along her exposed spine. Moving up to the base of her neck, he nipped her lightly and felt her shiver with pleasure.

"Sit up," he said.

When she did, turning to face him, her gown slipped down to her waist. The corset curved beneath her breasts, pressing them up invitingly, and he could not refuse. He set his hands at her waist, lowered his head, and feasted. His mouth moved first over one nipple, coaxing it to tightness, then the other. Back and forth, until she was gasping, her hands fisted in his hair.

When he stopped, her nipples were peaked and rosy. So

beautiful. He could spend years on her breasts alone—but more awaited.

Her gown pulled off easily, and her petticoats followed, tumbling to the floor. She sat, her hair pushed back, clad only in her undergarments. Feminine, and sensual beyond words. She met his gaze boldly, and smiled. The wolf inside him howled and leaped. He needed her, with a fierceness that could not be denied.

CHAPTER TWENTY

Clara's heartbeat sped, even as languorous heat spread through her. Darien watched her with heavy-lidded eyes, his touch nearly making her swoon. He still wore his concert clothes, his cravat loosened, his coat open.

"I think you're overdressed for the occasion, Master Reynard," she said.

It was titillating, using his formal title while she sat before him half clothed, her unbound hair caressing her back.

He must have thought so, too, for the fire in his eyes rose.

"I think you are not undressed enough," he said. "Come here and let me unlace you."

She rose, her fine cotton chemise whispering against her legs, and a moment later she was in his embrace again. Whatever his intentions of corset unlacing, it seemed that kisses were of paramount importance. His tongue traced her lips, his hands were warm against her naked shoulders, and she felt as though she were melting under the force of his heat.

Darien's tongue dipped into her mouth, and she opened to him, let her tongue touch his. Sparks of desire coursed through her, the place between her legs damp. She pressed closer to him and felt the hardness of his member against her belly—that mysterious male part that somehow had fit into her own body.

Just as he was turning her weak-kneed with his plunging kisses, she knew he would turn her weak-hearted when he entered her. She wanted it, wanted it fiercely. Wanted *him*, musician and man and, though he could never know it, mate of her soul.

If she could not tell him in words, she would let her body speak. She would open fully to him, give him everything of herself. All the secrets burning in her, all the secrets she could never say, transmuted to pure passion.

His hands tangled in her hair, he kissed her as though he were worshipping some pagan goddess who must be appeased by his kisses. It made her feel beautiful and powerful and humbled all at once. His mouth trailed a line of caresses along her jaw, down her throat, around the base of one ear.

She held tightly to his shoulders, her skin tingling from the brush of his lips. A soft moan escaped her and he lifted his head. Those green eyes regarded her, that firm mouth and sculpted features all the ladies sighed over—that *she* sighed over in the restless hours before morning. A wayward lock of dark hair fell across his forehead, and she could finally brush it back; an intimate gesture she'd been craving for weeks. His hair was black satin against her fingers, and she knew she would never forget the feel of it.

He smiled, and she caught her breath. It was a private smile, a smile made for bedchambers and midnights, full of promises.

"You are everything distracting," he said. "Turn around."

Even as he spoke the words, his hands turned her in place until she faced away from him. He held her by the hips, the male heat of him just behind her, then bent his head to lay more kisses along her neck. She closed her eyes and let her head fall back against his shoulder, giving herself up to the tickling shocks of his touch. She was dimly aware of him moving her, steering her a few steps to the right.

"Open your eyes." His voice was low and husky. "Watch."

They were facing the large mirrored wardrobe. Her eyes widened as she saw what was reflected there.

Lamplight played against her pale skin, gleamed on the long fall of her hair. Darien was tall and dusky behind her, one arm around her waist, holding her as the midnight sky holds a luminous moon. She looked like a goddess captured, unwary, by a masterful hunter. Unwary, but not unwilling. A wave of arousal swept through her, and her reflection mirrored it, lips parting, eyes half closing.

"Watch," he said again, a smoky undertone of wickedness in the word.

He brought his hand up to cup her breast, then ran his thumb over the pink tip. The sensation, coupled with the sight of him caressing her, made her gasp aloud.

"So lovely," he murmured.

He pulled her tightly against him and began teasing her nipple, all the while watching her reflection's eyes. His other hand grazed her hip, and he took a handful of her chemise and began to lift.

The light material inched up, exposing her calf, her knee. She swallowed, tasting the heady flavor of desire. It was scandalously exciting, as if she were watching another woman, a beautiful, sensual stranger, being undressed. He toyed with her breasts, while her chemise crept ever higher.

Past her ribbon-clasped garters to the pale skin of her thigh, the lacy edge of her drawers. Darien made an impatient sound. His hand moved beneath the chemise and she felt his fingers loosening the ties of her drawers. They slipped down, cambric and lace rumpling at her ankles. She lifted one foot, then the other, stepping free of the undergarment.

"Very good." He gave her a hungry smile.

She held his reflected gaze and dipped her head in assent. Here in his arms, he was the master and she would follow wherever he led.

He resumed the slow lifting of her chemise, and her heart pounded. She was naked now beneath it, nothing to shield her womanly places from his avid gaze. The smooth length of her thigh, her hip—and then the first glimpse of the golden curls wound tightly between her legs.

His hand stilled on her breast and she felt tension imbue his body. Here, now, the secrets of her body were revealed. And though she could not share her other secrets with him, she wanted desperately to share this. She reached back, lacing her fingers about his neck, and the movement raised her breasts even higher above the corset.

The woman in the mirror was deliciously wanton, a self she had never suspected, yet could not help but acknowledge. The proof was there before her in the glass—her pale hair unbound, her softly opened mouth and languid eyes, her breasts peaked and eager for his touch, her legs ready to be parted. Heat and a low throbbing pulsed from her center, and she let out a sigh. The kind of sigh the siren in the mirror would certainly give in the arms of her lover.

The sound spurred him to movement. Still holding her tightly, he leaned, snagged a nearby chair, and pulled it in front of her.

"Put your foot there," he said. "On the seat."

She obeyed, though it was a position that would expose her even more to him. With a low, guttural sound, he dropped his hand to her hip and pulled the rest of her chemise aside. Ah, she was still partially clothed, but naked everywhere it counted. The lamplight cast soft shadows between her breasts, shone faintly on the triangle of hair between her legs.

Darien was heat and powerful male at her back. The breath feathering past her neck was the only softness about him now. That, and the way his palm smoothed along her lifted leg. His hand slid forward to caress the sensitive skin of her inner thigh.

Breath hurried through her lungs now, and she was panting softly as his touch moved closer to the juncture of her legs. When he brushed her curls, she moaned—she could not help it. Her eyes fell closed, and his hand stopped.

Oh yes, she must watch. With effort, she lifted her heavy lids. He met her gaze in the mirror and gave her a nod of approval, then threaded his fingers through her curls and tugged gently. His knuckles brushed lower down, sending a shower of sparks tingling through her. Another moan escaped her lips.

"Very good," he murmured. "You are an apt student in the arts of lovemaking. Will you continue on as my pupil, Miss Becker?"

She summoned the breath to speak. "Teach me, Master Reynard."

Again, the formality of the words, contrasted with her shockingly explicit position, sent a wave of arousal through her.

"Excellent."

He laid his hot mouth against her neck, swirling his tongue in a pattern of pure desire. Lower, his hand brushed between her legs, lightly back and forth. Too lightly. She needed *more*. She tilted her hips forward and felt him laugh against her skin.

Taking his hand away, he brought his fingers up to her mouth. Slowly, he inserted his index finger between her lips. She flicked her tongue along it. He tasted of salt and man, slightly rough in the warm confines of her mouth. Experimenting, she sucked on his finger and felt a quiver run through him.

Finger slick with moisture, he brought his hand back to play between her legs. This time he boldly touched her, parted her, and slid his finger against the softness he found.

"Ah!" A sudden flare of excited relief surged through her. Yes—right there.

A feral light in his eyes, Darien continued to stroke her. The initial satisfaction quickly burned away, replaced by the fiery urgency she recalled from the night before. Need pressed close about her, pulled tighter than any corset.

"What do you see?" he asked, his voice low and unrepentant.

She had forgotten to watch, had been unable to watch, with such sensations running rampant through her.

"I..." She licked her lips and forced herself to look in the mirror again.

Her hair had fallen over one shoulder, partially concealing her breast, though the tip of it peeked out, the nipple still puckered hard with desire. His arm circled her waist, his fingers clenched around her bunched chemise, while his other hand moved relentlessly between her legs. She was spread open to his touch, to his gaze—indiscreet and reckless.

"I see a woman—"

"An incredibly desirable woman," he corrected.

"Being touched. Pleasured..." She faltered.

"Oh yes. Do you feel pleasure?"

She nodded, knowing that he could sense the sensation building beneath his hands in the trembling of her limbs, in the way her breath shortened as though she had just run up three flights of stairs.

"Let me give you more words," he said. "Stimulated. Erotic. Aroused."

Each descriptive sent another throb of heat through her.

He dipped his head and whispered in her ear. "Are you those

things? Let me hear you say them."

"Stimulated," she breathed, then shivered as he added a second finger to the one rubbing along her slit.

"Erotic." She felt as though the floor were tilting beneath her.

"Aroused." She could barely speak the word as the pressure of his fingers increased, sliding insistently back and forth. Back and forth.

Her head fell against his shoulder and she bit her lip, moaning.

"Yes, my beautiful one," he murmured. "Find your release for me—let me see it."

The feel of his hand closing about her taut nipple tipped her into a surge of sensation. Waves of fire clenched through her body, ripping a soft scream from her throat. Pulse. Pulse. Pulse. She was swept by tingling heat, every inch of her body suddenly, fiercely alive. If not for Darien holding her, she would have fallen in a fluid heap upon the floor.

The waves receded, leaving her trembling and languorous in his arms. He gently lifted her leg and set her foot back down on the carpet, let the chemise drop to cover the astonishing place between her legs. The place he coaxed such untoward sensations from. Oh, she'd touched herself before, curious, but had only ever felt a vague, dissatisfied tickle. Nothing like the surging, powerful sensations he evoked in her.

He took a step back and began unlacing her corset, dark head bent to his task. As the stays loosened, Clara took a deep breath. The corset slipped to the floor, and she shed her chemise on top of it. No modesty—not when she knew how the sight of her nakedness affected him. She could see the erratic pulse in his neck, the stark hunger on his face.

With a sideways look, she set one foot on the chair again and untied her ribbon garter. Slowly, slowly, she pushed the silken stocking down. His eyes followed the movements of her hands and he licked his lips. She repeated the action with her other leg, then turned to face him, naked and breathless.

"Now what?" she asked.

His smile was feral, with an edge of triumph. "Now we move on to the advanced course of study."

He untied his cravat, casually, as if he were alone, undressing after a concert. His fingers on his waistcoat were unhurried.

"Let me." She reached to help him with the buttons, but he brushed her hand aside.

"So impatient. But now it's your turn to watch."

Despite his studied movements, his voice was full of checked urgency, as if he were eager to tear his clothing off and only rigid control kept him from doing so. The deliberation tightened the coil of tension winding about them, set a spark of awareness low in her center.

He pulled off his waistcoat and began to unbutton his shirt at that same maddening pace. A sigh of impatience escaped her. At last the flat planes of his chest were exposed, his skin framed by the brilliant whiteness of his formal shirt. He shrugged the garment off over shoulders sleek with muscle.

Now the trousers. His hands paused on the flap, then he loosened them and his drawers together and let them fall.

Oh. Oh my. She had not truly seen him last night, but he was as imposing as she had thought. Her face must have reflected her momentary uncertainty, for he stepped forward and took her by the shoulders.

"Don't be afraid," he said.

"I'm not."

It was not fear. It was desire and anticipation and the knowledge that their bodies belonged together, in some deep, primal way she could not explain.

He pulled her against him. One hand under her chin, he tilted her face up to his kiss. Sensations ran through her like a melody, his lips over hers, his arm firm about her waist. And the scorching shock of their bodies standing skin to skin. She gasped, and he slid his tongue inside, tasting her mouth.

It was all heat, and softness laid over hardness. Gasping breaths, and her hands clutching his shoulders as he swept her up into his arms and carried her to the bed. The sheets were cool against her back, but he was a fever running deliriously through her. He knelt above her, his dark hair sweeping against his cheekbones, his skin gleaming in the lamplight.

When he spoke, his voice was roughened with passion. "I'm going to taste you."

She blinked. "Haven't you already?"

"No. Not fully." As if to demonstrate, he lowered his head and plundered her mouth again for a long second.

Leaving her gasping, he lowered himself, his skillful lips now at her breast, sucking and teasing. She arched into the touch, sparks scattering through her.

"Delicious," he said. "Yet not enough."

With a wicked gleam in his eyes, he slid down her body. He trailed kisses over her ribs, across her belly, licked the curve of her hip, then knelt between her legs, pressing them wide. His fingers played again, tickling and teasing sensations from her. Ah, he was a master indeed.

"But—"

"Shh. Remember, you are still a student." He set his hand over the mound of her womanhood and the pulse inside her grew more insistent.

Was he truly going to taste her *there*? It was scandalous and tantalizing, and suddenly she burned for it.

He moved his hand, then leaned over and blew softly against her skin. The caress sent a shiver through her. Her legs were wide, but he pressed them open even more, making a place for himself there between her thighs. Then, slowly, he touched her with his tongue.

Ah. Ah yes.

He explored her, his tongue slick and warm as he savored her secrets. She shuddered with sensation beneath his mouth. Then he slipped a finger inside her and she gasped, lifting her hips clear off the sheets. His laughter tickled against her. A second finger joined the first and he slid them back and forth, his tongue still caressing her until she thought she would go mad from the need burning through her.

A need left unfulfilled as he pulled back. She could feel him watching her, and slowly lifted her eyelids. The look in his eyes was possessive, his gaze moving over her as though she were a perfect score of music, written solely for him to play.

"Are you ready for the next tutorial?"

"Oh, yes."

She was ready. Beyond ready. And she welcomed it with everything in her soul.

"There is one thing." He slid to the edge of the bed, then returned a moment later, a packet in his hand. "French letters, to prevent conception and... illnesses."

He offered no further explanation. She watched, curious, as he removed a long sheath and pulled it over his member, fastening it tightly about the base with the attached ribbon. Then he knelt over her again, his hands to either side of her shoulders. She felt his manhood between her legs, pressing against her slickness.

It was easier this time. Her body opened to him and he slid in, deeper and deeper, stretching until he filled her completely. His gaze searched her face, clearly watching her for any sign of pain or discomfort.

There was none, only the slow sweet build of pleasure. And beyond that, the yearning of her soul, answered.

"Darien." She whispered his name, and left the rest unsaid.

Slowly, he began to move in her, stroking back and forth. She tilted her hips, finding the counterpoint to his rhythm. Together they strove, reaching for a song just out of hearing, reaching for the edge of the stars.

He quickened his pace, both of them breathing more heavily. It was a symphony of desire: the slip of the sheets against skin, the faint creak of the mattress beneath them, the rasp of pleasure in his throat, her own sharper gasps. Faster, closer. Brightness spun at the edge of her vision.

He threw his head back, neck taut, and together they whirled into that vortex of pleasure. A firework lit in her center, the explosion of light and sparkle flashing through her entire body until she felt she was made of nothing but sparks and air.

She clutched his shoulders and swallowed her cry of delight.

Darien shuddered, his movements slowing until they lay in a moment of stillness. Clara closed her eyes. She could almost feel the night sky heavy above them, the revolving earth carrying them breathless through space.

The immensity of it, the joy, was almost too much to bear. A tear stole from the corner of her eye, quickly cooling as it ran down her temple and into her hair.

"Clara." He brushed the moisture away with his thumb. "Are you all right?"

She opened her eyes and smiled up at him, at the concern and unexpected vulnerability in his expression.

"Yes," she said. "I am."

More right than he could imagine, cradled in that perfect moment under the spinning sky.

***

As the coach traveled through the Prussian countryside and into Austria, Dare watched Clara, and thought.

He had taken her innocence, though she had offered it gladly. Still, she was his now, in ways he could not explain even to himself. Hungry compulsion rose in him every time their gazes met.

When the musical competition was over, he would ask her to be his companion, and openly reveal their affair. Until then, they must be cautious. Nicholas was far too volatile. Any hint that his sister and Dare had been physically intimate could send the man spiraling out of control. Dare could not take that risk, though it was unfair to make Clara hide in the shadows.

Impatience made him curl his fingers into his fists. With a deep breath, he released them, leashing the emotions pulsing through him.

Less than a fortnight until the duel, and then everything would be laid bare, into the light. Until then, he must keep sight of his goal. He would be victorious—in all things.

CHAPTER TWENTY-ONE

Concertgoers of Europe! Will you acclaim the mawkish melodies offered by the second-rate composer Nicholas Becker? Or will you stand up and proudly applaud the true musical masters of our time? Consider well, as the course of history is in your hands!
-Varga Virtuoso (a street handbill)

The coach slowed through the crowded streets of Vienna. Clara watched out the window as tall, ornate buildings scrolled past, interspersed with gardens and statues. People wore heavy coats and thick pelisses against the chilly air, and there were far fewer umbrellas than in London during the spring.

"Worried that we'll be in another cold, provincial hotel?" Darien asked. "Never fear. We're staying at the Hofburg—the imperial palace."

Nicholas lifted his head. He had said little during the three-day journey from Prussia, spending much of the trip in reading. It had given Clara far too much leisure to think about Darien. Their gazes had tangled time and again, unsettling her until she had taken refuge in the corner of the carriage and closed her eyes.

Under pretense of napping, she replayed every touch, every caress of their nights together. Now a new melody was singing through her, clear and passionate. Her fingers itched to set it to paper. In her heart she called the piece *Amore*, though she could never reveal its truth to her brother. No, she must come up with a more innocent title.

"I thought Emperor Francis was a supporter of Varga." Nicholas closed his book of poetry and gave Darien a questioning look.

"That doesn't mean he will stint us his hospitality," Darien said. He stretched his arms along the seat. "Perhaps we can win him over. After some serious rehearsing, of course."

"Of course," her brother said, his voice thin.

Clara's breath tightened with worry. The last two rehearsals had been painful to overhear. Darien unrelentingly pushed Nicholas, which only served to make her brother more withdrawn and anxious.

She understood, though. Only too well.

Darien pressed Nicholas because of the night Clara had accompanied him. He heard the echo of what the music could be, but Nicholas could not, quite, give it, and so the rehearsals disintegrated into swamps of sullen notes and sticky passages. There was no lightness to the music—and that way lay failure. For all of them. Ten days until the duel. She tasted lead at the thought.

Still, they were in Austria now. Perhaps things would improve at the palace.

***

Dare set his violin case down and surveyed his suite. Sunlight filtered through thin curtains at the windows, the décor in the green and gilt rooms elegantly understated. Servants bustled in with his luggage, while others hurried to set the table in the sitting area with tea, coffee, and an assortment of pastries.

"It is comfortable," Henri said with a glance at the furnishings. "At least the Viennese understand good taste. Unlike that English Pavilion."

He gave an exaggerated shudder. Clearly his French sensibilities had been forever offended by the excesses in Brighton.

Dare noted the rich aroma drifting from the table. "Not to mention the Viennese coffee. Later we'll visit the Café Frauenhuber. I think Nicholas might like to take a cup of *schwarzer* alongside the ghosts of Mozart and Beethoven."

He hoped an outing just for pleasure would help ease matters. Their recent rehearsals had been fraught with frustration, and the music had suffered. Indeed, he ought to be less hard on Nicholas. After all, Dare had experienced one of the most transcendent musical evenings of his life because the man had been too indisposed to play. But even that could not excuse the composer's highly unprofessional behavior that night.

As for his own behavior… Dare tugged at his cravat, ignoring Henri's look of annoyance as he mussed the perfectly tied knot. He had not been able to resist Clara. He had not even tried. Their physical union had been a natural extension of their one night of perfect music—twining notes yielding to twining bodies, the two of them striving together and making something glorious.

Every night he wanted her there, between the sheets of his bed. Whether that bed was at an inn or a palace, it didn't matter. He burned for her.

But he craved more than physical passion with Clara. What had passed between them as they performed, their musical connection, had marked him. Marked them both.

He had asked her to accompany him again, and she'd adamantly refused, saying it would be a terrible blow to Nicholas if she usurped his place at the piano. Fear had flashed through her lovely, pale eyes, and he had not pressed her. Yet.

Dare blew out a breath. He must forgive Nicholas. To do any less would be the worst hypocrisy, after making illicit, passionate love to Clara.

"Monsieur." Henri gestured to the table. "It would be a crime to let these pastries languish. And even worse, the coffee is growing cold. I beg you, let me fetch the Beckers."

"Do so."

It had not escaped Dare's notice that their suite was just across the hall. Clara would be sleeping in her silken nightdress only a few stealthy paces away. Those lush lips and rosy-tipped breasts, the waterfall of her hair waiting to be unbraided and loosened, a spill of pale gold across her naked back…

"He is here!" Nicholas burst through the door, his eyes wide.

Clara and Henri crowded close behind, looking as unsettled as the composer.

"Who?" Dare asked, though he suspected he knew.

"Varga." Henri spat the name. "We spotted him just now, at the end of the hallway."

"Blast." Dare bunched his hands into fists and strode to the door, but there was no sign of his rival. "Paris, I can understand, but this—it's intolerable. He must be staying in the Hofburg, too. The emperor would insist on it."

"Varga is sly and devious, monsieur," Henri said. "We are so close to the duel, it does not surprise me that he would arrange things to give you the most discomfort."

Dare shot a glance at Nicholas, who looked pale. Another complication he could ill afford, another strain upon his already fragile composer. The possibility of failure insinuated itself, a clammy hand upon the back of his neck.

He shook it off. Self-doubt would only make matters worse. And *he* was the master, after all. Varga stood little chance of proving otherwise.

"We shall give him no satisfaction," Dare said.

He closed the door, then gestured them to the table, although the delectable Austrian pastries would now taste like dust in his mouth.

Varga, in Vienna. Nothing good could come of it.

CHAPTER TWENTY-TWO

The Café Frauenhuber was crowded, in a companionable manner. Dare took a deep breath redolent of coffee and smoke. Conversation filled the high-ceilinged room, a comfortable buzz of German, with a smattering of Italian and French.

"This way, Master Reynard, Mr. Becker." The white-coated waiter bowed, then led them across the parquet floor to a cozy alcove table. "May I bring you coffee?"

"Yes, two *schwarzer*."

Dare had sipped many cups in his travels, from the brown water the English served to the thick Turkish brew he'd savored in Morocco. But nothing rivaled the smooth, dark coffee of the Viennese coffeehouse.

Nicholas glanced about curiously. Dare followed his attention as it moved from a table of boisterous university boys to a lone man garbed in black, scribbling furiously in a notebook.

"Look." Nicholas's voice was thoughtful. "That might be another Beethoven, composing in obscurity."

"I think the next Beethoven is here," Dare said, then half smiled as his composer stared harder at the fellow. "No, not that gentleman over there. The next Beethoven may well be sitting across the table from me."

Nicholas jerked his gaze back to Dare. "Oh—I wouldn't say that!"

"Some are."

The waiter brought their coffee, two neat white cups each on their own silver tray, accompanied by a glass of water and a spoon.

Nicholas picked up the spoon and turned it between his fingers. "That's not all people are saying about the compositions. I try not to listen, but—"

"Then don't. Your worth is not measured by what people say, Nicholas, but by the music you write, which is magnificent. Don't allow them to judge you. Let your pieces speak for themselves."

Dare, too, had heard the criticism, which largely echoed what Varga had said in Paris—that Becker's compositions used overly emotional techniques to mask the fact the composer was a second-rate talent. Varga's supporters had taken to parroting his opinions, claiming the music was too sentimental, too lushly romantic.

Dare knew it was those very qualities of emotion that would make Becker's music live on and touch the hearts of listeners for centuries to come.

"I will try." Nicholas sounded unconvinced.

Dare drank his coffee, letting his mouth fill with the poignant flavor before swallowing. "What are you working on now?"

"Ah. A new piece."

"Have you a title for it?"

Nicholas dropped his gaze to the table. "Not yet, no."

"Our recent… troubles haven't impaired your composing, have they?" If the man had lost his muse, it would be ruinous.

"Of course not!" Fingers tight around his cup, Nicholas took a sip. "It's just… it's still in process. The newest work. But coming along well, I assure you."

"I'm relieved to hear it."

And would be more relieved still to actually *hear* the composition. Perhaps at one of their upcoming rehearsals, though he did not like the idea of working on new music anywhere Varga could eavesdrop.

Varga. As if thinking of the man had summoned him, Darien's rival strode into the coffeehouse. The waiter hurried up to him, but Varga brushed him aside. His dark eyes went unerringly to the corner where Dare and Nicholas sat.

"Hold fast," Dare murmured. "Varga's approaching."

Nicholas paled and carefully placed his cup on the table.

"Ah. Reynard. So, you are in Vienna." Varga's tone was overly hearty as he came to stand directly in front of their table. He gave a smile more akin to a sneer, then glanced at Nicholas. "And the little composer. Hoping for inspiration? You will need it. But where is the sister? Left behind to amuse herself at the palace, is it? I'm certain she will find many *amusements* there. The footmen are all quite handsome."

"You black-hearted knave!" Nicholas scraped his chair back and stood, his hands lifted into fists. "How dare you speak such insults? I demand satisfaction."

"Do you?" Varga smiled like a cat with a mouse under its paw.

"Easy now," Dare said, keeping his voice smooth, though anger flared through him. He rose and laid one hand on Nicholas's shoulder. "We've a duel already scheduled—and I assure you Varga will be the loser."

"Bold words, Reynard." Varga turned to him, hatred flaring in his eyes. "A pity your pet here isn't man enough to take matters into his own hands."

Dare felt Nicholas tense. Damn, the boy was about to do something rash.

"Nicholas." He weighted his words with warning. "Don't—"

Too late. The composer seized his glass of water and flung it in Varga's face.

"That should cool your evil tongue," he cried.

"Ahh!" Varga spluttered. He drew one arm across his cheeks. "You puppy! I should take you outside right now."

"Nothing would give me greater pleasure." Nicholas was breathing heavily, a wild look in his eyes.

The coffeehouse fell silent as the patrons noticed the confrontation. Even the scribbler set his pen down. Anticipation hung in the air, and Dare swallowed a curse. No matter how this played out, it would end badly.

Varga preened, despite the water dripping from his hair. It was the kind of scene he reveled in creating. Dare had seen it often enough.

Varga gestured to the door. "I would hate to keep you waiting."

Dare tightened his grip on his composer's shoulder and the silence in the air sharpened, a knife pointed directly at them. He saw

Nicholas's throat move as he swallowed, but the composer remained still.

"No?" Varga raised one eyebrow. "Well then, perhaps I shall go to the palace and renew my acquaintance with your sister. She did not seem particularly amiable when we met, but I will no doubt find a remedy."

Dare moved first. He released Nicholas and took a fistful of Varga's coat. Twisting it, he pulled his rival closer.

"Stay. Away. From her," he said, his voice low.

Varga's eyes widened. Clearly he had not been expecting the master to join the fight so quickly.

"Release me," Varga hissed. "I am not alone here."

Dare gave him little shake, then glanced behind his rival to see two brawny men hovering in the doorway. They looked as tough and scarred as professional brawlers, which they likely were. Of course Varga had come prepared for a fight.

"We will aid you, Master Reynard!" A fair-haired young man sprang up from a nearby table, gesturing to his companions to do the same. "Have no fear of Herr Varga or his minions."

"I don't think—oof!"

Varga had taken advantage of Dare's distraction to jab a surprisingly painful hand into his stomach. As Dare tried to catch his breath, his rival slithered free.

"Snake!" Nicholas yelled, and swung at Varga.

The henchmen pushed into the coffeehouse, and the earnest Austrian boys knocked their table over in their enthusiasm to join the fight. China and glassware clattered to the floor, and the café erupted with motion.

"Out! Out!" A man with large whiskers—presumably the proprietor—gestured urgently, desperate to move the conflict outside his walls.

The white-coated waiters did their best to contain the rapidly spreading fight and push the combatants out the door. Coffee splashed and another glass crashed to the floor. The entire establishment had taken sides—some for Varga, the rest for Dare.

The frustration and worry that had been building up inside Dare suddenly burst free like a dammed-up river released, pouring out of his fists and feet. Fierce glee filled him. He dodged around the university boys, only to meet one of Varga's brawlers. Quick as thought, Dare slammed his fist into the man's face. His knuckles burned, but it was his bowing hand—it could take a little damage.

The smell of coffee strong in his nose, he squinted, looking for Varga. There—darting out the door.

Nicholas lingered near their table, facing off against Varga's hired man. Dare winced as the composer threw a punch that connected squarely with the man's ribs. The brawler seemed unaffected, but Nicholas shook out his hand, a look of pain on his face.

"Nicholas, hurry," Dare called. "Varga's escaping."

He gave a swift elbow to the brawler. Leaving the man gasping for breath, Dare grabbed Nicholas by the shoulder and pulled him to the door.

They burst out of the coffeehouse to find the street knotted with men fighting. Word of the clash between the rival musicians had spread quickly. Chants of "Varga! Varga!" were met with "Reynard— Master Reynard!"

Dare bared his teeth in a grin, squared his shoulders, and waded in.

"Darien!" Nicholas dodged blows and tugged at his arm. "I don't see Varga anywhere. We must return to the palace—Clara is alone. What if he…"

Varga's taunts were designed to goad Nicholas, and Dare doubted there was anything of substance behind the words. Clara had Henri and a palace full of guards and servants to look after her. Still, it was wise not to underestimate his rival.

"Yes, let us see how your sister fares," Dare said, blocking a fist swinging too near his ribs.

He and Nicholas ducked into a quiet side street, away from the wild energy of the fight and back toward the high walls of the palace.

***

Clara hurried into Darien's sitting room, then halted in surprise.

"Gracious! The maid said I'd best come quickly, but whatever have the two of you been doing? Is Vienna such a rough city?"

Nicholas sported a bruise on one cheek and his cravat had come undone. He was holding his right hand awkwardly near his body, but when he saw her looking he straightened his arm. Still, she knew the guilty shadow in his expression that meant he was hiding something.

And Darien... When their eyes met, a jolt of sensation flew through her, hot and delicious. His hair was rakishly disheveled and he'd removed his coat. For a scorching moment she recalled the feel of his skin against hers, his strong arms around her.

His mouth curved into a devilish smile, as though he could tell what she was thinking. "Vienna is not usually dangerous. Unless one has made enemies."

"Varga attacked us," Nicholas said, his voice unsteady. He sank into one of the chairs. "There was a tremendous brawl at the coffeehouse."

"Yes." Darien grinned. "I wouldn't be surprised if it's spread to half the city by now."

"Why would it?" Clara asked.

"Because the musical duel is in less than a fortnight, and people love having a cause to champion. And fight over."

Nicholas scowled. "I cannot believe anyone supports that snake, when you are so clearly the better man. And musician."

"The rivalry is what makes it exciting," Darien said. "And will make my victory all the sweeter when I defeat him. Which, to that end, calls for more rehearsal. Tidy up, Nicholas, and I'll meet you in the parlor. Perhaps the temper of the afternoon will aid us in besting *Il Diavolo.*"

"Yes, master." Nicholas rose and, shoulders slumped, left the sitting room.

"Well," Clara said, "as long as you are both unharmed, that is the important thing."

She threaded her fingers together to keep from running her hands over his body to make sure he had taken no injury.

"Clara." Darien's voice was low.

He took a step toward her, and she backed away from his enticing heat.

Their nights of passion in Prussia must not be repeated. The duel was approaching so quickly, and if Nicholas found out, it would be a disaster. She must keep a proper distance from Darien, and try to erase the yearnings of her body. But she could not deny how every moment her blood sang with the notes of his name.

Her only respite was to set those feelings down on paper, to harness the fire and longing that swept her with every thought of him. Her newest composition scorched through her, unfurled in a storm of music, nearly complete. *Amore*. The memory of their bodies moving together in the night. The mysteries of two souls woven together. The beating of her own heart, echoing his name.

"I... I ought to see if Nicholas needs tending."

"You're not concerned for me?" There was a teasing light in Darien's eyes as he moved toward her.

"I am, of course! But you seem well."

More than well. Virile and overwhelmingly male. She took another step back and felt the panel of the door against her shoulders. She could turn, twist the handle, and flee. But he had captured her gaze with his, stalked her until she was cornered. Arousal shivered through her, and she could not make herself leave.

Darien closed the last distance between them and set his hands against the door, caging her between his arms. The heat of his body, the hot scent of him, pulsed over her. He was too close. He was not close enough. Clara's breath came in little gasps and her lips parted, as if to taste the air between them.

"Clara. You tempt me unbearably." He leaned forward, his dark eyes intent, full of hunger.

"I..." There were no words.

Only the taut peaks of her breasts, the warmth pooling low in her center. A single phrase of melody, high and sweet and trembling.

He made a sound somewhere between a growl and a moan, then lowered his head and took her lips in a searing kiss.

Yes, her body clamored. *Yes, this*. This heat and surrender. The feel of his tongue tasting hers.

Hot darts of passion sped through her, leaving her trembling for more. He clasped her hands, then lifted them above her head and pinned her against the door. His body covered hers, hard and insistent. She wanted nothing more than to melt into him.

Slowly, he ravished her mouth. Only the force of his body against hers, the link of their hands, kept her upright. Her blood burned as if it had been replaced by pure cognac.

At last he lifted his head. She took in a trembling breath.

"Darien…"

There were a thousand reasons this was wrong, but the words of protest dissolved on her tongue. She must lie to him about her deepest self, but she could not lie to him about this, about how he made her feel. Even if she denied it, her body betrayed her.

He uncurled his hands from hers and, eyes dark with sensual promises, spoke a single word.

"Tonight."

CHAPTER TWENTY-THREE

Frenzied Fighting in the Streets!

Supporters of Darien Reynard and Anton Varga clashed this morning, in a fracas that spread quickly through the streets. The conflict began in the Café Frauenhuber, long known as a hotbed of creativity and revolution. Several minor injuries were reported...

-Vienna Today

"**W**hat do you mean, you cannot play any more?" Dare set his violin in its case, then rounded on Nicholas. He didn't bother hiding the bite in his voice. "We've been rehearsing barely half an hour!"

"I know." The composer bent his fair head and stared at the keyboard in front of him. "I... during the brawl... my hand. I think I injured it."

"For God's sake." Dare let out an irritated breath. "Let me see."

Nicholas held out his right hand and Dare studied his bruised and swollen knuckles. "I'd say you've sprained your hand. No doubt when you punched that confounded brawler of Varga's."

"I'm sorry," Nicholas said, still not meeting Dare's eyes. "I should have been more careful."

"You should have mentioned it, instead of trying to play with an injury. Now you've made it worse, just when we can't spare any time from practicing." Annoyance pricked his temples. Still, no good would come of forcing Nicholas to play. "Have Henri tend to it."

"I..." The composer glanced up. "I could ask Clara to fill in for me. At least for today. She knows *Il Diavolo* well enough."

Anticipation flickered through Dare.

"Send her in."

Nicholas hurried from the music parlor, shoulders bowed. The strings of a nearby harp vibrated with the air of his passage, sending a faint, discordant hum into the air.

Watching him go, Dare frowned. Something was wrong with the composer, something more than his injured hand. Was he truly on the verge of plunging into melancholy, as his sister feared? Blast it. Nicholas had to hold together for ten days. Ten days! It should not be too much to ask.

He could not go easier on the man. *Il Diavolo* was still a challenge for them both. Dare must push himself and Nicholas to their limits if they were to be victorious in the musical duel.

"Master Reynard?" Clara stepped into the room. The light from the tall windows gleamed on her fair hair. "Nicholas said I am to rehearse with you this afternoon."

"He must rest his hand." Dare gave her a slow smile. "And I welcome the chance to play with you. I may require you tomorrow, as well."

The words carried a second meaning, as he had intended, and a pretty blush colored Clara's cheeks.

"Then we'd best begin." She settled at the piano in a very businesslike manner and began flipping through the manuscript pages.

He hid his amusement. Clara was a deer flushed from cover, but they both knew how the chase would end. If she wanted to pretend otherwise, he would indulge her. For now.

But first, there was the music to attend to. Dare lifted his violin and bow, and took his place beside the piano.

"We left off at the beginning of the second page," he said. "The *allegro* section—do you know the spot?"

She gave him a dry look, her fingers poised above the keys. "I am ready when you are, maestro."

Indeed, she was. Dare launched into the passage, his bow weaving and dipping, and the piano met him perfectly. Each note fell precisely where it ought, but more than that, the music carried an undercurrent of urgency. He had not felt that before, playing *Il Diavolo* with Nicholas. Perhaps it was the mutual awareness that moved between Clara and him, the knowledge of their secret intimacy filtering into the music.

Whatever it was, he prized it. The notes flew from under his fingers as they reached the *prestissimo*, the piano surging along with him. Sweat gathered at his temples and he felt the edge of the precipice dangerously near. They were going too fast, he could not quite control the *spiccato* bowing... and *Il Diavolo* tumbled to a broken halt as both he and Clara botched the intricacies of the passage.

She stared at him a moment, her silvery eyes wide. And then she laughed, a joyful outpouring of mirth, so at odds with her brother's sheepish reaction whenever he made a mistake.

"Ah, we almost had it!" She sounded jubilant. "Again. Please."

"A touch slower, perhaps." He couldn't help grinning back at her. "Let's take it from the arpeggios."

***

When Henri came to inform them supper was imminent, Dare could hardly credit it. Two hours had flown in a heartbeat. He reluctantly loosened his bow, pulled the velvet cloth over his violin, and closed the case.

Clara looked subdued as she shut the cover over the piano keys. Clearly she had enjoyed their rehearsal as much as he. And just as clearly, she was an incredibly talented pianist. A pity she had fallen into her brother's shadow.

"An excellent bit of work," Dare said. "I think *Il Diavolo* will yield soon."

"I've no doubt of it." Clara gave him a quick smile. "The octave shifts are nearly there. It's a devilish piece indeed."

"What was your brother thinking?" He shook his head in mock dismay. "Oh yes, I recall it now. It was a punishment for my sins."

She slanted a look at him. "Have you been adequately punished?"

"It depends on which sins we're counting." He held out his arm. "May I escort you to your room? I'd think you'd like to freshen up before dinner."

And he would like to steal another kiss. Or three. To add to his sins.

She hesitated for a heartbeat, then placed her hand on his arm. "If you insist."

"I do." He covered her hand with his and let his fingertips play over her bare skin.

When he slipped a finger between hers, he heard the breath tremble in her throat. Ah, Clara. So deliciously responsive. He was suddenly on fire for her, the echo of their music-making only adding to the fierceness of the flame.

They were nearly to her door when Nicholas hailed them. Blast the man.

"How did the rehearsal go?" he asked, hurrying down the hall toward them.

"Well," Clara said. "But what of your hand?"

He held his arm up, displaying the bulky wrappings. "Henri made me place it in a bowl of ice until I thought my fingers would turn blue, then bandaged me up. But I think my hand feels a bit better."

"Hm." Dare narrowed his eyes. "Perhaps you should rest it another day. Tomorrow, Clara can help me finish up the section of *Il Diavolo* we were working on. But by the next day, I expect you'll be able to play."

"When do we depart for Milan?" Clara asked.

"My agent, Mr. Widmere, will be arriving in two days. He'll accompany us to Venice, and then at last to Milan."

A tense silence followed this information. Nicholas glanced at the floor, chewing his lip, and Clara slid her hand from Dare's arm.

"Well then," she said. "I'll see you two at supper."

Before Dare could catch her she slipped into her rooms and closed the door, leaving him with her poor substitute of a brother. Stifling a sigh, he turned to Nicholas.

"Care to join me in a brandy?"

Nicholas looked up. "Yes, I would."

One brandy led to the next, at least for Nicholas. Dare watched over the rim of his glass as the composer imbibed.

"Tell me," Dare asked, "has your sister ever tried her hand at composing?"

"No." Nicholas took a hasty swallow of brandy, and commenced coughing. When he recovered, he poured another few inches into his glass.

"No," he repeated. "She tried a few compositions as a child, but Papa always discouraged her. It is not for women to compose."

Dare took a sip of liquor, letting it warm his mouth. "Your sister did an excellent job with *Il Diavolo*. I'm surprised she knew the piece so well."

"I am a very messy composer," Nicholas said. "She must copy the manuscripts out for me, numerous times. Whenever I make changes. So, you see, she hears the music in her head, and it becomes familiar to her."

Nicholas drained his glass, then poured another, his hand unsteady. Without a word, Dare capped the bottle and set it away.

"I see." The explanation made sense, and yet something about it did not quite ring true.

Supper was quiet, marked by Clara's frequent, worried glances at her brother. The more wine Nicholas drank, the quieter it became, until the clink of silver on china was the loudest thing in the room. Henri tried his best, yet not even his witticisms could revive the conversation. When Nicholas nearly fell sideways off his chair, Clara stood.

"Excuse us," she said, her tone strained. "I believe my brother would like to retire early. Nicholas, come with me."

She took him by the arm, and, despite his mumbled protests, led him away.

"Master Reynard," Henri said, "I do not like this turn our composer has taken."

"Nor do I." Dare thrust his plate aside. "Short of locking Nicholas in his room, what can I do?"

"Pray?" There was an ironic edge to his valet's tone. "And do not offer him brandy."

Dare folded his arms, his fingers tapping a restless tempo against the fine wool of his coat.

"Perhaps Clara will have some ideas." He rose, scraping his

chair back. "Good evening, Henri."

"Enjoy your consultation with Miss Becker," Henri said, his tone dryer than sand.

The man was entirely too perceptive. At least he was discreet. Henri might not completely approve of Dare's interest in Clara, but he would say nothing.

Clara. Dare might not know what to do with Nicholas, but his sister was another matter entirely.

He strode to her door and gave a single rap. After a long moment, it opened.

"Clara, we must discuss your brother."

She stepped back to let him enter. After a quick glance down the hall, she closed the door and led him to her sitting area. For a moment, they sat in silence. Clara perched on the front of her richly upholstered chair, her fingers laced so tightly together her knuckles were white.

Dare leaned forward and took her hands in his, smoothing her fingers flat.

"I…" She blinked, but did not pull her hands away. "I admit to some concern about my brother, but he will be ready for the competition. I'll see to it."

Despite her confident words, worry shaded her eyes.

"Can you?" He pressed her fingers more firmly between his own. "Nicholas cannot fail me now."

She nodded, perhaps unwilling to voice assurances they both knew would be empty.

"Enough of this," he said. "I am not here to make you miserable. Indeed, I plan to do just the opposite. Forget about Milan, about your brother. For now, there is only the two of us."

Standing, Dare pulled her to him. For a brief time they could set aside the worries swirling around the tour like dark fog—burn it away with the flame of their passion.

He kissed her, demanding. Clara moaned softly and leaned into him, her body warm and delicious, her tongue boldly tangling with his. She ruled his senses in ways no other woman had.

He slid his hand up to cup the back of her neck, plundering her mouth with an urgency that took him by surprise. He needed to lose himself in her. No schooling tonight, no games of mastery and provocation. Just Clara, spread out on the sheets, his for the taking.

Without breaking the kiss, he stepped her backward until they reached the large bed. At least the emperor didn't stint on the size of his mattresses, or perhaps he knew that his guests were prone to assignations.

Clara's mouth was intoxicating, and the sounds of arousal she made sent his control teetering. He forced his mouth away from hers, and released her trapped hands.

She sat on the edge of the bed to remove her shoes, her head bent close to his waist. His cock hardened even further at the sight. One day, he would teach her how to pleasure him with her mouth— her lips wrapped around the shaft, her warm tongue stroking...

Hastily, he pulled off his shoes, then took her by the waist and pushed her back into the middle of the bed. Her stockings were silky beneath his palms, her skirts a rustling wave of sea-foam green as he pushed them up, revealing her long, shapely legs. Pausing at her lace-edged drawers, he let his fingers graze the sensitive skin of her inner thighs.

"Ah," she sighed.

Much as he wanted to take her, *now*, he wanted her ready for him more. He would see the flush of passion and longing on her face, would drive her to the same precipice he stood upon. Together, they would leap into the void.

Her drawers untied with a simple ribbon, and he pulled them off, his attention on the blonde curls at the juncture of her thighs. Kneeling between her legs, he spread them wide. She did not resist, though he felt her trembling beneath his touch.

Heat and the musky scent of her arousal filled him as he bent to taste her. She was wet and sweetly salty, the nub of her pleasure already standing up for him. Every swipe of his tongue over her center made her quiver and moan. His cock strained against the fabric of his trousers.

Her moans turned to panting breaths, and Dare drew back. They would enter that pleasure together.

"Please," she said.

"Patience." He unfastened his trousers, then pulled on the French letter that had been waiting in his pocket.

Moving forward, he set the tip of his cock at her entrance. Then, with a single thrust, he surged inside her. The sensation of her warmth enclosing him made him close his eyes—half in utter relief, half with urgent need.

She gasped and tightened her legs around his hips. Dare let his body down, covering her, pressing her into the soft bed. Telling her in a language without words that she was wholly and undeniably his.

The pulse at her neck called to his lips, and he set his mouth there, trailing kisses up to her jaw, breathing in her scent. She let out a quiet moan, and he propped himself up on his elbows. Though his cock was begging him to slide in and out, fast and hard, she needed time to adjust. Not only was she unused to the sexual act, but he was of larger than normal size; a fact often remarked upon with delight by his lovers.

Her eyes met his, and he saw only desire in their silvery depths.

"Ready?" he asked. "I will not be gentle."

She licked her lips, then nodded.

He laced his fingers with hers, pinning her hands to the bed. With a groan, he began to move. Each slide of his cock sent liquid fire along his nerves. Clara sighed in pleasure at every stroke as he thrust harder, deeper. It was a composition: their breaths syncopating with arousal, the bedclothes rustling in high counterpoint, the increasing tempo of his strokes as he took her, over and over.

Her voice rose, her breathy moans climbing in pitch. His release gathered inside him like lightning, waiting to explode. Then she arched and trembled, crying out. It was enough to send him reeling into the abyss. A rough shout tore from his throat as fire rippled through him, hot white pleasure stunning his senses.

Finally, when the last aftershocks subsided, he unlaced his fingers from hers and rolled to his side. She turned her head and smiled at him with the look of a woman completely fulfilled. The lingering fear that he had hurt her with his forceful lovemaking evaporated. Clara was his match—in so many ways.

He did not want to lose her.

It was a startling thought. Before, he had always considered how his affairs would end, almost before he began them. With that one, fateful exception, of course.

But now…

He traced her lower lip with his thumb, keeping his thoughts concealed. There would be time after the musical duel to explore Clara's hidden depths to their fullest. Time then to think of promises. And futures.

CHAPTER TWENTY-FOUR

Maestro Reynard Dazzles!

Despite claims to the contrary from certain disreputable sources, Darien Reynard is in fine form as the musical competition in Milano draws nigh. The compositions of Mr. Becker are lush and splendid, and one must pity those poor listeners who cannot discern the genius of his music.

-Viva Venezia

Clara would have adored Venice under other circumstances. The canals gilded with sunlight, the graceful opulence of the buildings, the liquid syllables of Italian sifting through the air; all this was enough to fill her senses with delight.

But Nicholas was crumbling.

Although their concerts in Venice met with acclaim, Darien drove Nicholas in unrelenting rehearsals that left them both sharp-edged with frustration. Despite Clara's efforts to keep her brother and the bottle separated, Nicholas blunted his misery with alcohol. Short of locking him in his room—which he would not tolerate— there was little she could do. Her pleas were received with stony silence.

While Darien... A flush heated her body as she glanced at him across the breakfast table. He spent his frustrations in passion. Every night since they'd departed Vienna, Darien had come to her, or she to him. The dark hours were filled with heady desire, leaving her languorous and exhausted, and her heart ever more vulnerable to this man she had no future with.

Her nights glowed with joy even as her days remained shadowed with despair.

She could not continue like this. Finishing *Amore* had been her only true solace, and now the piece was complete. She had shown it to Nicholas under the title of *Viaggio*, voyage. The composition exemplified everything Varga belittled. She knew it, but she could not change it. Silently, Nicholas had scanned the music, then handed the pages back to her, his expression bleak.

"Three more days," Peter Widmere said, pushing his plate away. "The luggage is loaded and the coach is ready to depart when you are. Milan awaits."

"Yes." Darien set down his coffee cup and glanced at Nicholas. "We'll rehearse for an hour or two before leaving."

"I... I've completed a new piece," Nicholas said.

He did not look at her, though the tips of his ears were pink. The last bits of breakfast on his plate seemed of intense interest to him.

"You have?" There was a hint of disbelief in Darien's voice, as if he could not comprehend how such a morose fellow could continue to write new music.

After a too-strained silence, Peter cleared his throat. "A new piece—what excellent news."

Darien's agent affected a cheerful tone, but the furrow between his brows showed he disliked the undercurrents swirling just beneath the surface.

Darien pushed back his chair and stood. "Then we shall hear it. Nicholas, I'll meet you in my suite."

Peter followed his employer from the table, and Henri quickly excused himself as well.

"Nicholas," Clara said, once the two of them were alone, "it is only a few more days. You must—"

"Don't tell me what I must do." Nicholas threw his fork down with a clatter and met her gaze, his eyes red-rimmed and burning. "I am in hell, dear sister, and there is no escape. Not now, not in three days."

"Once we return to England—"

"Do you think Master Reynard will let his tame composer slip the leash that easily?" He gave a bitter laugh. "I am nothing but a trained monkey, dancing to a tune not of my own devising."

Clara swallowed. She'd removed all of the newspapers featuring Varga's hateful words, but clearly Nicholas had seen the comparison of himself to a pet.

"I will…" In truth, she had no idea what to do, other than somehow help Nicholas through the next handful of days.

"I'll tell you what you will do, sister mine. You will stop composing such overly romantic things as *Viaggio*! That bit of tripe will make me the laughingstock of Europe."

"Lower your voice." Anger iced her heart. "How *dare* you belittle the music? You and I both know its worth."

Amore was the best piece she had ever written—full of fire and passion, darkness and delight.

"False gold." Nicholas stood, his elbows stiff at his sides. "Excuse me. The master calls and I must obey."

"Stop it. If you despise the composition so much, I will come in and play it for Darien."

"So I may appear even worse by comparison? I don't need any assistance from you, Clara. My own failings are more than adequate to make me worthless in his eyes."

Her heart cracked. She rounded the table and took him by the shoulders. The muscles under her hands were tight with tension.

"Nicholas, no. He does not think you worthless. You are immensely talented, and have proven it time and again."

His expression softened, swinging into the despair she so feared. "I can't, Clara. I can't go on like this. There are days when…" He averted his eyes, his next words coming low and shaky. "When I would rather not live."

The words sent a knife through her, sharp and desolate. Even in his darkest hours in London, she did not think Nicholas had contemplated taking his own life.

She closed her eyes and drew in a deep breath. There was only one way to save them, to give Nicholas the strength to continue to Milan and play the way Darien needed him to. The solution had been there, crouching in the corner of her mind for weeks now, but she had been too selfish to bring it into the light.

"Then we will end this," she said. "I… I will stop composing."

The words scraped her throat. Scraped her very soul, leaving her raw and bleeding. "After Milan, you may tell Darien your musical well has run dry, and we shall return to London."

"Home." His voice held so much yearning she swayed from the force of it. "Truly, you would do such a thing? Stop composing?"

It would be like cutting off a limb: an essential part of her removed, forever. But her brother was equally essential. She had to change her course to keep from driving him to the pit of melancholy, and beyond.

"I must," she said. "Nicholas Becker will compose no more."

At least she had finished with a brilliant piece of music. *Amore* would live on, though all else in her life would wither.

She could not bear the gratitude on her brother's face.

"I must finish packing," she said, whirling for the door. "You'll have to rehearse without me."

"I will." Nicholas's voice was clear, and stronger than she had heard it for weeks.

***

As the coach left Venice, Clara pretended to be riveted by the passing scenery. She had not missed Darien's searching glances. He knew her well enough now to tell something was amiss. If she met his eyes, he would see too much; the signs of weeping she could not eradicate, the sorrow burdening her breath.

In marked contrast, Nicholas was giddily lighthearted.

"I can scarcely believe we're on our way at last to Milan," he said. "What a journey this has been."

Henri raised an eyebrow. "Your practice session must have gone well."

"Indeed." Darien left off looking at her, and gave Nicholas a half smile. "Not only is *Il Diavolo* in hand, Nicholas shared the first movement of his new composition. And it is superb."

The sun dimmed on Nicholas's face, but Clara was the only one to notice.

"I'm pleased your musical association is bearing such fine fruit," Peter said.

Clara recalled his doubts when he and Darien had first visited the Beckers in their drafty home in London. He had been right to fear, though not for the reasons he thought.

And his fears would soon come to pass. Nicholas Becker would have no more music in him.

She caught her lower lip between her teeth and turned back to the window. It would not be so very dreadful for Darien, who would continue on his brilliant career after winning the duel. Nicholas would be saved, and no doubt make a successful return to teaching, his reputation bolstered by his association with the master. Their family would be comfortably well off, debts paid, a handsome house in which to live.

And as for her?

She could not cease writing music. She'd been a fool to think that. No, she would continue to compose in private, never revealing her music to anyone. Truly, her life would little different from what it had been before Darien entered it.

Perhaps one day, decades after her death, her compositions would be discovered. It was not a happy thought. Who wants to be famous after they are dead?

Clara closed her eyes, taking refuge in the darkness, trying to let the rocking of the coach lull her to sleep.

She napped, roused in time for lunch, then slept again, an unhappy, restless doze full of half-heard melodies and shadows. When she woke she had an ache in her neck, and Darien's coat beneath her cheek as a pillow.

She shook it out as best she could, resisting the urge to bury her face in the fabric and inhale deeply of his scent.

"Thank you," she said, handing him the rumpled coat.

"You did not look terribly comfortable," he said, eyes glinting with concern.

She rubbed the side of her neck, and his gaze followed the motion to linger on her skin. Clara flushed and pulled her hand away. The last thing she needed was for Nicholas to realize she and Darien were carrying on an affair. Her brother must not discover it now, when she had finally pulled him back from the brink.

Three days. It would all be over in three days.

The curtains were drawn over the coach windows. Clara pulled one back to find that the gray blanket of dusk had fallen over the landscape. The lights of Milan glowed ahead, as if a thousand stars had come to ground.

"Ah," Peter said, following her gaze, "Milano. We will be staying at the Palazzo Reale."

Another palace, this one again the province of Emperor Francis. Clara let out a soundless sigh. She would not mention the name Varga, though doubtless Darien's rival would be in residence.

She glanced at Darien. He met her gaze, green eyes smoldering with promises.

It was dangerous for them—doubly dangerous—to attempt to meet. Not only must she protect Nicholas from the knowledge of her affair, the palace itself would be a hotbed of scandalmongers. Varga and his supporters would use every weapon they could to unsettle Nicholas and ensure victory over Darien.

Her pulse pounded in her temples, echoed by the sound of cobblestones under the coach wheels as they entered the city. Milan—where triumph and defeat awaited her in equal measure.

A growing crowd clamored behind them as Darien's distinctive black coach was recognized. At last, after traversing a tangle of winding streets, they arrived at the Palazzo. Peter disembarked, slipping out quickly and beckoning to the palace guards to hold back the onlookers.

Darien reached past Clara and twitched the curtain back over the window.

"You and Henri go first," he said. "Then Nicholas. I'll bring up the rear."

She nodded. Darien would be mobbed the moment he set foot outside the coach, and whoever remained in the vehicle would be trapped there for some time.

"An excellent plan," Henri said, swinging the vehicle's door wide.

The noise outside rose a notch, then dimmed as the crowd realized he was not Darien. It sounded like the surging of the sea.

Clara glanced at her brother. Nicholas was pale, but he met her gaze without flinching. *Three days.* The knowledge was writ on his face, along with the silent promise he would persevere.

Henri leaned back into the coach.

"Allow me, mademoiselle," he said, offering Clara his hand. "We shall not tarry. Peter will be waiting for us just inside the Palazzo."

As soon as Clara stepped down from the vehicle, the crowd surged again. The attention was avid, and she did not envy Darien his fame. Grasping fingers reached, eyes flashed hungrily in the lantern light, and Clara was grateful for the stolid line of palace guards marking their path.

"*Signorina! Signorina!*"

"… *la sorella…*"

"… no, no, his mistress?"

"Baciami!" a stout, dark-eyed man called out. "A little kiss, *per favore!*"

Henri took her elbow and tugged her forward. "Pay them no heed."

She quickened her pace, making for the gilt-edged doorway of the palace. When she stepped through, safely out of sight, the crowd let out a low sigh.

Peter waited, arms crossed, in the opulent palace entryway. His gaze measured her. Had he heard the crowd naming her Darien's mistress? Heat flamed in her cheeks. Surely any woman traveling with the master would be labeled as such, would she not? Still, his eyes on her were too perceptive.

A roar from outside made her turn and look. Nicholas stood on the coach steps. He waved—actually waved!—to the crowd, then hurried up the pathway, ignoring the calls to either side.

The throng stirred, with a sense of anticipation so strong it made her neck prickle. All eyes were focused on the black coach.

Then Darien stepped forth and the crowd erupted. Women screamed his name, men cheered, and several loud explosions shattered the air.

"Is someone… shooting?" Nicholas asked, his eyes wide.

"No, no," Henri said. "It is the firecrackers."

Clara peered out the doorway to see Darien poised on the top step. He removed his hat and made a sweeping bow. The noise, which was already deafening, increased, waves of sound buffeting Clara and echoing from the Palazzo's high walls.

Darien held up his hands and slowly the crowd quieted to a restless murmur.

"*Grazie!*" he called. "Thank you for the welcome. It is indeed a pleasure to be here at last in Milano." The words prompted a quick cheer, but Darien was not finished. "In two days, you will be witness to a competition the likes of which the world has never seen. Ladies and gentlemen, we are actors on the broad stage of time, and together we will make history! *Buona notte!*"

His "good night" was lost in cacophony. Flashing a smile, Darien leaped from the steps and strode up the guard-edged walk. He ignored the outstretched hands, the flowers and perfumed kerchiefs flung in his path, the cries of "*Maestro!*" and "*Ti amo!*"

The guards were jostled mightily, but held their ground against the adulation, even when Darien paused outside the Palazzo doors and waved one last time to the crowd.

"Hurry it up, man," Peter muttered. "I, for one, am ready to settle in to our rooms."

"The price of fame," Henri said with a wry smile.

Darien slipped inside and the palace attendants immediately shut the immense arched doors behind him. The noise outside muted to a dull roar.

"Will they all go home now?" Nicholas asked.

"No," Darien said. "Until the hour of the duel, the streets will be full of nothing but merriment."

"If you define merriment as argument, posturing, and drunken brawling," Peter said. "Much as your supporters adore you, Dare, Varga's love him as well. There are strong factions. It would be best for everyone to stay within the Palazzo's walls for the next two days."

Clara traded a glance with Nicholas. They had seen enough in Vienna to take the agent's words to heart. Indeed, this type of behavior in the streets of London would be called a riot, and quelled by force.

"Come," Peter said. "Our staterooms await."

The party followed one of the attendants, though clearly Darien, his agent, and Henri were all familiar with the palace. They spared not a glance for the long hallways glittering with chandeliers, the opulent art gracing the walls, or the intricately patterned marble floors.

Clara hung back until she was beside Nicholas.

"Are you well?" she asked in a low voice.

"Well enough. You?"

She nodded, giving him a false smile. Words would betray her, for she could not lie to him and keep her voice from shaking. He did not need her anguish to add to his own.

Their rooms were in a wing of the palace reserved for visiting dignitaries. The attendant ushered Darien to his suite, with Nicholas housed next door and Peter across the corridor. Clara was disappointed to find she was relegated to the far end of the hallway, though her rooms were sumptuous. She counted five doors between herself and Darien.

Still, what was the length of a hallway when faced with the barren expanse of decades without him?

First, though, there was a formal banquet, then a musicale that spanned several drawing rooms. Varga moved like a hawk through the throng, but Clara found him easy to avoid, since he was constantly surrounded by admirers. As was Darien.

One raven-tressed *signora* in particular clung far too frequently to his arm. She was clad in apricot satin that accented her voluptuous curves, and her smiles and laughter were full of delight at being so close to Master Reynard.

Clara tried not to watch, tried not to imagine who would take her place once she was gone from Darien's life.

As if feeling her gaze, Darien lifted his head and scanned the partygoers. His moss-green eyes met hers, held, and the heat in them scorched her down to her embroidered slippers. He raised one brow, and she nodded, ever so faintly.

Tonight she would go to him.

The knowledge eased her heart enough that she could breathe. Though she could not laugh, nor even smile.

Nicholas extricated himself from a nearby eddy of Italian nobility and made his way over to her. He held a glass that was nearly empty, and Clara tried not to look too closely at it. One glass of brandy—surely she could not begrudge her brother that. If, indeed, it had only been the one.

Extravagantly dressed ladies and gentlemen swirled about them, but she felt as though she and Nicholas stood in a pool of shadow. Music drifted from two different directions, jarring and discordant. The air was too warm, and yet she was chilled.

"Don't frown so fiercely," Nicholas said.

"I'm not frowning." She made an effort to smooth her expression, but could not keep her gaze from flicking to his brandy glass.

"And I am not drinking." He held up his tumbler. "If I don't carry this about, people will insist on pressing drinks upon me. But I'm weary, and you look to be, as well. Shall we retire for the evening?"

"Yes—though I rather suspect it is morning by now."

If Nicholas were leaving, there was no reason to stay, beyond watching beautiful women flirt with Darien, and she had no stomach for that. He would notice she was gone soon, and judging by his smoldering look, would welcome a visit to his bedchamber. At least she could lose herself in his bed, in him—plunge into passion and leave her worries behind.

Her brother consulted his pocket watch. "Indeed, it's past time for me to seek my bed, especially as Darien wants to spend much of tomorrow rehearsing. Clara—will you attend the rehearsals? Your insights always make the music better."

"I…"

"We need you," he said, the pleading in his eyes eroding her will.

Nicholas was right. She must do everything within her power to help Darien win the duel.

"Very well." Though it would be as painful as swallowing

razors.

***

Clara undressed with the assistance of the same palace maid who had gowned her for the soiree, then sent the girl away. She paced restlessly before the dim coals in the hearth, her dressing gown swishing with each turn. The ornate clock on the mantel ticked the minutes away too slowly, but she had resolved to wait a solid hour before going to Darien.

The melody of *Amore* twined through her thoughts, a bright flame of music to keep her company. To warm her once she was no longer by his side.

At last the hour hand fell heavily upon the three. Clara took up the flickering candle by her bed, then stood beside the door, listening. There had been no noise or movement in the hallway outside for some time. Carefully, she lifted the latch and peered out.

Darkness veiled the hall, though her candle flame picked out glints of gold from the wall hangings. The palace slept, the air heavy with dreams. She closed the door behind her and softly made her way down the corridor. Past one door, then two.

"Well, well." The low, sinister voice came out of the darkness.

She bit back a shriek, her candle trembling violently. Shadows skittered along the walls.

"Who's there?" she asked, her voice high and quick from fright.

A figure appeared, the light revealing the mocking features of Anton Varga. Clara darted a glance down the hall, but all the doors remained firmly shut. She took a step back toward her rooms.

"It seems the Beckers are a restless lot," Varga said. "I saw your brother slipping out some minutes ago. And now it is your turn. Where, I must ask, is the pretty sister going?"

"I simply—"

"An assignation, of course." His lips twisted into a smile, though his eyes were untouched by mirth. They fastened on her, dark and knowing. "With whom, I wonder?"

He stepped forward and Clara moved back again, their

movements parodying a dance. Only one door lay between her and the safety of her rooms. If she turned and bolted would she reach the threshold? Or would Varga spring upon her the moment she turned her back? A cold shiver prickled her skin. She did not want to find out.

"I was in search of fresh air," she said. "How unfortunate that the hallway bears such a stench."

"Don't pretend to insult me," he said.

In two long strides he was upon her. Clara pulled back, but he took her chin in a strong grip. There was a wild look in his eyes, malice and triumph twined together. He bent his face close to hers, and she smelled wine and onions on his breath.

"Release me at once," she said.

"Does Reynard's pet composer know that his sister is having an affair? Ah, your eyes widen like a trapped doe. What is it worth to you, Miss Becker, to keep that knowledge from him? And what coin will you use to pay?"

His gaze dropped to her neck, then her breasts, covered only by her nightclothes and the thin satin dressing gown.

"I will pay you nothing," she said. "And Master Reynard will defeat you."

She brought the candle up, holding it beneath Varga's wrist until, with a muffled yelp, he pulled his hand away. Before he could reach for her again, she whirled and wrenched her door open. Her last glimpse of him showed him scowling as the shadows descended once more.

Pulse pounding in her throat, Clara threw the lock. Then, to be safe, she dragged her trunk in front of the door as well. She would not be visiting Darien tonight after all, not with Varga menacing the hallways.

Sleep was elusive, then ragged when she finally slumbered, her dreams filled with the ashes of failure: a broken violin, Darien turning his face from her, a river weeping silently toward the sea.

CHAPTER TWENTY-FIVE

Nobility from throughout Europe fill the hotels of Milano to bursting as the hour of the musical competition rapidly approaches. One cannot set foot inside the Palazzo Reale without tripping over a crown prince—though Master Reynard and Anton Varga have kept well to themselves, no doubt in preparation for the imminent duel...

-Il Pettegolo

"**A**gain," Dare said to Nicholas. "The passage is almost perfect."

The salon they had taken over as a rehearsal space was filled with slanting sunshine and rich colors—indigo and burgundy and gold. Various musical instruments lay about the room: a harp, two old wooden flutes, a richly inlaid guitar, and, of course, a piano. The acoustics were muffled by the swags of draperies and layered carpets, but at least the piano was in tune.

Though Dare focused on the music, he was still—always—aware of Clara. She sat curled on the settee with her feet tucked beneath her, her shoes abandoned on the carpet before her. It was an endearing pose, made possible by the fact that the doors were locked, with just the three of them inside.

Nicholas, his face weary, lifted his hands to the keyboard. The introduction to the *Air in E minor* was strong. Taking a firm grip on his bow, Dare launched himself into the melody.

When they reached the second section, however, the piece faltered once more. Dare bit back a curse and lowered his violin. He was driving Nicholas too hard, but the competition was tomorrow.

In one day, all his dreams and fears would be poised, waiting on either side as he took the stage at La Scala. To his right, darkness and perdition. To his left, brilliant triumph. Which way would he fall?

He was not a man to entertain thoughts of failure, and yet…

"Enough," he said.

"But—" Nicholas began.

Dare cut him off with a curt gesture. "I have said we are finished rehearsing. Tonight, there will be no carousing into the wee hours. I want you well rested, Nicholas."

Clara looked up sharply at his words. "I believe we sought our beds before you did, Darien."

"The fact did not escape my notice."

Nor had the cold, empty sheets, when he retired less than an hour after Clara had departed the soiree. He'd waited in vain for her. Had even opened his door twice, thinking he heard a noise in the hall—for nothing. Resigning himself to her absence, he had respected it, believing she had been too weary, or too unsettled, to come to him.

She met his gaze, her silvery eyes clear. "I tried."

"Tried what?" Nicholas asked.

"To shepherd you away at a reasonable hour," she replied. "I agree with Darien. We must all retire early tonight."

"Indeed." Dare gave her a smile filled with private heat. "After the banquet, I expect everyone to seek their rooms."

Nicholas rose and straightened the stack of music on the piano.

"Wait." Dare strode forward and fanned the pages again. "Here—the *Viaggio*. We have been so busy rehearsing for the duel, we've not yet played the second movement. It will be a refreshing change of pace. Come, let us play it."

They both needed to play for enjoyment, without the specter of the competition shadowing every note.

Nicholas's shoulders slumped further. "I…"

"I'll play it with you, if Nicholas agrees." Clara slipped her feet into her shoes and came to stand beside the piano. "He deserves a rest."

"And I do not?" Dare pressed back the smile he felt edging his lips.

He didn't want to show his pleasure too much at the prospect of playing with Clara again. Not in front of Nicholas, not on the very cusp of the duel.

"Nicholas?" Clara touched his arm.

He passed one hand across his eyes. "Go ahead. Although, if you don't mind too much, I will go back to my rooms."

"Take care not to be seen," Dare said.

At his request, Emperor Francis had provided this little-used salon for their rehearsal, sending a palace official to guide them along the servants' corridors. Dare was determined to give no specifics away to curious fans—or Varga's spies.

"Rest well," Clara said.

Nicholas nodded, gave his sister a strained smile, and slipped out the side door leading to the maids' passage.

Dare stared at the wall a moment, where the paneled door had closed. He wished he did not have to work his composer so hard. He wished the sheer musical brilliance on the page translated more fully into Nicholas's fingers. And he especially wished to be free of the suspicions that had begun shadowing his mind whenever he thought of how well Clara performed her brother's music.

She moved to the piano, her slender body concealed in a gown of pale green silk. Still, he could imagine her naked limbs in perfect detail: the sensitive hollows behind her knees, the small scar on her left arm from a childhood mishap, the sweet indentation of her waist.

"I missed you last night," he said.

"Varga caught me in the hallway, coming to you." She shivered.

Rage flashed through him, sudden and searing. "If he touched you, I'll—"

"No. He questioned me, and I fled back to my rooms. He may suspect, but he has no proof."

Dare cursed his own thoughtlessness for exposing her to danger.

"No more wandering the halls for you," he said. "Tonight, I will visit your bed."

Her eyes opened a shade wider. "You will risk it?"

"Of course." The words revealed too much, uncovered a younger, eager part of himself he kept hidden from the world.

Banishing it, he lifted his violin to his shoulder. "The second movement, if you please."

Wearing a small, cautious smile, Clara set her hands to the keyboard and began to play. Instantly, Dare was swept into the music. In some indefinable way the notes reminded him of making love with Clara. Yearning spilled from the fluid arpeggios, the twists and turns of melody that spiraled up, nearly reached their goal, then fell short. His bow vibrated across the strings, pulling the music out, pulling the emotion from the depths of his soul. *Just once*, the notes whispered. *If only…*

He leaned forward and played his heart into the music. Clara met him there, the piano sure and clear, her trust in him shining through the phrases. No matter what happened tomorrow, they had this—the pure, perfect music holding them in its center.

***

Dare rotated the stem of his wineglass between his fingers and endeavored to appear interested in his dinner companion's listing of her lapdog's attributes. At least it was better than the banquet the night before, when he'd been seated between a young lady struck mute by his fame and an older woman who would not cease setting her hand on his thigh beneath the cover of the tablecloth.

"My Poco does like to yap a bit, though he is so darling. I'm sure you understand." The lady on his right smiled at him. Her brown hair was curled into a fair imitation of sausages.

"Undoubtedly," Dare said.

The conversation lulled on their side of the table, and a woman's laugh filled the quiet, the sound rich and sweet. He knew that laugh.

Searching across the wide table, past the candelabras and platters of flower-bedecked fruit, Dare finally spotted her, seated some distance to his left. Francesca Contini. Once the most celebrated opera singer in Italy.

She was still beautiful, though it was strange how the years had laid a veneer of unfamiliarity across her features. As if feeling his gaze, she lifted her head and met his eyes. A brief, sad smile crossed her features. Dare lifted his wineglass to her, then set his Chianti down untouched when she turned back to her dinner companion; her husband, Baron Antonio de Luca.

The man was handsome, in a stately way, but even more important to Francesca's goals, he possessed both a steady income and a large villa outside Milano. Of course they would be at the palace. Dare should have anticipated it.

Seeing Francesca again stirred the ashes of his old sorrow, and the bittersweet strains of what might have been curled about his heart.

Years ago, when she began touring with him, Dare was certain his life was complete. He'd been young and full of brash confidence, certain that he had met the woman with whom he'd share the rest of his life. But within a handful of months his dreams had tarnished, then shattered.

After a performance that had not gone as well as it might, Francesca had paced the polished floors of their suite, her steps agitated.

"Darien, *tesoro mio*, I cannot continue."

"What?" Throat tight with premonition, he tossed his cravat aside, then went to take her hands. "Do not worry about the concert tonight. Some performances go that way. Tomorrow will be better."

"That is the problem—I do not want to have another performance tomorrow, or the day after, or the day after that! I can find no lasting joy in it."

Though he'd seen the signs of her discontent, he'd been confident they could overcome anything. He'd lifted her chin and searched her eyes, dark with unhappiness.

"Not even with me? Francesca, I *love* you!"

Inside him, the young boy who had craved a scrap of tenderness began to howl. He had at last let his guard down, only to feel the knife slip deep into his heart.

"No." Her voice was low and anguished. "Not even with you. Remember, though we do not speak of it, that I am older than you and have already tasted of fame. This is not the life I want."

"What *do* you want?" The knife was stabbing, over and over, bleeding his heart cold.

"I want things that would make you equally miserable. A quiet villa in the country, a few performances a year. A family, children."

"I want that, too." Just, not now—not for years in the future.

"Perhaps the family, but for the rest?" She shook her head sadly. "You are made for greater things, Darien. And I cannot follow you there."

Words of entreaty dried in his throat. She was serious, and he knew, deep in his soul, that she was right, though his mind raged against the knowledge.

"If you leave, I shall have to cancel the rest of the tour."

Although he could not afford to. His bank accounts already strained with the cost of producing his tours, but eventually the profits would pour in. If, that was, he continued to perform.

"You would disappoint your audiences so? You would let the other dogs yapping at your heels vie for the title of maestro, which you have only so recently won?" She pulled her hands free of his. "No, you must continue without me."

A part of him cried that he could not.

"Francesca, this is the life I want. With you. On the stage."

"You cannot have both, and I will not yoke you to misery all your days. You have made your path—it is clear beneath your feet."

She spoke the truth. All his life he'd known he would have to fashion his future with his own hands. His only means of doing so was his talent on the violin. Even his drunkard of a father had recognized Dare's gift, enough to find him a teacher during a rare sober period. And luckily Signor Ghiretti had been willing to provide lessons for no pay, when he heard Dare play. Once Dare had gained some prominence, he'd seen his old instructor rewarded.

But one could not build a secure existence by relying on luck and happenstance. Every accolade, every sold-out performance, came from his own hard work. He could not abandon what he had wrought over years of struggle, and she was not asking him to. No, she was only leaving him. Forever.

"Why must I lose you?" The words grated against his throat.

216 ~ ANTHEA LAWSON

"Because you cannot have everything, love." She set her hand to his cheek. "Some day, perhaps, you will find the woman who can match you in every way—but I am not that woman."

She left the tour the next morning, and he had been alone ever since.

Plenty of willing women had warmed his bed, but he had learned not to give too much of himself. His music could not coexist with love. The final proof of that had been hearing of Francesca's marriage, six months later, to the Baron de Luca. Apparently she had three children, performed four times a year around Lombardy, and was happy.

The banquet dinner came to a close. Dare bowed over the hand of his chatty companion, then went to find Clara and Nicholas. He must banish the melancholy in his heart, and remember that he'd achieved his aims. Fame and fortune were securely in his grasp. He had everything he needed.

Not everything, his soul whispered.

He caught a flash of blonde hair. Clara. Dare pushed his way forward, his breath easing as he drew up in front of her.

"Darien—are you well?" The smile on her face faded as she sought his gaze.

She wore a gold and burgundy dress that flattered her figure, but beyond her physical beauty, Dare could see the light of her, shining from within.

Her eyes were luminous, and he wanted to take her into a crushing embrace, there in the emperor's formal banquet hall, consequences be damned. *When had Clara become the most important part of his world?*

He did not know; but Nicholas was right behind her, and the duel was tomorrow. He reined in his emotions, and gave Clara a tight smile.

"Just ensuring we're ready for an early evening," he said.

"Oh, don't go," said a low, sweet voice behind him.

He closed his eyes briefly, then, with a deep breath, turned.

"Baron and Baronessa de Luca," he said, bowing over Francesca's hand. "What an unexpected pleasure. You look well."

She was shorter than he'd recalled, but still lovely. Faint smile lines fanned from the corners of her eyes. Her husband stood at her elbow, his expression unruffled. Surely he knew of Francesca and Dare's former liaison, but the knowledge did not seem to bother him. Of course, he was the one who married her.

"Darien," she said, "no need for such formality. I am here to wish you the best of luck tomorrow. And is this the composer of whom we've heard so much?" Her gaze went to Nicholas and she held out her gloved hand.

Nicholas bowed, the tips of his ears pink. "I'm Nicholas Becker. It is an honor, baronessa."

She gave her throaty laugh. "The master's supporters have arrived in force, as you've no doubt noticed. I am looking forward to hearing your compositions tomorrow. And I'm certain Darien will retain his title."

"I am, too," Clara said, moving up to stand next to Dare. The scent of lavender soothed his senses.

"Allow me to introduce Miss Clara Becker," Dare said.

"An honor," Clara said, her voice cool and reserved. She dipped Francesca a slight curtsey.

Dare slanted a look at her, to see that her chin was lifted, her mouth firm. In the way of women, it seemed she recognized the former connection between Francesca and himself. Without thinking, he drew Clara's arm through his.

One of Francesca's elegant brows arched at the sight, and her expression turned thoughtful.

"It is a pleasure to meet you, Miss Becker," Francesca said. "You are a fortunate woman, to keep such company."

She put a slight emphasis on the word "keep," so subtle that only Dare heard it. He tilted his head at Francesca, an unasked question.

"I know my own fortune well enough," Clara said.

"Do you, I wonder?" Francesca's gaze went to Dare. "I hope, maestro, that you succeed tomorrow. And in all things."

"Come, my dear," the baron said. "We do not want to keep Maestro Reynard or his company any longer. Good luck, signors."

Francesca's smile was indulgent as she laced her arm through her husband's. "We shall be applauding loudly from the audience tomorrow. *Buon notte.*"

"Good night," Dare said, but she was already turning away.

"She is correct," Clara said. "We'd best be going."

He folded his hand over hers and, with Nicholas following, led her from the emperor's hall.

After the competition was finished, whatever the outcome, Dare was going to bring matters into the light. He was done with the secrets tangled between the three of them.

Without Clara, his life would be empty and cold beyond bearing. He glanced at her, and the constriction around his heart eased. She was music, and love, and he was the better for it.

Francesca's words echoed through him. There was no doubt she'd been speaking of love, as well as fame. Could he succeed in *all* things?

He had every intention of doing so.

CHAPTER TWENTY-SIX

Clara did not glance behind her as they left the banquet room, though the hubbub of conversation followed them into the landscape-lined hall. She tilted her head up at Darien, and he must have seen the questions in her eyes, for he smiled faintly.

"The Baronessa de Luca," he said, "was once known as Signora Contini."

"The opera singer?" Nicholas asked. "The one who toured with you?"

"Yes, though she accompanied me for only a few months. Life on the road did not agree with her."

There was the faintest catch in Darien's voice, and Clara knew the story was not so simple. She suspected he and the singer had parted bitterly, after being more than colleagues. Was Signora Contini the reason he had initially opposed Clara's presence on the tour?

What she had once thought was Darien's arrogance masked a vulnerability he almost never showed, and certainly would not admit to. But she had seen through the layers he wrapped himself in, to the true man within. The man she loved.

Her heart clenched. Tonight would be their last night together.

Darien bid her good night and left her at her door, but the look he gave her sent a thin flame racing down her spine. She nodded imperceptibly. She would be ready.

Clara prepared for bed and dismissed the maid. Clad in her nightgown and a fanciful Chinese silk robe that Henri had insisted she purchase in Paris, she sat before the mirror, brushing out her hair. It shone in the low-burning lamplight, more luminous than the yellow silk she wore, and she felt beautiful. Beautiful and tragic, like any opera heroine.

But she must not let Darien know; must breathe no hint that their affair was ending, until after the duel was over. She would plunge herself into their lovemaking this night, seize every moment, every taste and caress, until tomorrow dawned.

Only an hour had passed before a single tap came at her door. She opened it, and Darien slipped in, quick and quiet as a shadow.

He took her in his arms without a word. The heat of their bodies pressing together blazed like the rising sun in Clara's bones, like certainty and truth and home.

She could not bear it.

"Kiss me," she whispered, lacing her fingers through his thick, dark hair.

Darien bent and took her mouth with his, his lips sensuous and firm, his tongue dipping in to touch hers. She opened her mouth, inviting him in. It was not enough.

After a moment she pulled back.

"Clara?" He searched her eyes.

She took his hand and led him into the bedroom. The sheet was turned down, the pillows plumped, the lamplight a cozy circle of gold on the bedside table.

"Lie down," she said, pulling him to the edge of the bed.

His lips tilted into a rakish smile. "As my lady desires. Clothed, or naked?"

How daring did she feel? Despite the heat rushing to her face, she held his gaze. The master was hers to command.

"Naked."

A devilish glint shone in his eyes. He slid his hand from hers, and slowly began undressing. Shoes first, and then his coat, folded and laid on a nearby chair. As was his habit at formal events, he wore a black shirt. Contrasted with his skin and hair, he was a study in darkness and bronze. She caught her breath. *Darien.*

His scarlet-embroidered waistcoat closed with gold buttons. Deliberately, he unfastened each one, then pulled his waistcoat off. His shirt followed, opening to reveal the taut planes of his chest. He shrugged the fabric off, baring his shoulders, and she nearly went to him to run her hands over that gleaming expanse of skin. But not yet.

Clara's pulse thrummed in the hollow of her throat.

Still holding her gaze, he unfastened his trousers and let them drop, along with his underclothes. His manhood jutted out proudly, and she swallowed, shy at the sight of his arousal.

Shy, yet intrigued. When he set his mouth between her legs, it gave her such pleasure. Was the reverse true? She intended to find out.

"That's a rather intriguing smile," he said. "What are you thinking?"

"I'll show you."

She pulled back the coverlet and gestured to the soft expanse of sheets. Darien climbed into the bed, the play of muscles under his naked skin riveting, and lay on his back, arms folded beneath his head. For a long moment she simply looked at him—handsome and assured and masculine. And in her bed.

"Well? You know I'm not the patient sort," he said, his mouth curving up on one side.

"I know."

Slowly, she lifted the yellow silk robe and the thin cotton of her night gown beneath. He watched, leashed desire in his green eyes. But she did not undress. Instead, she bared her legs to the thigh, then climbed onto the bed and settled over him, one knee to either side of his hips. Her nightgown covered his nakedness, but she was all too aware of the heat emanating from every inch of his bare skin. Bracing her arms, she leaned over until the silk of her robe whispered against his skin. The pale curtain of her hair fell down, surrounding them.

She brushed her lips over his, keeping the caress light, tantalizing. She wanted to sear the memory of this night into both of them.

She wanted him never to forget her.

"Clara," he breathed, running his fingers through her hair.

She lowered herself to lie on top of him, the silk of her robe providing a provocative barrier. Heat tingled at the juncture between her legs, and she slid up and down, savoring the sensation. Darien's hands went to her shoulders and he pulled her into another kiss, his tongue hot and demanding, tangling with hers.

Every inch of her was alive, intoxicated by the feel of his body beneath hers. She pressed herself harder against him and he gave a low groan of pleasure.

At last she broke the kiss and sat up. His hands slipped over her breasts to play with her nipples, which were pushing against the fabric of her nightgown. The touch sent tiny sparks flaring through her.

"Undress," he said.

His fingers tightened over her breasts, and she nearly complied, her skin aching to be naked beneath his hands—but she was not quite ready to relinquish her power.

"Wait," she said, moving to his side. "Spread your legs."

Heat flushed through her, that she would say such things. And that he would obey.

She ran a tentative finger down his shaft. It jumped at her touch, and she quickly pulled her hand back.

He laughed. "You've found my sensitive spot. Don't stop."

Catching her lower lip between her teeth, she reached again. The skin of his manhood was so soft, yet covering a hard rigidity. He twitched again, but this time she let her finger continue stroking. It was good to know that he had a place on his body she could gently tease.

She wrapped her hand about the length of his shaft and he let out a low groan of pleasure. Lightly squeezing, she stroked up and down, and he moaned again.

One more experiment, and then she would give in to the rising desire pulsing through her.

"Close your eyes," she said. She did not think she would be able to be so bold if he were watching.

As soon as his lids shut, she knelt between his thighs. Her hair brushed across his legs, over his shaft, and he shuddered with unmistakable pleasure. She swept her hair back and forth over his skin, delighting in teasing him. Then she leaned forward and placed her lips on the spot she had discovered.

"Ah, Clara." His hands fisted the sheets.

When she touched him with her tongue, he moaned. She licked

the velvet-smooth skin, kissing his shaft as she would kiss his mouth. After a moment, she grasped him with one hand and moved her mouth to the tip. A drop of moisture met her tongue, slightly salty, and she savored it as proof of his arousal.

She opened her lips and took him into her mouth, and he groaned in pleasure. Sliding him in and out between her lips, she felt him grow even more rigid, encompassed in the hot wetness of her mouth.

"Clara," he gasped after a mere minute of this treatment. "You're driving me mad."

She smiled and sat up. "Good. Do you want me to stop?"

"No. Yes." He let go of the sheets and reached for her. "I want you."

His urgency sent hot waves through her center. She pulled off her nightgown and robe, then straddled him once more and slowly lowered herself. The tip of his manhood touched, then parted her, but she controlled the pace. And she intended it to be deliciously deliberate.

Darien caught his breath, his fingers closing convulsively over her bare shoulders, but he held still. She slid lower, letting his shaft stretch her wide. Even lower, until their bodies met, hip to hip.

She drew in a deep breath as her body became accustomed to his length, his hardness. Beneath her, she could feel him trembling with leashed desire.

"Are you ready?" she asked.

"For you? Always."

The answer drove a sliver of sorrow into her heart. Banishing it, she began to move up and down, enfolding him, surrounding him with her body. It felt very different, being on top. She caught a rhythm and he set his hands at her waist, urging her on.

They lost the beat, found it again, then lost it. Clara leaned forward. Before she could say a word, he wrapped himself about her and rolled them over.

He smiled down at her, that devilish grin she loved so well.

"Delightful as it was having you over me," he said, "you were driving me to distraction. We can practice it again, another time."

There would be no more times.

"Take me," she said, grasping his shoulders.

His gaze holding hers, he began moving over her, sure and strong. The feel of his shaft sliding in and out made her breath speed. Heat built in her center, that delicious tension of need and desire winding through her.

No more thoughts, no more sadness. Only the plunge and pull of two bodies striving together, the mad dance to unheard music. The sweet pounding pleasure that surged over them both, a wave breaking, and breaking again.

She wrapped her arms around him as he stilled, and held on tight. The aftermath of fulfillment pulsed through her, each beat quieter than the last.

Then the last trembling echo of bliss slipped from her body, and was gone. *Darien*, her heart whispered, *I love you.* But her lips remained silent.

CHAPTER TWENTY-SEVEN

Milano hums with excitement as the city prepares for the much-anticipated Grand Duel between Maestro Reynard and Signor Varga. Betting is heavy in the streets, with the odds slightly in Reynard's favor. Florist shops have been denuded of their blossoms, and coveted tickets to the event are selling at several times their face value. Tonight there will be fireworks!

-Il Pettegolo

Clara woke, alone—as she would always wake. The cold sheets beside her held only the faintest scent of Darien, dissipating even as she clutched the pillows against her face. She rolled over and sought the soft darkness of sleep once more, unwilling to open her eyes and let the day fully begin.

Two hours later, head foggy with wisps of dreaming, she woke again. It was no use staying in bed any longer; she must rise and face what the future brought.

The maid fetched her a cup of morning chocolate and a light breakfast of pastries and fruit. Clara had little appetite. The food was tasteless in her mouth, but she made herself eat. She would not be able to support Nicholas, or keep up a façade for Darien, if she felt light-headed with hunger.

After she was dressed, she went and rapped on her brother's door. There was no answer—likely he was already working with Darien. She nearly turned her steps to the maze of servant's passages leading to their rehearsal room, but she did not think she would be able to watch him play without giving in to the tears pressing, hot and uncomfortable, against her chest.

Instead, she returned to her rooms and tried to compose a letter to him. She sat at the writing desk and stared at the cloud-flecked sky outside her window. The room was quiet, but for the ticking of the ornate clock on the mantel.

Pen in hand, she considered the creamy sheet of vellum, trying to think what to write as the ink dried on the nib. No words would come—but music would. A sweet, elegiac melody moved through her. With a heavy breath, she bent her head and began to scribe the notes of her farewell.

A half hour later, someone rapped loudly on her door.

"Clara?" Darien's voice sounded through the thick wood.

"One moment!"

She shoved the composition under the other loose sheets of paper on the desk, smearing her most recently inked notes, then went and opened the door to Darien.

"Is Nicholas here?" he asked.

"I thought you were rehearsing." The first whisper of worry coiled about her heart.

"He was supposed to meet me over an hour ago to run through the pieces for the competition." Darien ran his hand through his dark hair, disheveling it. "We don't have any time to waste."

"He's not in his rooms?" She stepped into the hallway, making for her brother's suite.

Oh, Nicholas, not again. Please. Her heartbeat pounded in her throat.

"If he's there, he's not answering," Darien said, following her. "And the door is locked."

Clara tapped on her brother's door and called his name. When he did not reply, she knocked harder. There was no response. She beat her fist against his door, refusing to give way to her rising panic.

"Stop." Darien took her hand and frowned at her reddened knuckles.

"But—"

"Come." Without releasing her hand, he led her down to his rooms.

As they entered his parlor, Peter Widmere left off pacing the ivory-hued carpet. She glimpsed Henri in the bedroom, brushing out one of Darien's coats.

"Did you find Nicholas?" Peter asked.

"No. Fetch the palace guards to break down his door." Darien's voice was tight.

Clara felt dizzy with fear. Where was her brother?

"Is that really necessary?" Peter frowned.

"Yes." There was no arguing with Darien's tone. Without another word his agent left the room.

"I..." Clara swallowed past the dryness in her throat. "I don't think Nicholas has done himself harm."

She prayed the words were true.

"Perhaps not willingly," Darien said, "but we've both seen what your brother is capable of."

Tears pricked the corner of her eyes. "No. He would not have... He swore to me he had stopped drinking."

Had her brother faltered and fallen, on the very eve of the duel? She had trusted him, believed in the strength of their bargain. Had Nicholas seen the truth—that she was desperately in love with Darien Reynard?

Darien had not released her hand. His clasp was warm over her chilled fingers.

"We will find him, Clara."

In the corridor outside she heard men calling her brother's name, and then the splinter and crack of wood. They truly *were* breaking Nicholas's door. She hoped the emperor would not be too displeased.

A few moments later, Peter re-entered the parlor.

"Not there," he said, his brows creased in a worried furrow. "It appears his bed was not slept in, either. Perhaps he... found other accommodations for the night."

He shot a glance at Clara, his meaning clear.

"No." She was certain of this, at least. "Even if he had, my brother would not be so remiss in his absence. Not on this day, of all days."

Peter folded his arms. "Might he have left the palace and encountered some trouble? Varga's faction is none too gentle."

"They would not stoop to foul play," Darien said. "They believe their champion is the best, that Varga needs no assistance to win the duel on his own merits. Harming Nicholas wouldn't serve their ends."

"What shall we do?" She felt cold, all the way through.

"I'll speak to the emperor immediately," Darien said. "There will be no duel until Nicholas is found."

"Varga will not like that," Peter said.

"He will have to stomach it, if he wants a competition." Darien squeezed Clara's hands, then released her. "Stay with Peter and Henri in my rooms until I return."

She was a string tightened to the point of snapping. She could not sit, she could not stand still. At last Henri brought her a cup of tea and made her settle into a chair. The warmth did little to ease her and the beverage was bitter in her mouth.

After an eternity, Darien strode back into the room. He shut the door, then turned to face them.

"Emperor Francis has sent his men to search the city," he said. "And he has agreed to postpone the musical competition for twenty-four hours."

"But what if Nicholas is not found before then?" Henri asked.

Clara clutched her teacup tightly. They would find her brother within a day. They must.

Darien paced to the settee and gripped the back, his hands betraying his tension.

"Then either I choose to compete without Nicholas, or I forfeit the duel."

"We could find you another accompanist," Peter said. "It's short notice, but—"

"Varga was there, with the emperor." Darien's mouth twisted. "He said that he would be happy to perform solo, without any accompaniment obscuring his genius on the violin, and challenged me to do the same."

Henri steepled his hands beneath his chin. "He has thrown down the gauntlet. I do not like this."

"We must pray that Nicholas is found," Clara said, her voice catching on the words.

Darien had spent all his time recently on Becker's compositions. Although he was the maestro, she did not think he had three solo pieces prepared to perform at a moment's notice. Certainly none that would showcase his musical genius as *Il Diavolo* did.

She set her half-full teacup on the side table and rose.

"Where are you going?" Darien asked.

"I must join the search for my brother."

"No." Darien's eyes were dark on hers. "We have already misplaced one Becker. You will remain here, in the palace. I will join the search."

"Monsieur." Henri's eyes widened. "You cannot be thinking of looking for him yourself. The streets are dangerous."

"Nicholas is out there somewhere," Darien said. "I cannot abandon him."

The words stabbed through Clara. After all the strife and difficulty between Darien and Nicholas, Darien was still willing to risk himself to look for her brother. A muffled sob escaped her lips.

"No." Peter folded his arms. "Don't be an idiot—you can't go."

Stubborn lines formed around Darien's mouth, and Clara moved to his side. She set her hand on his tense forearm.

"Please," she said.

She could not bear to lose him, too.

No, she refused to let such thoughts lodge within her ribs, icing her lungs and seizing her blood. Nicholas would be found, safe and well.

Darien regarded her for a long moment. Then his lips eased from their tight line.

"You are right. I will not leave the palace."

Peter blew out a breath of relief. "I'll go, and send word with any news."

Darien gave a short nod, then turned to his valet. "Henri, please escort Clara to her rooms and stay with her while she rests."

"I don't—" she began, but Darien cut her off.

"You will rest. I'll come fetch you for dinner, but until then remain in your rooms."

She wanted to suggest she help him rehearse, but she could not play with such dread coiling about her fingers. Besides, Varga had made it plain there were to be no substitutions.

"I will send word the moment we hear anything," Darien said.

Despite the fact that the others were watching, he brushed a kiss against her cheek. She leaned into his warmth and solidity, wishing she could curl up against him and stay there until the sun burned out and the moon ruled the sky, until the seas ran dry. Until her brother was found, safe and whole.

Instead she straightened and, Henri behind her, made for the cold protection of her rooms.

***

The banquet hall of the palace was full of visiting nobility, but unlike dinner the night before, the gathering was subdued. Buzzing whispers filled the air, and Clara tried not to overhear the speculation about what might have happened to Nicholas.

Candlelight glimmered, hundreds of tiny stars illuminating satins and silks, sparking against jewels, and shining off the fine china and silver gracing the emperor's table. The meal was extravagant. Ever-attentive servants delivered course upon course of delicacies and circulated with carafes of wine, keeping the diners' goblets full.

Clara had no appetite, but Darien, who insisted on being seated beside her, kept sliding morsels onto her plate.

"You must eat," he said.

Clara lifted her fork and poked at a slice of partridge breast. He was right. If... no, *when*, they found Nicholas, her brother would need her to be strong.

She chewed and swallowed, tasting nothing.

"Good." Darien set a baked apple on her plate, followed by a neatly curled prawn.

She turned to him. "I am perfectly capable of selecting my own food."

"Then stop shaking your head in refusal when the servants offer, or I'll keep feeding you."

He gave her a teasing smile, though the concern in his eyes

contradicted the effect. They both understood that arguing over something as trivial as dinner was only a distraction from the looming absence of Nicholas.

"You are insufferably overbearing," she said.

"It's part of my charm."

Beneath the table his leg pressed hers, not in a suggestive way, but a simple confirmation of his presence. Had it not caused talk, she would have leaned against him. But already she could see the avid eyes noting his solicitousness of her. The gossips would fasten upon it.

But it did not matter. She had no future at Darien's side.

After dinner, the emperor stood and invited his guests to repair to the public parlors for more music and celebration. Clara did not think she could bear it.

"I'll escort you back to your suite," Darien said, clearly reading her mood.

She took his arm and let him lead her from the overly warm banquet room. In the relative quiet and cool of the hallway outside, Clara drew in a deep breath. There was so much she wanted to say to Darien, but the words were tangled in her heart, with no hope of unraveling.

They traversed the corridors in silence. Months ago she would have been overawed at the abundance of gold leaf, the rich carpets beneath their feet, the sparkling crystal sconces and rich oil paintings lining the walls. Now the opulence was merely a blur. She would be glad to never see such splendor again, as long as Nicholas was returned to her, whole and well.

Darien ushered her into her suite and followed her in, closing the door firmly behind him. Without a word, she went to him, and he folded her into his arms. The tears she had been choking back all day fell freely, and she shook in his embrace.

He held her, one hand stroking her hair, until her misery had spent itself, then offered his kerchief. Clara wiped the scrim of tears from her cheeks.

"Come, lie down," he said, leading her to the bedroom.

The tall bed was neatly made, the dark blue coverlet and mass of pillows inviting her to rest. Aching and tear-stained, she perched on the side of the mattress and let Darien remove her slippers. His touch was comforting, and though she felt the strength and heat of him, he did not demand her affections or press her for more than she could offer.

Instead, he held up her dressing gown and helped her don it, then pulled back the sheets.

"Stay with me," she said. She could not bear to be alone with her thoughts, her regrets.

"I will."

While Darien slipped off his shoes and shrugged out of his coat, she slid across the soft white sheets to make a place for him. The bed gave under his weight, and she gratefully rolled against him, coming to rest with her ear pressed against his chest. He pulled her even closer, one arm circling her waist. His heartbeat was steady, an even rhythm she matched her breath to.

"Sleep." He dropped a kiss on her forehead.

Embraced in his warmth, Clara took a long, shuddering breath. Exhaustion crashed upon her, the weight of fear and worry heavy as iron. She closed her eyes, and fell into the blessed relief of slumber.

***

When she awoke the next morning, Darien was gone. Unlike the morning before, the sheets where he'd lain still held the warmth and scent of him. Clara burrowed into them, inhaling deeply. But there was no escaping the day.

Throwing off the covers, she rang for the maid. She would face whatever came, and hold fast to her hope.

After dressing and taking a small breakfast in her rooms, Clara went in search of Darien. He was pacing like a caged panther in his parlor. At the sight of her, his expression lightened.

"I trust you slept well?" he asked, the secret between them gleaming in his eyes.

"I did, thank you." She glanced at Peter, who sprawled, rumpled and weary, in a nearby chair. "Any news?"

"No, and I was up half the night helping with the search."

"Get some sleep," Darien said, in a voice that brooked no argument. "I will need my agent in a better state than you are now when we go to La Scala this evening."

Peter hoisted himself from the chair and scrubbed one hand over his face. "We'll depart promptly at seven."

The musical competition was scheduled to commence at eight o'clock. Less than twelve hours. Clara folded her arms across her ribs. *Oh, Nicholas, where are you?*

"We'll be ready." Darien swept up his violin case and tipped his head at her. "Clara, come assist me. I must warm up and run through the pieces. With a piano. Nicholas will appear in time." He sounded so confident.

"But..." She could scarcely bring herself to say the words. "What if he does not?"

"Then I need your musician's ear to help me arrange the pieces for solo violin." He gestured at the door. "After you."

She was grateful for the distraction. For a few hours she would be able to lose herself in the solace of music—pour her grief and worry out, into the notes. It would be a welcome respite from the heaviness weighing every breath, the constant mist across her eyes.

In the corridor, Darien took her arm and led them through the circuitous route to the practice parlor. The room was empty, a certain peace in the wan light slanting through the windows, far removed from the bustle at the heart of the palace.

Darien unpacked his violin and Clara slid onto the polished mahogany piano bench. She sounded an A, clear and sweet in the still air, and Darien matched it.

"Let us begin with the *Air in E minor*," he said.

Clara nodded. She made no pretense of needing the music. Setting her fingers to the keys, she began the introduction.

***

Dare watched Clara play, the notes dancing beneath her fingertips. Even burdened with sorrow, she was truly a gifted musician.

Nicholas and Clara reminded him of another brother and sister he'd encountered in the musical world: Felix and Fanny Mendelssohn. Both were talented pianists, though the brother was the one known as the composer. Still, it had come to light, in a bit of scandal involving royalty, that Felix had lent his name to some of Fanny's compositions. The man had been impeccably honest about it, to the point of jeopardizing his own career.

For some time now, Dare had suspected Clara of being a composer. She knew too much about the music allegedly written by her brother; played it from the depths of her being as Nicholas never had. Was every note he touched, every composition hailed by audiences and critics, written by her—but claimed by her brother?

If a famously lauded composer like Mendelssohn faced disgrace from such an admission, how much worse would it be for a complete unknown? If his suspicions were correct, the Beckers should have told him the truth from the beginning.

Oh, certainly, his inner voice mocked. *Expose their most vulnerable secrets to the maestro, risking scandal and ruin, simply because of his so-called genius?*

Not at first—but it burned that Clara had not confided in him. And it explained so very, very much.

He pressed his bow to the strings, playing his frustration out into the open, taking the swooping melodic lines of the *Air* and turning them angular and jagged. Clara tried to match him, but the chords were too sweet for his mood.

"Enough." Dare tucked his violin beneath his elbow, the bow dangling from one finger.

"I'm sorry," Clara said, folding her hands in her lap.

"It's not you." Although in so many ways, it was. "Let us try *Il Diavolo* instead."

As the sun slowly tracked across the carpet they dismantled the composition, section by section. Two hours later they had pieced it back together for solo violin. Dare made Clara abandon the unyielding wood of the piano bench and sit instead on the comfortable sofa while he performed the new version for her.

He launched into the piece, fingers and bow flying. It was still a brilliant work, despite the now-missing accompaniment.

The last notes sprayed into silence, and Clara leapt to her feet, applauding wildly. For a moment the despair lifted from her expression.

"That was magnificent! Varga has no chance."

Dare did not reply, only swooped in to steal a kiss from the sweet curve of her lips.

He had his doubts. Not about *Il Diavolo*, but the other pieces, which did not lend themselves nearly as well to solo work. With every passing hour, his hopes for Nicholas's safe return dimmed.

To keep Clara distracted, he kissed her again. Of a certainty, now was not the time for lovemaking, but she softened in his arms.

After a long, delightful moment, she sighed and pulled back.

"Hush," he said when she opened her mouth to speak. "We have one more piece of music to play today."

"We do?"

"The final movement of *Viaggio*. Play it with me, Clara. For your brother's sake."

"Yes." She all but whispered the word. "Darien. That is not the true title of the piece."

"No?" Somehow he was not surprised.

"It is called *Amore*."

Love. The word sent a jolt through him. Of course. He searched her eyes, begging her to reveal herself, but she pulled away. Wordlessly, she went to the piano and sorted through the pages, then handed him the violin part.

Her music spoke her entire soul and, at last, he could hear it.

He lifted his violin. "Count us in."

They hit the downbeat together in perfect unison and the music unfurled like a silken banner, snapping and dancing in the breeze. Despite the glorious melody, Clara played with a melancholy lilt Dare could not help but echo. The triumph of the piece swerved into lament, an aching elegy for her missing brother.

When they finished, Clara sat immobile at the keyboard. A line of tears shone on her cheek.

"Ah, love," he said. "Your brother will return to us. Have faith."

"I cannot." Her words were choked.

Dare drew her into his embrace, holding her as if he could absorb all her sorrow. He wiped her tears with the back of his fingers.

"The *Amore* is a masterwork," he said. "You must be very proud."

Her silvery eyes went wide and she stilled in his arms. *Tell me*, he thought fiercely. *Tell me it is your composition.* She held his gaze for one heartbeat. Two.

Then she flushed and looked away, and Dare swallowed a curse. He could not force her to trust him, though he wanted to take her by the shoulders and stare into her eyes until she confessed.

"Is it yours?" he asked, his voice rough.

Still not looking at him, she shook her head.

"Clara—"

"I cannot speak to you of this!"

She wrenched away and, before he could stop her, flung the door open and fled the room.

Damnation.

It was a bitter start to what would no doubt be the most difficult evening of his life.

CHAPTER TWENTY-EIGHT

The city is abuzz over the disappearance of Nicholas Becker. Did he fall victim to foul play, or has he, in a rash of madness, fled the country? Search parties comb all of Milano, but there is no sign of the composer—and Master Reynard's odds of winning the grand competition are plummeting rapidly. Place your bets while there is still time!

-Il Pettegolo

Clara hid in her rooms for the remainder of the day. She alternately paced, cried, and tried to write a letter to Darien—none of which eased her mind or spirit in any way.

"Miss Becker?" Peter's voice accompanied a knock at her door. "We'll be departing for La Scala in an hour."

Hoping her eyes were not too reddened from weeping, she undid the lock and opened the door a crack.

"Please send the maid to assist me," she said.

"I will." His expression was unreadable.

He made no mention of Nicholas—not that she expected him to. Had her brother been found, they would have notified her immediately.

She nodded and shut the door in Peter's face.

When he returned for her, she was ready, though she pulled up the velvet hood of her cloak and did not meet anyone's gaze. Especially Darien's. She was gowned in silver tissue embroidered with pearls and sequins, a truly extravagant creation that, again, was Henri's fault. He had said she looked luminous as the moon, bedecked with stars, but tonight Clara was grateful for her black cloak to shroud that brilliance.

She said nothing during the carriage ride, though Darien's

regard lay heavy upon her. This was supposed to be his night of triumph, and instead she felt as if they were traveling to an execution.

La Scala was lit against the night, the building's façade pale and lovely against the dark sky. Lines of carriages clogged the streets, and the air hummed with excitement and speculation. Darien and his party disembarked from the black coach, and for once the crowd showed restraint. A few voices cried out encouragement as Peter led them to the back entrance.

Clara drew in a deep breath, scented with dust and perfume, as they entered the theater. The audience up front sounded like the surging of a wild sea, a contained turbulence ready to break into storm at any moment. Darien paced to his dressing room, nearly as elemental in that small space as the crowd in the theater. Clara could not bear to be near him.

Instead, she took a seat on the divan at the far end of the hall. She could wait in Nicholas's dressing room, but being surrounded by his absence would be even worse.

She slipped her hand into her beaded reticule and fingered the envelope waiting there. During the eternal hours of the day, she'd composed a letter to Darien. Each word had been a drop of her heart's blood. And although her original plan with Nicholas—to depart for London this very night—was in tatters, she knew the hour would come.

Oh, Nicholas. Her heart was rent in two.

She could not return home and face Papa without her brother. It had been her responsibility to protect him, and she had failed miserably.

"Ten minutes!" the director called, poking his head out of his office.

Anton Varga stepped from his own dressing room. He caught sight of Clara sitting in the hallway, and smiled unpleasantly.

"Miss Becker." He sauntered forward, his bearing full of arrogant confidence. "Are you certain you don't want to take the wiser course and desert the maestro as your brother did? Reynard faces nothing but ignominy tonight."

Clara clenched her hands. "It is you who will be the loser."

"A pity, that you cling to such illusions." He shook his head. "No matter. The entire world will soon know the truth."

Truth. Such a sharp-edged word.

Darien's door opened and he strode into the hallway, making straight for Clara's side. She was relieved to have his solid presence beside her.

"Varga." Darien nodded to his rival.

"Reynard. Good luck this evening. You will need it." Varga laughed, a hollow sound with no shadow of mirth.

He made Clara a tight bow, then spun on his heel and stalked away. The air seemed darker in his wake, as if his presence stained it.

Darien set his hand on Clara's shoulder. "Peter has reserved one of the boxes for the performance. Would you like to join him?"

"No."

She needed to be close to the stage, not trapped in a theater box if her brother made a miraculous reappearance. And she would be there for Darien, in either victory or defeat.

"Two minutes!" the theater director called, this time emerging from his room.

"Come." Darien led her to the shadowed wings where a handful of chairs were set, concealed from the audience by the heavy crimson curtain.

The expanse of the stage was illuminated with footlights, the dark bulk of the piano gleaming. The audience sounded less like the sea here. Clara could make out high laughter in counterpoint to the low rumble of male argument.

The director stepped onto the stage. Silence percolated through the theater, so filled with anticipation she could almost taste it; rich and complex as chocolate, sweet and bitter in equal parts.

"Ladies and gentlemen," the director cried. "Welcome to the performance of the century!"

The crowd did not hold back their cheers. Even Clara felt her heart rise. When the audience quieted, he continued.

"This evening, we are privileged to watch two of the finest musicians in the world battle for supremacy. Signor Varga and Maestro Reynard will each take the stage three times. Your applause will be the measure of their success. With the conclusion of the third round, the victor will be declared, and crowned the musical maestro of all Europe!"

Shouts erupted, and it took several long moments until the director could be heard again.

"And now, to begin our competition… Signor Anton Varga!"

The director gestured toward the wings and Varga swept forward, passing Darien and Clara without so much as a glance. The applause was loud and strong, though not—yet—overwhelmingly in Varga's favor.

He bowed to the crowd, his violin tucked under his arm, and waited.

"My dear audience," he said, when he could be heard, "thank you for your patience. As you know, due to the unfortunate absence of Mr. Becker, there have been changes to our competition. Not the least of which is this inconvenient postponement."

There were a few bitter calls at this, and Varga tipped his head.

"Yes," he continued, "it was not an easy wait, but Emperor Francis is magnanimous. Where royalty leads, we aspire to follow. Too bad the wayward composer has not seen fit to make an appearance."

More catcalls, and a few boos, rang out. Clara glanced at Darien, to see he was frowning.

"Don't let Varga upset you," she whispered.

Darien tightened his lips, but said nothing. They both knew his insistence on finding Nicholas, and the emperor's subsequent delay of the concert, had cost Darien some measure of popularity. Enough to lose the duel? Clara wove her fingers tightly together.

Varga strutted to the front of the stage. "Tonight, it is my pleasure to perform for you Tartini's *Sonata in G minor*."

Clara sucked in an anxious breath. It was a piece intended for unaccompanied violin, and renowned for its difficult trills. Not only that, Tartini, being an Italian, was certain to be a fan favorite. Oh, Varga had chosen well.

He tucked his violin beneath his chin, the lights gleaming on the reddish hue of the wood, and began to play.

It was an ambitious choice—full of darkness and demanding chords on the violin.

Despite herself, Clara was drawn into the music. Varga did not have the control and musicality of Darien, but he played with a muscular quality that suited the piece. Instead of dancing with the notes, he sparred with them, wrestling the melody into submission. There was a raw appeal that she understood, though she far preferred Darien's more nuanced approach.

Varga fired the last passage into the audience as if the notes were bullets. They met their mark, and the crowd applauded madly. Flushed and triumphant, Varga took multiple bows.

It did not bode well for Darien. Without a word he rose, fetched his instrument and gave it a quick re-tune, then waited beside the draperies for his rival to exit the stage. Clara wished she could hold Darien, knead the tension from his shoulders—but he was narrowing his focus. In a few moments only these things would exist: the smooth wood of his violin beneath his fingers, the pull and sway of the notes, the music spinning inside his soul.

Varga stepped into the wings and paused before Darien.

"Well done," Darien said, no hint of sarcasm in his voice.

"Good luck, Reynard." With a single laugh, Varga disappeared into the shadows.

As long as he stayed away from her, Clara did not care where he stood to watch Darien perform.

The director announced Darien and the crowd clapped and cheered. Darien gave Clara a single, penetrating glance, then lifted his head and strode on stage. The lights gleamed on the glossy midnight of his hair and picked out golden hues from the violin beneath his arm.

"Thank you," he said, bowing to the audience. "Although Nicholas Becker is not here, his music speaks for itself. For my first piece, I will play his *Air in E minor*."

The crowd quieted, and Darien launched into the opening lines, playing the swooping melody Clara had written that cold winter night.

How their fortunes had changed. And changed again. *Oh,*

Nicholas. The thought of him was an arrow through her lungs. She shivered in the dim light and swallowed her sharp grief as Darien played.

Most of her compositions relied on the intermingling of piano and violin, and the *Air* was no exception. But Darien had been adamant about performing only pieces by Becker. They had spent much of their rehearsal trimming and reshaping the music, until it was lovely even when voiced by a solo instrument.

Yet lovely would not be sufficient. She had been blinded by the echo of the piano part, but she saw now—or rather, heard—that the spare simplicity of the melody alone was not quite enough.

He played it masterfully, of course. The air shivered with tension and sweetness, and Clara knew that some members of the audience would be as enthralled by the music as she was. Far more, however, would prefer the angular brashness of Varga's performance.

Oh, why had they not chosen differently? Or begun with *Il Diavolo*, as she had suggested? Her heart, already leaden, sank until it lay at her feet, a useless lump of base metal.

When Darien finished there were enthusiastic cheers, but the audience did not respond as they had to Varga. Darien took his bow, then strode back to Clara.

"Darien—" she began, but he made a sharp movement with his hand.

"It's all right," he said. "Wait until the next round."

She pressed her lips together in worry, and to keep unspoken the words he did not want to hear.

"Attention!" the director bellowed into the audience. "Winner of the first round is Signor Varga!"

The crowd cheered again, and Clara tried not to wince under the onslaught of sound. She glanced at Darien, but he faced the stage, his expression revealing nothing. His handsome face was set, his lips tight, and Clara ached with yearning, with loss, with all the secrets lying jagged against her heart.

CHAPTER TWENTY-NINE

On stage, the director again held his hands up for quiet. Clara bit her lip. If Darien lost this round, the competition would be over. Her blood turned heavy and slow with misery.

"The loser of the last round will begin the next," he announced. "Once more, welcome Master Reynard!"

Darien strode back out onto the vast stage of La Scala, into lights so bright Clara had to squint from the dimness beside the stage.

"*Il Diavolo*, by Becker," Darien said in his loud, firm voice.

With a dramatic move, he swept his instrument to his shoulder, then froze, bow poised. Not until the crowd had become an almost silent breath, a huge animal waiting in the warm darkness beyond the footlights, did Darien begin.

She had been a fool to doubt him. Clara leaned forward on the edge of her chair, her fingers curled tightly into her palms, as he demonstrated what it meant to be the maestro.

The notes careened from his violin, sprays of brightness flung so rapidly she felt dizzy. The *spiccato* passages were flawless, eliciting spontaneous shouts and the crack of applause, quickly hushed so that the audience could hear again.

Darien took all the frustration, all the impossibility that every human faced when confronted with life, and spun it taut, winding and winding and winding, until Clara's chest was tight. Then he threw the final melody up into the air, past the gilded proscenium of La Scala. Past the scrim of clouds covering the city. Past the diamond points of the stars. A pure, exultant shout straight to the heart of the divine.

Clara swallowed, tasting the salt of her own amazed tears.

The audience surged to their feet, their ringing applause a tribute to the genius they had just witnessed.

Movement on the other side of the wings caught Clara's eye. Varga stood there, an ugly scowl on his face as he watched Darien bow before the crowd. There was no disputing that the master had won this round, although Varga had not yet played.

Smiling, Darien strode offstage, followed by stagehands bearing armfuls of bouquets. The scent of hothouse roses and orange blossoms lingered in the air as the assistants hurried to deposit the flowers in Darien's dressing room.

"That was wonderful," Clara said as Darien laid his violin back in its velvet-lined case.

"Thank you," he said, "but I couldn't have done it without your help on the arrangement."

His eyes were full of such brightness she wanted to fling her arms around him in a joyful embrace—but Varga was still watching, his expression dark. When the director announced him, he stalked onstage and nodded stiffly at the crowd.

Vargas's performance was as stiff and angry as his demeanor. The raw power he had demonstrated in his playing slipped into roughness. His notes were edged with grit, and he began to snap his bow hairs from the force of his overplaying. By the end of the piece, Clara counted five hairs dangling from the tip of his bow, swaying in the over-perfumed air of the theater.

The applause was loud, but nothing like the acclaim given to Darien. Varga bowed and wrenched his stray bow hairs off, letting them fall at the edge of the stage.

Eager onlookers in the first row scrambled to claim them, and a tussle broke out. The thin strands of horsehair might still prove to be trophies from the most preeminent musician in the world.

Or not.

The two were tied now, Darien Reynard and Anton Varga. One more performance each and the musical duel would be over.

What then?

Clara shook her head, trying to keep any thought of the future from taking hold. There was only now—*this* now, poised at the edge of the greatest stage in the world, beside the man she had given her soul to, if he but knew it.

Varga left the stage, heading for the opposite wing, and the director took his place.

"Ladies and gentlemen!" he cried. "We will take an intermission before the finale of this thrilling spectacle. Refreshments can be found in the lobby. And please, do not attempt to reach the performers backstage until the competition has ended. My men have been instructed to use force." He nodded at the pairs of ushers who stood guarding the doors from the house to the backstage.

A commotion at the left side of the theater made the director shade his hand with his eyes. Slowly, the lights rose to reveal a knot of people crowded around one of the side exits.

"Becker!" someone cried, and the name was taken up.

Clara's heart seized, the blood stopping in her veins before rushing again, hot and immediate. Heedless of the audience, she ran to the edge of the stage. She paused, eyeing the drop—but Darien vaulted down, then held his hands up to assist her onto the floor.

The uproar was spreading, the entire theater craning to see what was happening. Could it really be Nicholas? Alive, unharmed? Hope clutched her so tightly she thought her bones might break.

Holding firmly to her hand, Darien plowed through the crowd, making for the center of the hubbub. Clara could not see over his broad shoulders.

"Move aside," he commanded, and the audience fell back, murmuring his name.

At last he halted, and Clara stood on tiptoe, scarcely daring to breathe. Darien pivoted, pulling her in front of him. And there Nicholas stood—her own brother, surrounded by grinning men in laborers' clothing. Tears blurred her vision as she threw herself forward.

"Nicholas!"

"Clara, take care with my arm," he said, catching her in an awkward embrace.

"What happened?" She drew back, hands on his shoulders, and studied his face.

246 ~ ANTHEA LAWSON

His eyes were circled with exhausted shadows, and his hair was dusty and uncombed.

"I was set upon in the palace itself. I tried to fight, but there were five of them," he said, and the listeners murmured in sympathy. "They knocked me unconscious and transported me out of the city to an abandoned farm. When I woke, I found my arm was broken. I was locked in an old hayloft with only a blanket, a jug of water, and a loaf of hard bread for company."

Darien muttered a curse under his breath. "Do you know who took you?"

It seemed clear to Clara that only one villain could be responsible. Anton Varga.

"No." Nicholas frowned. "I'm not certain I'd be able to recognize my assailants, either. They all wore ornate masks. At first I thought I'd been caught up in some kind of celebration, until they started dragging me away."

"How did you escape?" Clara asked.

"These good gentlemen here," Nicholas nodded to the homespun-clad men, "heard me banging on the walls. There was an old broomstick under the hay, and once my voice gave out from shouting, I started hammering away. They broke open the door, fed me, and, as soon as I discovered it was the day of the competition, rushed me into the city."

"I'm so glad you're safe! I feared…" Her lungs caught on the horrible imaginings she'd tried her best to keep at bay.

He was not lying dead by his own hand, or another's, in some moldering alleyway. His body was not floating, bloated and lifeless, in the river.

Clara shut her eyes briefly, taking a firm grip on her emotions. She refused to dissolve into a weeping mess of gratitude in the middle of La Scala. Not now. Darien's warm hands came to rest on her shoulders, and she drew in a shaky breath, glad of his strength behind her.

"Yes," Darien said, all the force of his relief and gladness vibrating in that single word.

"But I cannot play." Nicholas nodded to his left arm, wrapped in a linen sling.

"That doesn't matter," Darien said. "Henri, fetch a doctor."

Clara glanced to the side, surprised to see the sprightly figure of the valet.

"I already have," Henri said, "with instructions to meet us in the dressing room. This is no place for such examinations."

"See to rewarding these good men," Darien said, "while I escort the Beckers backstage. Come, I'll clear a path back to the door."

Clara squeezed Nicholas's shoulders. "Follow Darien. We'll keep you between us."

She refused to take her eyes off him. The miracle of his presence was still too new for her to quite believe.

The audience did not press in on them as she and Nicholas followed Darien, though excited murmurs spread like ripples from their passage. At the door to the backstage, she saw Peter barring the way. He grinned when he caught sight of them, and moved aside.

"Thank God," he said.

When the heavy door closed behind them, a trembling joy seized Clara. The tears she had battled surged to victory and, careful of his arm, she grasped Nicholas in a tight embrace. He smelled of wood smoke and mildewed hay.

"We must get your brother to the doctor," Darien said.

Clara let Nicholas go, unsurprised to see that his face, too, was wet with tears.

"I'm sorry," he said. "If only I could play—"

"Don't regret what you can't change," Darien said, holding open the door of his dressing room. "It's enough that you are here, and relatively unharmed."

There was a wild light in Darien's eyes, a spark Clara had not seen before. Clearly he was overjoyed to have his composer returned.

She turned her face away, heart weighted with the knowledge that she had no more excuses to stay by his side. Now that Nicholas was safely back with them, she must fulfill her promise.

The doctor waited inside, and set to work immediately, tsking and humming as he bent over Nicholas's arm.

"The competition isn't over yet?" Nicholas winced as the doctor unwrapped his crude sling. "Is Darien winning?"

"He and Varga are tied," Clara said. "Varga took the first round, but Darien won the second. He played *Il Diavolo* flawlessly, without accompaniment."

"Solo?" Nicholas glanced from her to Darien, who stood behind the doctor, his eyes watchful.

"Varga insisted upon it," Darien said. "We're both performing without our pianists."

"Oh." Nicholas twitched the fingers of his left hand. "Perhaps I could manage—"

"Nonsense," Darien said, and Clara had to agree.

There was no way her brother could play accompaniment. The doctor snorted in disapproval of the idea, though his hands were gentle as he splinted and bound Nicholas's arm.

"Maestro?" A rap on the door, and then the director stuck his head into the room. "Two minutes, if you will. The crowd is restless for the conclusion of the duel. Signor Varga will perform first, as he lost the last round."

Darien set his hand on Nicholas's shoulder. "Come join us in the wings when the doctor has finished."

He offered his arm to Clara, and they made their way back to the hushed shadows flanking the stage.

When the director announced him, Varga strode onto the proscenium to thunderous applause. Clara bowed her head at the sound. Fear lodged in her throat, eclipsing her joy at having her brother safely returned. Now all her worry was for Darien. What if he lost the competition? She had never let herself believe it was possible, but now...

She squeezed her eyes closed, willing Varga to fail.

Instead, he stood there, absorbing the adoration of the crowd. At last he raised his hand for quiet.

"My dear audience," he said, a smug note in his voice, "as many of you know, Nicholas Becker has managed to reappear—just in time for the conclusion of the competition."

There was robust clapping at his words, and Clara's heart lifted at the sound. Darien still had many sympathizers in the crowd.

Then Varga beckoned to a figure standing in the wings. His accompanist, a tall, thin man with an extraordinary reach on the keyboard, stepped forward, and Clara felt her eyes widen.

"Since Reynard has his accompanist back," Varga said, "I'm sure you will be pleased to welcome mine onto the stage, won't you?"

The crowd shouted their approval, but Clara jumped to her feet.

"He can't!" She turned to Darien, anger pumping hotly through her. "We have to stop him. There's no comparison. Nicholas can't play a note! The director must—"

"Too late." Darien took her elbow. "The audience has decided. Trying to change things now will only earn their ill will. Look, Varga is about to begin."

"But, Darien—"

He laid a long, nimble finger over her mouth.

"All will be well," he said in a low voice. "Trust me."

He stroked his finger across her lips, his green eyes alight with excitement, challenge, and something she could not name. She could say nothing, though Varga's duplicity scorched her nerves.

The accompanist launched into the opening chords. Slowly, she sat, her skirts rustling like brittle stalks. It was, indeed, too late.

The addition of the piano carried Varga's notes to the very top balconies of La Scala. He played with a technical brilliance that could not be denied, his earlier, brutish style now melding with the accompaniment to create a music that strutted boldly forward. Varga performed with utter confidence, as though victory were assured. Listening to him holding the crowd rapt and still, Clara almost believed it was.

Too soon, he finished. Applause cracked through the air, thunder and lightning rolled into one, and Varga took bow after bow, his accompanist a thin shadow behind him. Flowers, flung from the audience, littered the stage.

The director finally ushered Varga offstage and sent one of his crew to retrieve the blossoms scattered over the shining wood.

Now it was Darien's turn. Her heart beating like an over-tightened drum, Clara met his eyes. He took her hands and stood, drawing her up with him.

She must speak. No matter what happened, it was time to release the secret scarring her soul. She owed him that honesty. After tonight, things would never be the same.

And perhaps knowing that she had penned the notes he was about to play, perhaps that might give Darien wings. She thought he loved her. Would that be enough?

"Darien." Her voice rasped her throat. "Before you play, there is something I must tell you."

"No." He tightened his grip on her hands, then released her. "You must come onstage as my accompanist. Now. Look, the director is announcing me."

He strode the few paces to his case. Scooping up violin and bow, he turned and held up a sheaf of pages for her to see. The violin part for *Amore*.

The applause from the crowd took on an impatient edge. Clara glanced to the stage, where the director beckoned urgently.

"But—"

Darien's gaze was insistent. "Come with me, Clara. Please. I need you."

She could not refuse him.

"Yes." The word was a mere breath, but it was enough.

He strode forward into the light, into the eye of the world. Trembling, she followed.

CHAPTER THIRTY

Clara blinked at the heat and brightness of the footlights, and kept her gaze averted from the front of the stage. She could not ignore the audience, however. Whispers shivered through the crowd, prickling her nerves, and she braced herself for the boos and catcalls that must surely follow.

When she reached the piano, she drew in a shaky breath and tried to calm her rushing fear. Black and white keys stretched before her, a familiar world she could gratefully immerse herself in. There could be no room for the panic hovering over her fingers, no entry to the hollow terror that wanted to curl into her chest. She must be steady for Darien.

Darien offered no introduction, no word of explanation to the audience. Instead, he swept his violin up to his shoulder and waited. Two heartbeats later, the audience stilled. Anticipation flavored the air. Everything, everything hung upon this. Clara felt the crowd lean toward the stage, waiting. Watching.

She watched Darien, too, ready for the preparatory rise of his bow, the descent that would propel them both forward. Into the music. Into the future.

When he pulled the first long, sweet note from his violin, she was there, the piano meeting him in perfect harmony.

Keeping her focus only on him, Clara let everything else fall away. There was no watching emperor, no theater waiting to judge the outcome, no continent spreading out from this single point of music.

There was only one man, playing the melody she had written for him, playing her heart out into the open. The notes spiraled and

252 ~ ANTHEA LAWSON

twined, their breaths rising and falling together, violin and piano singing in sweet, lush counterpoint.

The second movement quickened, fiery passion sparking from the violin, tossed back and forth between them. Clara felt her face flush as she met Darien, matched him, their notes striving together, pushing and pushing into harmonic brilliance. The echo of their nights of lovemaking infused the music, the desire and racing of the blood as bodies touched and tangled, ascending into a perfect climax of sound.

A breath of silence, and they plunged in unison into the third section. The notes she had played earlier, the elegy for a lost brother, were now transformed. Shadow gave way to light, despair to hope.

The melody rose from the piano, seeking, questioning. I have been searching, alone, for so long. Is there love for me, in this world?

The violin answered, a line of notes steady as the stars. *If there is love, then we share it. I have found you at last.*

Weeping turned to aching sweetness as she and Darien melded to one musical whole. Two lives, two souls, finally revealed to one another.

Amore. Love.

Darien reached the final, pure, high note of the piece. It spun out into darkness, asking a question. *Will you be mine, now and forever?*

Clara played the concluding chord, her fingers strong and sure. *I am yours. Now, and forever.*

The music was complete.

Silence.

For one icy moment, Clara imagined that the audience had left, departed while she and Darien were caught up in the throes of the music—the theater was that still.

Then applause crashed down, so loud it vibrated the stage beneath her feet and set the piano strings to humming. Varga had played with technical genius; he had played for fame and immortality. But Darien had played for love. His mastery of the instrument was married to sheer emotion, surpassing Varga's skill.

The proof of Darien's victory shook the gilded walls of La Scala.

Deafened by the noise, Clara locked eyes with him. The knowledge she saw there split her heart in two, and healed it.

He knew. Within the music, and outside it, he knew *she* was the composer.

Darien motioned for her to join him. When she reached his side, he took her arm and together, they bowed before half the courts of Europe.

From the corner of her eye, she caught movement in the wings: Varga, snatching up his violin case. The duel was over, and the cascade of applause was not for him. Knowledge of his defeat was clear in the set of his shoulders, in the way he hurried away, not once glancing back to the brilliantly lit stage.

At last Darien held his hand up for silence. It was a long time coming.

"Thank you," he said, his voice projecting to the back of the theater. "Tonight, I wish to introduce you to the composer—the *true* composer—of Becker's glorious music."

Ignoring the sudden buzz of consternation in the crowd, Darien turned to her.

"No," she said in a low, strained voice. "Darien, are you mad?"

He bent to speak softly into her ear. "Clara, you deserve this recognition. You deserve so much more than you give yourself."

"You can't tell them!" Panic raced through her. "You can't risk your career for this, for me."

"Too late." He lifted his head and raised his voice. "Ladies and gentlemen, nobles and commoners, I give you Miss Clara Becker!"

There was no applause. The air stilled, hardened, and cold pressure gripped Clara's lungs. Oh, he had ruined them all. She could not look at his face, nor the audience who had turned from friend to foe in a heartbeat. Staring at the floor, she willed herself not to weep. Willed her feet to carry her back to the sheltering shadows of the wings.

Her family was ruined, Darien's fame tarnished—possibly beyond repair. What had he done?

Before she could turn away, Darien caught her arm. Humiliation burned through her as the silence continued, with her and Darien pinned on the stage.

Then, out of the darkness beyond the footlights, came the sound of a single person clapping.

The audience stirred and murmured like fallen leaves, the rustles growing louder as they turned to see who would do such a thing.

Her mouth dry as sand, Clara lifted her eyes, searching. The sound was coming from the most opulent box at the front of the theater, the stage lights reflecting off the standing figure of a woman in a pale dress. Diamonds glinted at her throat and from the tiara in her dark hair, and Clara could just make out her strong features.

Caroline Augusta. The Empress Consort of Austria.

Beside her, Emperor Francis gave her a look from beneath his stern brows, then rose to his feet, adding his heavy applause to his wife's. A gasped breath later, the entire theater followed suit, the air once again pulsing with applause.

Clara glanced into the wings, her heart squeezed with worry for Nicholas. How would this acknowledgement affect him? He stood just at the edge of the shadows, and she saw a slow smile spread across his face as his world righted itself. All was well.

Then Darien did the unthinkable.

There, before the assembled nobility of Europe, in front of an enormous crowd, he went down on one knee and grasped Clara's hand.

"Clara," he said, shouting over the applause. "Clara Becker, I love you. Would you do me the utmost honor of becoming my wife?"

She looked down at him, and the crowd quieted once more. Such a spectacle! The musical duel nearly paled in comparison to Darien's revelation that she was the composer. And now, consummate performer that he was, the audience was witness to his shocking proposal of marriage.

Yet there was no calculation in his expression. His eyes were full of determination and sincerity. And love. It was the only thing that could save them.

"Yes," she said.

"Louder." He squeezed her hand.

"Yes." More strongly this time, but it was not enough. Clara gathered air into her lungs and, in a most unladylike way, shouted her answer.

"Yes!"

The audience exploded into cheers, a huge wave of acceptance washing over her and Darien. She blinked back tears, to see Nicholas yelling approval from the wings, Henri and Peter beside him.

A moment later, Darien was on his feet. He set his violin on the piano bench, then swept her into his powerful embrace. Her heartbeat was the pounding of hands and feet, her breath the cries of approbation careening up five stories of balconies and echoing off the painted ceiling.

His lips met hers in a passionate kiss. A kiss full of love, full of fire, resonating with the perfect harmony of two souls who have finally found one another.

EPILOGUE

Last night's performance by the Reynards in King's Theatre marked the triumphant close of this musical family's latest European tour. As usual, Maestro Reynard compelled the audience with his sublime mastery of his instrument. His wife, ethereally lovely in silver satin, premiered a new composition commissioned by Queen Victoria, to the monarch's enthusiastic praise.

The couple's ten-year-old daughter, a violin prodigy in her own right, took the stage with her father to perform Telemann's Canonic Sonatas *with breathless virtuosity. And their young son's command of Bach on the keyboard promises great things.*

Indeed, the Reynards will leave the world a lasting musical legacy.
-The London Times, April, 1841

Clara curled up on the divan, sipping her tea while Darien read the latest reviews out loud. It was good to be home. Although the children enjoyed traveling and performing, eight-year-old Benedict was prone to mischief, and Annabel to poutiness.

It was easier to knit their family together in the months they did not tour. Not to mention giving the children some semblance of a normal upbringing, although Annabel spent hours a day practicing her violin. She kept demanding new pieces from her mother, searching for an elusive melody that Clara was unable to capture.

She would not be surprised if her daughter turned to composing her own music within the year.

Just as Nicholas had, at last, embraced his poetic muse and begun publishing his own works to some acclaim, Clara knew that her children would have their own paths to follow. No matter what their parents might think, or demand.

"Well." Darien folded the newspaper away and took a sip of his coffee—a taste she had never managed to acquire. "The reviewers liked our concert well enough."

"I don't care what the reviews say. It's the audience that matters."

She smiled at him. It had been over a dozen years and hundreds of successful concerts since their marriage, yet his features were still most beloved to her. The brush of silver at his temples and the lines at the corners of his eyes bespoke the years passing, but when they played, time had no meaning. Together, they reached the pure, perfect heart of the music.

And together, they always would.

HISTORICAL NOTE

Sonata for a Scoundrel is set in 1830-31, midway through the era now called the Romantic period in arts and music, which roughly spans the years from 1800-1850.

Although there were a few women composing music during that time, they did not have the societal approval to do more than "dabble." Penning a few small pieces was acceptable, but it was unthinkable for a woman to aspire to become a professional composer.

Fanny Mendelssohn (1805-1847) was actively discouraged from composing by her father, who believed that being a housewife was the only suitable calling for a woman. Musical scholar David Montgomery has said of Fanny: "Only the lack of compulsion (or perhaps opportunity) to publish more often seems to have prevented her skills from developing to match those of any major European composer of the day." In other words, Fanny Mendelssohn may well have been one of the most talented composers of her era, had her gifts been allowed to flourish.

Like Clara and Nicholas, Fanny allowed her compositions to be published under her brother, Felix's, name. The story of the near-scandal alluded to in *Sonata for a Scoundrel* is true, although I took some artistic license by placing the siblings a decade early. Felix Mendelssohn was a great favorite of Queen Victoria and Prince Albert, and the queen made a show of learning and performing one of his songs. Felix confessed that the composition was actually his sister's, and only his high standing with the royals allowed him to emerge relatively unscathed from this social blunder.

Clara's namesake, Clara Schumann (1819-1896), might also have been a great composer had she lived in a different time. Her husband, famed composer Robert Schumann, wrote in his diary: "Clara has composed a series of small pieces, which show a musical and tender ingenuity such as she has never attained before. But to have children, and a husband who is always living in the realm of imagination, does not go together with composing. She cannot work at it regularly, and I am often disturbed to think how many profound ideas are lost because she cannot work them out."

It was not until the early 1900s that women composers began to be recognized as capable of creating more than small-scale parlor music. Even today, the musical contributions of women throughout history are often overlooked.

Darien Reynard is loosely based on one of the most famous violinists to ever grace the stages of Europe, Niccolo Paganini (1782-1840). Paganini was such a master on his instrument that he was frequently accused of selling his soul to the devil in exchange for his musical brilliance.

Unlike Dare, Paganini was also a talented composer. For decades, his music was thought unplayable due to the immense difficulty of his pieces. It is only with intensive modern violin approaches that performers are able to attempt Paganini's pieces.

Clara's compositions are partially inspired by the music of Frederic Chopin, who composed his works about a decade later than this novel is set. Baroness Dudevant, whom Clara observes at the salon in Paris, is the famous novelist George Sand, who carried on a tumultuous affair with Chopin from 1837 until shortly before the composer's death from tuberculosis in 1849.

Franz Lizst is also introduced at the salon. He was, indeed, a halfhearted player, until he was inspired by a meeting with Paganini in 1832. From that point on, he applied himself to practice and composition, and became one of the great musical superstars of his age.

Pieces mentioned in the novel include:

Beethoven *Violin Sonata No. 9* (Kreutzer), played at Darien's first concert in London.

Telemann *Fantasia No. 7*, played in Brighton.

Handel *Chaconne in G minor*, also performed in Brighton.

Beethoven *Sonata in D major Four Hands, Opus 6*, played by Clara and Nicholas at the inn.

Amis, la matinee est belle from *La Muette de Portici* by Daniel Auber, performed by Henri at the inn.

Tartini *Sonata in G minor*, Varga's opening piece for the duel.

Mozart *Sonata in E minor K. 304*, Varga's second piece.

Telemann *Canonic Sonatas*, played by Darien and his daughter Annabel, mentioned in the epilogue.

Bach *Prelude and Fugue BWV 849*, played by Darien and Clara's son, Benedict, mentioned in the epilogue.

Additional recommended composers:
Fanny Mendelssohn
Clara Schumann
Paganini (especially his *Caprices*)
Frederic Chopin
Felix Mendelssohn
Robert Schumann
Franz Liszt
Hector Berlioz

THANK YOU!

Thank you for reading SONATA FOR A SCOUNDREL! If you enjoyed it, please consider helping other readers find this book:

1. Lend this book to a friend!

2. Leave a review on Amazon, Goodreads, or any other site of your choice. It makes a difference, and is greatly appreciated!

3. Request that your local library purchase a print copy, so that other readers can discover Anthea's romances.

Be the first to know about new releases and reader perks by subscribing to Anthea's newsletter at tinyletter.com/AntheaLawson.

ACKNOWLEDGEMENTS

This book owes much to the music teachers I've had over the years, and a childhood filled with music—including the long symphony rehearsals and concerts my brother and I were forced to sit through. Though some of it might have felt torturous at the time, my life has been immeasurably enriched as a result. Thank you: Mom, Kathie Jarrett, Willa Dean Howell, Shelley Clark, Dale Kempter and Ron Teare, Jim Bonnell, Betty Whiton, Tim Brock, Robin Boomer and all the founding members of the OCO, and the many musicians I've had the pleasure of playing with over the years.

The novel itself was greatly improved by the input of my critique partner Peggy, my editor Laurie Temple, my beta readers Chassily, Sean, and Ginger, and the copy-editing skills of Arran Nichols at Editing 720. Additional thanks go to Anne Victory's Oops Detection service.

Once again, Kim Killion proves her incomparable talent in cover design. Many thanks for a gorgeous cover, and thanks, too, to models Jimmy Thomas and Jax Turyna for a romantic pose that perfectly captures Dare and Clara.

ABOUT THE AUTHOR

Anthea Lawson's first two novels were co-written by Anthea and Lawson, a husband and wife creative team living in the Pacific Northwest. Their first novel, *Passionate*, was released from Kensington books in October 2008, and was a finalist for the prestigious RWA RITA award for Best First Book. Booklist has named Anthea one of the "new stars of historical romance."

Since 2010, Anthea has branched out solo, continuing to write historical romance, as well as award-winning YA urban fantasy under the pen name Anthea Sharp. Anthea is still happily married and living in the Northwest with her husband and daughter, where the rainy days and excellent coffee fuel her writing.

Discover more at anthealawson.com and on Facebook/AntheaLawson. To find out about Anthea's upcoming releases, please subscribe to her mailing list at www.tinyletter.com/AntheaLawson. Thank you!

Made in the USA
Lexington, KY
28 April 2015